Six Years in Heaven

A True Story of Human Credulity and Unexampled Devotion, Embracing a Complete Expose of the Abominable Practices and Monstrous Professions of

George Jacob Schweinfurth

THE FALSE CHRIST

Whose Main Heaven is near Rockford, Illinois, with a Biographical Sketch of this Most Remarkable Religious Pretender of the Century

Alex. McCleneghan
With an introduction by Frank C. Lauder

Solis Press

ISBN: 978-1-910146-27-9

Published by Solis Press, PO Box 482, Tunbridge Wells TN2 9QT, Kent, England

Web: www.solispress.com | *Twitter*: @SolisPress

Contents

	Introductory	5
I	A Mysterious Figure	7
II	The Landlady's Story	11
III	Schweinfurth as a Youth	15
IV	In the Church Triumphant	20
V	The Trail of The Serpent	24
VI	The Wolf and the Lamb	31
VII	In the Toils	37
VIII	A Stern Chase	42
IX	The Lord's Will Be Done	50
X	The Law Invoked	58
XI	In Heaven	67
XII	A Disappointing Reception	73
XIII	He Couldn't Fool the Messiah	80
XIV	Prosperous, Beautiful Zion	88
XV	The First Death in Heaven	93
XVI	The Doctor Disappointed	101
XVII	A Vain Woman's Blighted Life	106
XVIII	A Certificate of Moral Character	113
XIX	Another Holy Ghost Child	120
XX	Out of Bondage	127
XXI	A Ghost of The Past	134
XXII	Music, Tights and Tableaux	140
XXIII	Humiliation	148
XXIV	An Astonished Detective	153
XXV	Diabolism	161
XXVI	Surprising Disclosures	167
XXVII	Seeking the True Way	173
XXVIII	A Beautiful Angel	179
XXIX	Higher Salvation and Fresh Vegetables	186
XXX	Out of the Slough of Despond	191
XXXI	Hearts Reunited	199

Introductory

IT IS HIGHLY GRATIFYING that one has been induced to turn his talents to the preparation of this work whose journalistic experience in Rockford has given him unusual advantages for close observation of the institution whose infamy he discloses, and it must be confessed that, with consummate skill, he has woven the weft of fact and the warp of fiction into a tale fraught with alluring interest for the casual reader and philosopher alike. No pen could more vividly portray the shrewdness, cupidity, hypocrisy and heartless selfishness which characterize the professed Messiah, whose deeds and words, faithfully chronicled, form the basis of this narrative.

Various students of mental phenomena have imputed the pretender's claims to hallucination, and his power over his worshipers to hypnotism, but when his marked acquisitiveness and sensuality are also considered, the inevitable inference pronounces him an arrant and audacious knave. Utterly destitute of pity or remorse, this moral monster's scruples not to enter happy homes, bringing beggary, disgrace, and even the midnight mists of madness, in his train, while at best but a wretched serfdom awaits the weak man or weaker woman who avows his divinity and consents to minister to his greed and lust. It is to be regretted that an establishment as vile as the one described should be permitted to flourish and abide, scornful of law and popular indignation, in the shadow of a city of churches, as Rockford is truthfully designated in this recital; but the author supplies a most reasonable explanation. In a busy, prosperous city people are apt to be too deeply absorbed in their immediate concerns to vex themselves with affairs in which they are not directly connected, and this mundane heaven has developed so gradually from an annoyance to an enormity that its growth has not severely shocked the sensibilities of the devout Christians who constitute the majority of the inhabitants of "The Lowell of the West." Sacrilegious doctrines are now openly proclaimed, and base ceremonials regularly observed which, at the outset of the pretender's career in this vicinity, were cautiously advanced and secretly celebrated. Many abominations were concealed with diabolical craft until so sure a foothold has been obtained that dislodgement seems almost impossible, as the difficulty of obtaining direct and reliable evidence makes legal procedure futile.

Apart from the romance clustering about the lives of Clara McCoy and Arthur Fitzroy, this work leaves nothing untold that could serve as a solemn admonition to the earnest seeker after divine truth, who might be led by plausible pleas to acknowledge the hateful pretensions of the head of the so-called Church Triumphant. In the light of past events it would be idle to expect that this book, or any other exposition of his methods that might be made, will influence the actions of this impostor to any extent for good; but could that hope be indulged, this work would start upon its warning mission backed by the fervent prayers of every Christian man and woman who knows aught of the sinful communal life of Mount Zion.

The author's aim will doubtless be achieved if through the perusal of his story some wavering brother or sister be restrained from plunging into the iniquitous Hell he depicts, whose only doors are death and disgrace. The authenticated evidence of George Jacob Schweinfurth's blasphemy and vice should be carefully noted; and the book deserves to be read, not only by the curious who seek entertainment, but also by the thinking moralists who hold in deep detestation the pernicious principles and practices of this odious personage, which menace the welfare of society by enticing the weak to wear the shackles of his miserable and shameful servitude.

F. C. L.
Rockford, Ill., Dec. 20, 1893

Chapter I
A Mysterious Figure

ONE PLEASANT DAY IN September, in the year one thousand eight hundred and ninety-two, a bright young man named William Hatfield, fired with a laudable ambition to excel in his chosen profession, found himself on horseback on the cliffs of the Kentucky river. The young man was there in the capacity of a reporter, having been assigned by the paper he represented the task of acquiring and writing in the best manner he could, the details on a very mysterious affair that had happened in a little village, in the neighborhood of which he was now inquiring his way. The circumstances may be briefly stated as follows:

Some six years before, the daughter of a well-to-do farmer, of attractive personality and rare accomplishments for one in her station of life, had mysteriously disappeared from her home on the outskirts of the village. The peculiar disappearance had almost passed into tradition, when the facts were vividly brought back to mind by the return of the unfortunate young woman in the last stages of consumption, the dews of death already gathering on her pale brow. She dragged herself to the home of her childhood—no one knew from where—leading by the hand, her little daughter. The child was about four years of age, with a delicate but bright and intelligent face. Soon after reaching home the young woman sank quietly from earth into the gray twilight of the tomb, and the little one was left to the care of the grandparents. Vague rumors of the extraordinary experiences of the unhappy young woman set all the tongues of the quiet little village to wagging furiously; and finally these rumors reached the keen-scented representative of a large city newspaper. He promptly reported the matter to his chief, who regarded the affair of sufficient consequence to assign to one of his brightest and most ambitious young men the duty which brought the solitary young horseman onto the cliffs of the Kentucky river.

A garrulous countryman pointed to Hatfield, a neat country house at a distance of perhaps half a mile from the shore of the river, "where," he said, "they keep tavern and you can be accommodated with supper, if you do not want to go down to Shelbyville to-night." Rather amused with the simple loquaciousness of the man, Hatfield handed him a small sum of money for his information, bade him farewell and ascended by a winding path the towery cliff.

The sky was brilliant with the tints of the setting sun. Beyond the numerous and variegated farms which the elevation overlooked, the distant hills lost their tops in the blue mists of heaven. All nature was hushed to a solemn stillness, save the hollow echo of the countryman's song. Even the impetuous stream, as it dashed along between the stupendous masses of calcareous rock, which presented an insurmountable barrier on either side, seemed fearful of disturbing the general repose.

As Hatfield rode along the brink of the precipice toward the tavern to which he had been directed, he discovered on his right a small country church, to which he involuntarily turned his horse. He had always admired the appearance of a country church and graveyard, and could not resist the inclination to pause on his road and look for a few moments at the one so near at hand. In the copse near the road stood a neat wooden building, the undergrowth for some distance around having lately been cleared away, while the majestic trees of the forest waved their green foliage in silence over the clay tenements of those who were "gathered to their fathers."

The graves, scattered around the church, were quite shut out from the rays of the sun by the boughs of the overhanging trees. There were no costly monuments, but occasionally a willow or an evergreen, planted by some kindred spirits, awakened a train of emotions beyond the power of the finest marble to impart.

The little rural temple was built of hewn logs, one story in height and almost concealed by the surrounding forest. As Hatfield drew near, his attention was arrested by the commanding figure of a man who, with downcast looks, was standing near the foot of a recently made grave, over which was scattered a profusion of evergreens. His face, manly but sun-burned, portrayed a depth of woe the intruder thought he had seldom seen depicted upon a human countenance. His long, dark hair hung in graceful curls below a broad, cheap straw hat, while his general appearance was that of one who had become most noticeably negligent in the matter of dress. Sitting upon the sod a few feet from him was a child, a little girl of about four years of age. The child was silent and subdued, but occasionally glanced up into his face, as though she understood and would commiserate in her childish way the sorrow of the strong man before her.

The path led near the side of the churchyard, where the man was standing with folded arms, seemingly petrified with grief and as insensible to the surrounding objects as a statue of marble. Hatfield's feelings were deeply interested in the personage before him, but, unwilling to appear intrusive, he passed on to the tavern, which was but a few hundred years distant. He had no sooner seated himself in the portico than he observed the object of his attention leave his position, take the child up in his arms, and with a slow and measured tread pursue the path down the steep declivity.

Just as he was disappearing from view the landlady approached. Hatfield called her attention to the strange figure he had been contemplating and inquired if she knew him.

"Yes, sir," she replied, with a serious look; "that is, I know him by sight. I am a comparatively recent arrival here and have had no opportunity to become personally acquainted with him. But I understand he was formerly the pride of the neighborhood and the most promising youth who dwelt upon these hills."

"Indeed; can you not tell me something about him? I have a penchant for hearing peculiar experiences, and I sometimes make them useful to me in my business."

"I am not familiar with the details, about which the relatives in the village are inclined to be reticent, because of the notoriety which has already been given the affair. His history is a sad one, and, if you care to hear it, as soon as supper is over I will relate to you all the facts in my possession. You may be able to learn more from the friends in the village afterward, if you intend going there, which I suppose you do."

"I am not going down until morning," returned Hatfield, "unless you find yourself unable to keep me over night."

"I shall be glad to accommodate you, sir. That is the purpose for which I am here."

"Thank you; and after tea, if you are still disposed, I shall be glad to hear the story."

"Is there anything you would especially desire for your tea?"

"Whatever is most convenient to prepare will be quite satisfactory."

"And you will want breakfast?"

"If you please."

The landlady at once retired and busied herself in the preparation of the meal for her visitor, and when she had gone Hatfield fell to reflecting on the peculiarity of the task to which he had been assigned. For some reason, for which he could find no plausible explanation, he fancied the strange and dejected person he had observed in the churchyard was in some way connected with the unusual work he had undertaken. He was endeavoring to form a theory to fit this singular notion when the landlady approached and announced that supper was ready, and, entering the large, old-fashioned dining-room, he partook of a plain but very palatable meal.

Hatfield then returned to the portico, and in a short time the land-lady followed and took a seat near him. He was really anxious to hear what she had to say, and she was no less eager to impart all the knowl-edge she possessed regarding the mysterious man in the grave-yard.

Chapter II
The Landlady's Story

WHEN THE LANDLADY HAD begged Hatfield to excuse what she called her country-like manner of relating a story she began her narrative:

"As I have already said, my acquaintance with the details is very limited. The name of the unhappy young man of whom you desire me to speak is Arthur Fitzroy. His parents, though poor, belonged to a highly respectable family in Virginia, and were among those who emigrated to this state, making the improvements on the farm which they yet own about two miles from the opposite shore, and afterward opening a general store in the village. Arthur, the only child, was born soon after their arrival, and breathing nothing from infancy but the salubrious air of the mountainous cliffs, and exercised by the labors of the farm, his person attained the size and manly beauty which it now exhibits. Meanwhile his intellectual faculties, improved by the ablest teachers that could be procured hereabouts, gave, at the age of twenty, indications of a mind vigorous in its perceptions and replete with the noblest feelings of nature. I might say that at the age of eighteen he received an invitation from a wealthy uncle in Virginia to spend a year east of the mountains. Consent was given by his parents, who were greatly desirous of his improvement. During this year he visited some of the principal cities, reading works of general literature and improving his mind. When he returned he was gladly welcomed by the whole population, male and female, with whom he was always a great favorite.

"Before going away he had grown to be very fond of a bright young woman named Clara McCoy, and they corresponded regularly during his absence. On his return their intimacy was renewed. She was the daughter of James McCoy, who still resides a short distance from the village. She was then just turning her seventeenth year, and to a mind well cultivated there was added a degree and elevation of fancy which occasionally seemed bordering on the romantic. And less as an infant, divested of envy and suspecting none in others, she was esteemed by all who knew her, while the continued sprightliness of her manners and the brilliant coruscations of her wit gave a zest to the enjoyment of every circle in which she mingled. Nor were the attractions of her mind surpassed by those of her person. Cast in the finest mold of her sex, grace characterized every movement and loveliness sat enthroned upon her face.

"In Arthur Fitzroy, her enthusiastic mind found a congenial spirit, and it was not long ere they both discovered that the society of each other was essential to complete their happiness. The result of a protracted interview, which soon took place, rendered him the happiest of men, and emotions of a new kind were awakened in the breasts of each. Heaven was called upon to witness their declarations of unshaken constancy.

"Not long after this there was some kind of a religious revival. A man came along inculcating some new and peculiar doctrine, the tenets of which I never learned. Clara, being religiously inclined and very impressionable, was soon brought under the influence of this new belief. No public services were held by this man, as is the custom, I believe, with most of those engaged in the work of evangelization. Quiet meetings were held at the house of some friend, where this man, who called himself an apostle, expatiated with magic eloquence on the beauties of the new doctrine, and there were those besides Clara who seemed to imbibe his dogmas. Her parents, though strongly impressed, did not become entirely convicted; while Arthur, being less susceptible and having a broader knowledge of the world than most of the unsophisticated people around him refused to the influenced by the fervid obsecrations of the so-called apostle. Though Clara supplemented the persuasiveness of this man with her own tender appeals, Arthur remained obdurate. He utterly refused to be led by the new light.

"It is impossible to say to what extent this difference of opinion might have affected their engagement had not an unexpected and deplorable circumstance intervened. One morning, shortly after the departure of the apostle, Clara was missing. Her bed was found not to have been occupied during the night, and from this it was assumed that she had left the house of a comparatively early hour in the evening. Her unhappy parents, well nigh distracted with grief, used every means in their power to discover her whereabouts, but their anxious and continued efforts were unavailing. She had gone entirely from them in the darkness of the night, and not a trace of her remained.

"Arthur was scarcely less distressed than the agonized parents, and spared no effort to learn what had become of his betrothed. His hopes were disappointed and his feelings cruelly lacerated. The remembrance of the beloved object of his affections dissipated and his former gaiety, and in vain were his books and other means of diversion resorted to in the hope of restoring some of his wonted cheerfulness. His mind became more oppressed daily and his moods more gloomy. Finally he absented himself from the neighborhood entirely, and, though he sent a message to his parents from different places occasionally for a time, he did not return, and his absence was protracted into years. It was agreed that his mind had become affected from the loss he sustained in the disappearance of her he cherished more than all else on earth, and that he was wandering about from place to place in the hope of finding her. In the meantime the parents of Clara felt themselves reluctantly forced to believe that the unfortunate girl, her mind unsettled by the new religious notions she had acquired from the apostle, had ended her life in the dark waters of the river; and when every human effort to find her had proved futile they mourned her as dead.

"The circumstances of her peculiar and mysterious disappearance had long passed from the minds of most people when, two months ago, or perhaps less, she returned as unexpectedly as she left. She was a mere shadow of her former self. Accompanying her was the child you saw with Arthur this evening. Poor Clara dragged her emaciated form over the cliffs to the home of her happy childhood. What she said to the parents regarding her absence I do not know, nor do I suppose they could be induced to tell, though they have permitted it to be understood that she had been for some time a widow and had suffered keenly from privation. She lingered until a few days before the return of Arthur, and at the close of her mortal career, with the name of the Messiah constantly upon her lips she bade adieu to the ever recurring sorrows of this life and gladly welcomed death as the harbinger of eternal happiness.

"The little girl thus became the care of her grandparents, and they lavish upon her all the love they formerly gave their daughter. Arthur is attracted to the amiable child by an irresistible impulse, and does not permit a day to pass without visiting her, frequently bringing her to the grave of her mother, where you saw them to-day. He seems to be peculiarly affected by the loss of the idol of his heart. There is nothing dangerous to himself or others in the strange malady which has seized him; but life seems to have become an uninterrupted waste of joyless existence, without the intervention of a single enlivening ray to cheer his gloomy path, unless he finds it in the presence of the child of her he loved so well. The woebegone aspect of his countenance, which you doubtless observed, seldom leaves him, and at the close of each day since his return, he has sought consolation in weeping over the dark and narrow tenement which contains the mortal part of the lovely friend of his youth."

"Madam," said Hatfield, when the landlady had finished, "I am deeply interested in your story, the more so, perhaps, because it is to make inquiry into this very affair that I am here; and, notwithstanding

I am so greatly indebted to you for the valuable information you have so kindly imparted, my interest prompts me to ask if there is nothing more in relation to this strange case that you can tell me? For instance, do you know or imagine there is anyone who has any knowledge of now this unfortunate girl's time was passed during her absence from home, or what motive if any, other than possible mental aberration from religious excitement, induced her to leave home in the first place?"

"I do not."

"That is strange."

"It is very strange. You understand no information has been vouchsafed by her parents on either point. If they know they are not disposed to make the facts public, and none of their friends have possessed sufficient lack of feeling to further lacerate their torn hearts with curious questions. It may be that Dr. Shannon, the village physician, who attended the unhappy young woman during here last hours, has some knowledge of these things beyond that given the public, though he might not feel himself at liberty to divulge them. However, you can see him when you go to the village in the morning and very speedily make this discovery for yourself."

"Do the family belong to any religious society?"

"Yes, I think so. They attend the Baptist church—the only church in the village."

"Do you think the minister," persisted Hatfield, with the perseverance characteristic of his profession, "would have any knowledge of the affair?"

"I am sure I cannot say, sir. I have told you all I know, all that is generally known."

"For which I am indeed deeply indebted to you, madam."

"No at all."

"Now, if you will kindly give me the name of the minister, I will retire and not provoke you with further useless questioning."

"Reverend James Brown."

"Brown, eh?"

"Yes, sir. Will you rise early?" she asked, as Hatfield prepare to retire.

"I'll be up with the lark, if there's one round here, and off to the village at the earliest moment. You see I am interested."

The strange story he had heard possessed Hatfield's mind until sleep overtook him. With a faculty that belongs to a natural journalist, he discerned much more in this mysterious affair than the landlady had any idea of, and he meant to know more about it before he ceased his investigations.

Chapter III
Schweinfurth as a Youth

"CHRIST LIVES! HE HAS come to earth the second time! Behold the Savior! He is the pure one—the perfect one! He knows no guile! He is God become man. By believing in him we are made pure and sinless as he is, and out salvation is assured. O, how grateful and happy are we who are redeemed! Blessed be God, that we have found him!"

Such were the utterances, delivered in a quiet but intensely earnest tone by one of the angels in the terrestrial heaven of George Jacob Schweinfurth.

Who is this Savior? Where may he be found?

He is the head of the peculiar sect originally known as the Beekmanites, and is believed by a numerous following to be Christ risen again from the dead.

Whence came he?

George Jacob Schweinfurth was born at Marion, Marion County, Ohio, in the year 1853, of German parents. At the age of six years he was regarded as a remarkably obedient boy, loving his mother so ardently that his devotion and attachment had no parallel in the neighborhood. To know his mother was happy seemed to be sufficient reason for the affectionate lad to make the woodland resound with the songs which his clear, strong voice often carried full a mile away. He sang and spoke mostly in the German language, his favorite songs being those of a devotional nature. Before he reached the age of twelve his mother's heart was gladdened by these words from an aged minister:

"Your son George is destined to become a Levite. Verily, God has chosen him."

The boy, when but eleven years of age, was seen to possess a degree of inspiration almost divine. His earnest soul frequently impelled him to begin a song of praise in the special services held in those days. The responses which he often made in services of testimony were forceful and clear. He seemed to long for association with the good and pure.

At the age of thirteen he lost his mother. Her sufferings were almost unendurable to the loving and sympathetic son. He seemed to divine her approaching demise, and it brought an inexpressible sorrow to his heart as he contemplated the inevitable separation. But the example and instruction of the mother he mourned, added to his own extraordinary power of selection, kept him free from contamination by the vices which inflict all grades in society.

Until eighteen years of age he was a constant attendant at the village school, devoting his vacations to labor in the harvest field. He was ready to do "whatsoever his hands found to do." He was engaged at one time as a book agent. At another time he worked in a smithy, and was for a time a clerk in a general store.

His life up to this time had been spent mostly in seclusion. He had not yet found the society which suited him. The ribaldry of the villagers was intolerable to him; hence his friends were few, and they were the only ones who really knew him. He was painfully conscious of limitations when his soul sought to use its yet unfledged opinions. In those days he used to say: "The direct battles that man can fight are those which are waged on the arena of his own soul." He was, however, living in a hope whose wings were growing. Ministers sought to tame his heart of fire by telling him that limitations are identical and coeval with the physical existence. A phrenologist one of those days said: "This young man is aiming toward the sky. He may not reach it, but he will rise higher than if he did not so aim."

In the summer and autumn of 1873 he served in the humble capacity of sexton of a Methodist church at Jackson, Michigan, for which service the church failed to pay him. Here was the incipiency of a series of struggles and conflicts in which he had tremendous odds against him. He had been taught that the Methodist church was the most nearly divine of any of the Christian segregations. He was gradually ceasing to think the church and God akin to each other. The church was declining in his estimation. It would soon lie far below his soul's vision.

The period of these struggles covered several years, during which time he taught school and afterward attended Albion college. The professors of this institution esteemed him as a model young man. He was believed by all who knew him to have a bright future before him. Dr. Perrine said to him: "Young man, you have a good head on you, and your forte is composition."

In the autumn and winter of 1873 he attended two terms of school of Evanston, being assisted through the last term by a kindly minister of the Methodist church who took an interest in the frail but fervent young man. After a trip around the lakes from Chicago to Detroit, taken for the benefit of his health, Rev. A. R. Bartlett, presiding elder of the Saginaw district, appointed him minister of an unsupplied circuit in Tuscola county, Michigan, with headquarters at Kingston, a small place near Vassar.

"I asked God," he said to a friend, "'What wilt thou have me to do?' Then I watched for the answer, and it came: 'Enter the Methodist ministry now. Do your further studying in connection with your future ministerial labors.' My soul answered: 'I will obey.'"

Regarding his first pulpit effort he wrote to a friend the subjoined letter:

"Dear friend:—I commenced my ministerial work to day. That the good Lord has brought me hither and commanded me to work directly for him I have no more doubt than I doubt that I am here. I preached here this afternoon from the words: 'What wilt thou have me to do?' I felt a little misgiving before going into the pulpit, but, while thinking about the matter, suddenly there came over me a heavenly tranquility and an elevation of soul; and in this state of mind and heart He bore me through the ordeal.

"Yours in the Lord,

"GEORGE JACOB SCHWEINFURTH."

In the church to which he was assigned the sentiment prevailed that the greatest blessing it ever had was "in securing Brother Schweinfurth for a pastor."

Outside the church it was said: "This community is unworthy of such a man." When the year was up the church made known to the pastor that it desired his return. He said: "This will be, or will not be, as God shall direct." A petition for his return was placed in his hand as be started for the conference, with these words from the speaker of the committee: "Hand this to the presiding elder." The elder never saw the petition, nor did the young minister return to that charge. He was asked more than once where he desired to go, and his unvarying answer was: "I desire to go where I am sent."

As he entered his second field of labor at Alphena, Michigan, he was in the spirit of rapidly becoming more a citizen of heaven and less a denizen of earth. He was entering into closer kinship with the super-earthly. He was becoming more a minister and less a Methodist. He desired to bring heaven this side of the stars, and so he said to himself: "I shall be no more a Methodist than the Savior was a Methodist. I shall be free as truth can make a man. I will belong to no body of men; I will belong to God."

So he labored to make his people like God, not like John Wesley, preaching that "sin is the only thing that is keeping Christ and heaven out of this world, out of our lives. Sin in the church and out of the church is damnable, and the former more than the latter. All unrighteousness is sin. Now, what is it that is not right? What are those upright things that are obstructing our friendly God in coming to his own?" Mr. Schweinfurth turned the light of inspiration upon this subject, and as he became of more service to God he proved to be of less service to the church.

In December, 1877, he met Dorinda Helen Fletcher Beekman, and "through the window of her soul he saw God." She was the gateway of his future. She was his spiritual Mary—the mother of his soul.

The sect of which he is now the head, and which acknowledges his divinity, has been in existence about seventeen years. Mrs. Beekman, the wife of a Congregational minister, originated the body of strange believers. She preached that in her own person were the attributes of the risen Lord. She was the woman Christ inspired and made sacred by the indwelling of his spirit. The band of believers grew slowly but steadily. They first located their central church at a village named Byron, Illinois, and by dint of besieging the meetings of all the other churches, and declaring their doctrines at all seasons, kept the poor clergymen and their flocks in continual hot water. Her husband did not believe in the new faith, and as a result is now in an insane asylum. Schweinfurth preached the new doctrine in the country churches around and drew good audiences. He preached well, and was especially popular with the young ladies. It is related that they often made a pretense of conversion merely to kneel at the altar where he could place his hand upon their brows and sweetly whisper: "Dear sister, have faith; only have faith."

But alas! For the faith of the devoted little band. Mrs. Beekman died and became cold, inanimate clay, as every other mortal must. Her heart-broken believers kept her body for a week, expecting that she would rise, as she had promised and prophesied. They placed her body on a raised platform and worshiped about it hourly. There were expectant believers standing around it every moment, in the hope that life would return and they would witness the resurrection. At the end of the week the corruption of the body grew so great that interment was ordered by the public authorities.

At this juncture Schweinfurth came before the comfortless little band, and declared to them that "just as Mrs. Beekman was dying he saw a glimpse of heaven through the window of her soul," and from her lips came the words: "You are Christ, the Holy One, My spirit passes into thine, and by this act transforms thy whole being. Go forth pure and sinless, the only son to God. Thou shalt bring all nations to worship thee, and put to rout the evil one and all the hosts of darkness."

The credulous company believed and rejoiced in the real Savior brought to them from the dead.

From that day the growth of the organization, both in financial resources and membership, has been simply wonderful. The new Messiah has developed remarkable business acumen and is a keen observer of human nature. As a result of his shrewdness, unlike Him who had "not where to lay his head," the later lord has an accumulation of this world's goods that would seem astonishing were the figures given.

"I am Christ."

Chapter IV
In the Church Triumphant

IN THE PRECEDING CHAPTER the reader has been given a biograph- ical sketch, necessarily brief, of the new Messiah up to the time he abandoned the church and became the head of one of the most remark- able religious sects of all the queer theological schools. It will aid in understanding and appreciating the romantic part of this narrative if the personality of the head of The Church Triumphant is more ful- ly elucidated. It will also be well to know something of the manner of life of this community of "saints," and of the proselyting methods employed by the Messiah and his agents. Nor will it be uninteresting to note how he contrives to maintain the new Zion practically undis- turbed in a community of upright, reputable citizens, having no sym- pathy whatever with his remarkable doctrines, and be designated by those in his immediate vicinity as "the best neighbor they have or ever had."

Physically "the perfect man" is rather insignificant. He is a trifle below the medium height and delicately formed. Still to many, on first seeing him, the impression is one of astonishment. He has a surprising resemblance to the generally accepted pictures of the Savior of man- kind, and the observer might easily fancy a life-size production of some of the old masters. His eyes are brown; his complexion florid. He wears all around his face a flowing auburn beard, the same color as that which Christ is said to have worn. He has a white brow, with veins plainly indicating refinement. He wears his hair brushed back from a forehead indicative of intellectual force, and has a sharp, penetrating eye that can look meek and pathetic when circumstances demand humility. His clothes are always in style and materials the best that can be procured. Everything he wears always fits him elegantly. His deportment, at least beyond the confines of heaven, is that of a humility bordering on the abject. Being once denounced by a clergyman as a lecherous mocker of holy things and assailed with opprobrium, he answered calmly, quietly and respectfully, without a shadow of anger. Just here it might be well to let a Presbyterian clergyman, Dr. Samuel L. Conde, of Rockford, Ill., who has met him a hundred times or more, express an opinion:

"He is a dangerous man. He hardly ever fails to convert those who go there to listen to his teachings. His sophistries are hard for any one to meet unless thoroughly familiar with the teachings of Scripture on the second coming of Christ. There is not a particle of insanity about him, and I am convinced he is perfectly free from any lust of the flesh, for I know of the most thorough tests. I have been told by women whom he has had under his sway that there is some magnetic power in his eyes which forces them to do his bidding and speak of a belief in him when their whole nature is antagonistic to it. Outwardly no meeker, more patient, more perfect man has ever come under my notice. I honestly believe he is possessed of the devil, who has come to the world in the garb of an angel of light."

That is the new Messiah as he appears to-day, and has appeared since he assumed divinity. Now what of the terrestrial heaven where he holds such absolute sway?

Among the converts which Schweinfurth made immediately following his defection from the Methodist church was a good old farmer named Weldon, who possesses eight hundred acres of well-cultivated and valuable land five miles south of the city of Rockford, Ill. One of the first things this infatuated farmer did was to make over his entire property to Schweinfurth, as head of the Church Triumphant, and there the central community, or heaven, is now and has since that time been located.

The new Zion is a large mansion standing in a spacious enclosure. It is some distance back from the main road, from which it is part-ly hidden amid the shelter of numerous large trees. To the west are spacious barns, carriage buildings, sheds and other appurtenances of a well appointed farm. There are a large number of imported horses and the finest cattle in the land. All the other stock is of the same superior grade, and the place is supplied with all the latest approved appliances for carrying on the operations of the extensive farm. The house will easily accommodate one hundred persons, and there are usually about fifty women and half that number of men about the place. The male disciples do the heavy work, some of them being mere drudges. They live on the plainest food, two meals being served daily, and sleep in the attic. But they count themselves happy to be permitted to suffer and labor for their Lord, having given up all their earthly possessions when they took up their abode in heaven. Some of the women are com-pelled to drudge as well as the men, but they are the ones who have not attained and angelic condition, or who have fallen from grace.

Visitors are generally ushered into the reception parlor, in which room the Sunday service is also held. The furnishing is elegant and tasteful. A low ceiling gives the room a most cozy appearance. Winding down into the room is an oaken staircase. The organ in the room matches the staircase and the rest of the woodwork. The fireplace is of pressed brick with polished brass facings. A handsome lamp is suspended from the center of the room. The carpet is soft and of tasteful design. Several beautiful pictures adorn the walls. Indeed, the general effect produces the conviction that the furnishing and decoration were the result of a refined taste. And not alone of the reception room may this be said. The furnishing of the house from top to bottom is elegant. The furniture, the pictures, the lace curtains, the carpets and the bric-a-brac are all such as would adorn the costliest of Metropolitan homes of wealth and refinement. The Lord has a library which any man of letters might envy. It is lined with books in solid walnut cases, tastefully veneered with French varnish. It is quite evident that Schweinfurth is something of a student.

Of the domestic life of heaven it is unnecessary to say more at present than to give an idea of what the Messiah himself claims it to be; what it really is will appear later on.

In an interview a few years ago, Schweinfurth said: "We live here a large family. There are several married couples, but most are unmarried. The charge that we indulge in evil practices shows how little the world knows of the purity and sinlessness of our lives. I am the type of the sinless one, and those who live with me and believe become pure even as I am pure, and in them there can be no guile. Our marriage ceremony is binding, and there can be no divorce. The gratification of animal passion is considered sinful. As for myself, I never experience the passions of man, for I am God. I know that I shall be reviled and persecuted, and men will say all manner of evil things against me, but I am holy, and the world will yet know it. The whole world is impaneled as a jury to try us, but those who now persecute us will be utterly destroyed. All will have to believe in me before they can be saved. I might add that the Church of the Redeemed will supplant all others on the earth.

"We shall subdue that whole earth. The so-called orthodox churches are the beasts of Daniel and must be destroyed."

It will thus be seen that Schweinfurth has all along arrogated to himself the attributes and powers of divinity.

The growth in membership of this remarkable sect has been astonishingly rapid within the last few years, and branches now exist in some of the principal cities in the United States and Canada, all of which are tributary to the central community over which the Messiah himself presides. Schweinfurth has complete charge of all the finances and uses the means at his pleasure, being compelled to make no account of anything. The membership numbers about a thousand at the present time. All members who are not inmates of heaven or some of the branch communities are required to pay tithes—one tenth of all their accumulations. Were they incapable of earning an average of more than one dollar a day, the receipts gathered into the exchequer of Zion would not be entirely insignificant. But, indeed, most of the converts are persons of means, and, what is not a little surprising, people who seem to be possessed of more than ordinary intelligence. There are clergymen, lawyers and doctors who have given up all to follow the new Master. Poor apostles are received when they can be made available upon the farm or at some of the branches, when it is shown that they are sincere in their professions; and women without means are accepted upon the same conditions. If they are personally attractive and give promise of attaining future "perfections" they do not find it difficult to obtain a place in the heavenly household.

Conversions are made through the instrumentality of silver tonged and trusted apostles. There is quite a number of traveling men, colporteurs and agents in various lines, who are sowing constantly the seeds of the new religion. Schweinfurth makes a special effort to attract this class, as they are capable of selecting the more likely subjects for the purposes of the Messiah. Some of these emissaries have been ministers of the gospel, and all are men of education and refinement who have themselves been brought to feel the mystic power of this man.

Services are held at heaven once each Sunday, and Schweinfurth always preaches. The sermons occupy from two to four hours. Stenographers take down his every utterance, and typewriter copies are made and sent to all the branches, where they are read to the faithful the Sunday following.

Many who visit the central community seem to see nothing there but a happy home life. Those who have gone from curiosity have returned with the impression that there is something fascinating about the man and the place.

Chapter V
The Trail of The Serpent

"YOU WILL FIND THIS an extremely interesting work, I can assure you, and I hope I may be able to induce you to take a copy."

These were the words to a debonair, timid man who had found admission to the home of Mrs. McCoy, at a time some six and a half years previous to the events recorded in the opening chapters.

"I am sure," he continued, "you will find the history of the Franco-German war almost as interesting as the heroic deeds and achievements of our own deplorable internecine struggle of a few years ago. While we wasted so much blood and treasure for the preservation of the Union, we have the satisfaction of knowing it was not in vain—that our great country is now one and inseparable, in the enjoyment of peace and unexampled prosperity; while France—la belle France—overwhelmed by force of numbers and superior discipline, was soon laid prostrate at the feet of the foe, the best blood of the nation shed in fruitless carnage, and the resources of the country well-nigh exhausted."

"Were you a union man, Mr.—"

"Mamby is my name."

"Mr. Mamby, were you a union man?"

The suave agent, who usually took the precaution of first making himself familiar with the sentiments of those upon whom he contemplated calling, before doing so, in order that he might not imperil a sale by unpleasant references, had not thought of the possibility of dropping in upon a family who might still be in mourning for the "lost cause" of the Southern Confederacy, and for a moment he was in doubt what to say. But his hesitation was of sufficiently short duration not to be noticed, for his keen, sharp mind instantly grasped the situation and he replied:

"Madam, I am compelled to confess that during the days of fratricidal strife my sympathies were with the people of the South, whom I conceived to be contending for a principle dear to their hearts, though at that time I was resident of Canada and took no active part on either side. I have been a citizen of this country but a short time. I am a man of peace, and I should be immeasurably distressed to see another such struggle for Southern independence, realizing, as I do, the horrors involved in a great war, the bloodshed, the suffering, the broken hearts and desolate homes, the waste of treasure and the demoralizing influences of barbarian and brutalizing warfare. May God spare this united, prosperous and happy country a repetition of such scenes as the late war of the Rebellion witnessed."

"Those are our sentiments here, Mr. Mamby. We, too, were sympathizers with the cause of the South, but we have accepted the results of the war, and our fervent prayers go up for the continued peace and prosperity of our united country."

"A very beautiful sentiment, Mrs. McCoy," said the agent, feeling that he was again on safe ground. "You do well to pray for every blessing upon all our people. I wish all the people of this country were praying people, and that their prayers might be rightly directed."

"Are you a praying man, Mr. Mamby?"

"I certainly am."

"I am glad of that, sir. I am now prepared to regard your book more favorably."

"And I am glad of that."

"If you will kindly call this evening I think it extremely likely you will be able to dispose of a copy of your *History of the Franco-German War*. I will speak to Mr. McCoy about it."

"I am much obliged, I am sure, Mrs. McCoy, and I shall be most happy to call at the time you have set. At the same time, if Mr. McCoy and yourself have leisure, it would afford me much pleasure to discourse for a short time on religious matters. It is always a source of pleasure to me, whenever it is possible, to meet those of a sympathetic nature, to exchange views on those affairs of the soul which should most deeply concern us all."

"We shall be too happy, Mr. Mamby, to enjoy an evening to religious converse. My daughter Clara and her—well, her future husband, we expect—will be here this evening, and I doubt not a season spent in exchange of thought on these important matters will be agreeable and profitable to them as well."

"You do not know what pleasure you have given me," said the agent, with every indication of satisfaction at the prospect before him.

Having asked Mrs. McCoy if she was not a member of the Baptist denomination, to which she returned an affirmative answer, the agent took his departure. As the reader must have already surmised, Book Agent Mamby was none else than one of the numerous sleek apostles sent out from the new Zion to make converts to the peculiar faith of the sect who acknowledge George Jacob Schweinfurth as the Messiah. The McCoys, while people of but modest fortune, would nevertheless be very desirable acquisitions. It appeared to him that Mrs. McCoy was a person whose susceptibility would render her very receptive to his religious teachings. He hoped the other members of the household would be as easy to handle. If not, the penalty of obtuseness or stubbornness would be theirs. He had already settled in his own mind that some one of the family could be made a contributor to the material resources of Zion; and having driven the entering wedge, by insinuating himself into the favor of Mrs. McCoy, he would not desist until success had crowned his efforts. This apostle had already made numerous converts, and in several instances had completely disrupted family relations in doing so. But he did not charge himself with blame because of that. It was surely not his fault if his seductive words and promises were insufficient to convince and entire family. It was enough for him if any one member, fully believing in the Messiah, desired to be "saved." That one should not be eternally lost because the others refused to heed the call.

Mamby was a type of the other apostles with a roving commission to proselyte. He was a man of perhaps forty-five years of age. His face was covered all around with a luxuriant black beard, fringed with streaks of gray on either side. His high forehead denoted intellectuality, and was white and clear. His small eyes, shaded with long dark lashes, occasionally showed a passing gleam of cunning, though they were very nearly always cast down in a way that gave his face an expression of meekness and humility, a trick he had doubtless acquired from the master he served so faithfully. He spoke in a well-modulated voice, his intonations being mellifluent and winning, while his whole demeanor was humility personified. These characteristics were indubitably the result of assiduous cultivation, but they were not forgotten for a moment, even when his meek eyes would brighten and his smooth tongue grow eloquent in advocacy of the doctrines he lost no opportunity to inculcate. His language was simple and well chosen, and even those who could not bring themselves into sympathy with his ideas invariably gained the impression that he was an honest and earnest advocate of the doctrines he professed. His dress was generally what might be described as semi-clerical black and always fitted him nicely, while his headgear was invariably a black felt hat. He was always neatly but not showily dressed.

Such was Apostle Mamby when he made his first appearance in Shelbyville, and the same description would need little or no correction to-day. He is still selling books, as he did before "the great light" came to him, and is as eloquently pleading the cause of the Messiah as of yore. His services have been great, and he has been the recipient of many "heavenly" favors; but it may be said in his behalf that he was himself as true a convert as any he ever made.

When Mamby left the McCoy home he made his way directly to the next house, and then to a dozen or more others before evening, spending a good deal of time wherever he found those with leisure or inclination to talk with him. This he did often, for the population of small places, male and female, are not infrequently disposed to extended chats when they meet a stranger, well informed on general topics, and an entertaining talker; and some of them have even been known to spend a good deal of time in confabulation with those who were not especially entertaining. He disposed of some of his books, for he was a successful agent as well as an efficient evangelist; but he found no one he was able to interest to any great extent in the matter of religion, old or new. All the ladies he met attended church on Sunday, and sometimes found their way to the prayer-meeting and nearly always to the church sociable. They were willing to agree with all Mr. Mamby said respecting the benefits and beauty of a devout life, but they never grew very earnest in this direction, unless perhaps for a few days at the annually recurring revival season. It is therefore doubtful if any of them remembered what the apostle said on the subject of salvation a half hour after he took his departure. These apathetic, or easy-going, Christians may be found everywhere, and they possess at least one advantage over the more fervent and earnest ones—they are seldom influenced or injured by such dangerously insinuating teachers as Apostle Mamby.

At the appointed time in the evening he repaired to the house of the McCoys. He found, as Mrs McCoy had assured him would be the case, that besides her husband there were present her daughter Clara and Arthur Fitzroy, with both of whom the reader has already been made acquainted.

It has been noted that Clara McCoy possessed, in addition to a mind devoid of every form of guile, a most attractive personality. Mamby, ever argus-eyed, at once observed the beauty of face and figure of the young girl. He saw a wonderfully fair complexion, and a sweetly innocent face, with eyes in which the keen observer could read purity, affection and devotion. Her form, slender and willowy, only lacked the fullness of maturity to make her a perfect specimen of youthful womanhood—a being "a little lower than the angels."

Mamby's mind was made up at once. She, no matter how the others regarded him and his teachings, should become a convert. More than that, he would bear her away to the earthly Zion, that the Master might see he was not unmindful of that which most pleased him. He saw at once he could control her without difficulty, binding her senses so effectually that chains would be no more than a temporary bondage when he called her to fly to the bosom of the later Lord. This much the apostle was convinced of the moment he looked into her eyes. His chief concern now was to what extent the other members of the family, and more especially Arthur Fitzroy, could be influenced. He would satisfy himself on that point before the evening was over.

After a few commonplace remarks Mamby devoted himself to the sale of his book, which was really a handsome one, well bound and typographically neat, and a work, moreover, that might be profitably read. The agent extolled it and all admired it, and the sale was soon effected.

The company then engaged in pleasant conversation on general topics, the McCoys, and young Fitzroy also, being gratified to find their transient guest a man of learning and discernment, well informed and having positive opinions on the living questions of the day. Arthur, better equipped intellectually than most of those in the community in which he lived, found especial pleasure in the converse of the stranger, and for a part of the time these two did most of the talking.

After a while Mamby cleverly turned the conversation to religion, upon which subject Arthur had little to say—not that he was skeptical, but his mind upon these affairs was in transitory state. His ideas were being constantly changed or modified. Therefore his opinions, such as he had, were not very clearly defined, and he preferred not to discuss a matter upon which he was not prepared to advance ideas of some sort. He was not willing to uphold what did not appear to him to be reasonable, and to express a doubt of what he had not fairly investigated he conceived to be a species of impiety in which he was not inclined to indulge. Thus in religious matters he presented a contrast of contrarieties, and was content to listen while others talked.

When, however, the apostle spoke in glowing periods of the divine attributes of the new Messiah, he began to question either the honesty or sanity of the speaker. He listened in silence for some time and then asked:

"Do you mean to tell me, Mr. Mamby, that your people believe the head of the Church Triumphant to be Christ risen again from the dead?"

"We believe the perfections of the Nazarene to be focalized in his personality."

"Why do you believe this?"

"Because of the effects which have been produced upon our lives by his teachings."

"May not the same results be accomplished by the simple teachings of the Scriptures? If it be the perfections of the Nazarene that are, as you believe, focalized in the personality of Mr. Schweinfurth, how can the stream rise higher than its source?"

"He is himself the source. He is more than Christ. He is the perfect man and also God. He possesses the attributes of Jesus, and has his spirit; and, more than that, he is the Almighty himself."

Arthur was amazed at the calm, deliberate manner in which the apostle made this statement, and he looked searchingly into the man's eyes with the expectation of detecting symptoms of insanity. There were no such signs. The meek eyes had undergone no change; they were as calm as the voice and demeanor of the man who had spoken these extraordinary words. He could not have given expression to the most indifferent remark with less perturbation. The others, Clara especially, sat as though petrified in the presence of a superior being.

"It would seem to me," said Arthur, when he could finally find language, "that most people, in the light of Scripture, would regard what you have just said as an unpardonable offense—that of blasphemy of the Holy Ghost."

"That is because they, like you, my dear friend, do not comprehend. God gave his only begotten son, that by believing in him the world might be saved. Is it not possible for God to reverse his judgments? You are aware the Scripture says he repented having made man. Now, having found the means of redemption inadequate, provided when he gave Christ to the Cross and Calvary, he has determined to make another effort to rescue a perishing world. To accomplish this he has raised up from among the people one whom he has clothed with divinity and power from on high. Thus the head of the Church Triumphant is not only the second person of the Trinity, but is delegated with the power and authority of God—in fact, is God himself."

Arthur did not reply; he had made up his mind he was in the presence of a lunatic, as harmless as he was eloquent in advocacy of his strange ideas, and soon after he took his leave. The apostle remained for some time with the members of the family, impressing them with his earnestness, charming them with his eloquence and transporting them with the beautiful pictures he painted of life in the new Zion. He told of the calm, peaceful existence the saints there led, the perfection of life, and the joys experienced in the fullness of redemption and the benign presence of the Messiah. Clara was peculiarly moved by these apostolic recitals of the glories of the terrestrial heaven. She was especially impressed with the divine purity of heart and life of those who had gathered there to foretaste the ecstatic bliss of the more glorious heaven beyond the skies. Mamby had read her aright when he told himself she would be an easy convert.

When it was about time for him to take his departure he changed his position so that he sat facing Clara and could look her full in the face. In a moment he caught her eye. For perhaps twenty seconds he gazed steadily into those beautiful orbs. That look penetrated her very soul. Then he turned his head and chatted pleasantly with the others for a few moments, but Clara did not speak again while he remained. Before leaving he shook hands cordially with the members of the family. He first greeted the father, then the mother. Then he walked over to Clara, who rose as he approached. As he took her hand he said, in an almost inaudible whisper—"Meet me at ten to-morrow"—at the same time making a quick downward motion before her with his left hand, purposely standing so that this movement was not observed by either of the parents. He then bade her good evening in his usual tone of voice, as he had the others, and took his departure.

Neither father, mother nor daughter saw the trail of the serpent, but it was there.

Clara, when she shook hands with Mamby, felt a strange. Inexplicable sensation, much like a person suddenly awakened from sleep. She did not attempt to account for this, for her mind at once reverted to the absorbing topic that had engaged so much attention during the evening. The new Messiah was the last thing in her mind when she lost consciousness in sleep.

Her parents, too, when they had retired, debated long upon what had been told them before they fell asleep, the only conclusion reached being a resolve to have the apostle again visit them, if he would, and further enlighten them regarding the remarkable man in whom they already felt so deep an interest.

But, think you, will Clara meet the apostle on the morrow, in compliance with his whispered behest? Will she jeopardize her reputation, in a community much given to gossip, by an assignation with a stranger of whom she had never heard before that evening, though he did charm and impress her by his apparent devoutness? And, if willing, where would she meet him? He had given no intimation of where he would be found. But that was entirely unnecessary with one under so potent an influence as that which the apostle exercised upon this hapless young woman.

Chapter VI
The Wolf and the Lamb

ANIMAL MAGNETISM, OR MESMERISM, is a science that, while undoubtedly practiced centuries ago, is yet but imperfectly understood. It is generally known, however, that it is a force that may be made productive of incalculable good if properly directed, and also, like every power for good, may be made a power for mischief.

It is well understood that sleep may be induced in some persons by passes slowly made with the slightly curved open hands of another person, at a distance of from half an inch to an inch, from the crown of the head downwards along the face and chest to the pit of the stomach. Subjects so susceptible have been found that they have been put to sleep with one pass. Others, again, sorely try the patience of the mesmerizer. There is no end, perhaps to the varieties in the degrees of susceptibility in different individuals to the influence of these magnetic manipulations known as passes.

Hundreds of persons have witnessed the phenomena of the human will operating upon sensitive male and female subjects. Many and many a time have persons been made to travel considerable distances by the force of the silent will of another.

This mention is made of one or two well authenticated scientific facts in order that a variety of occurrences herein-after mentioned may not seem incredulous and thus be set down as inventions of the writer pure and simple.

All the morning following the discussion, in which the apostle made so deep an impression, Clara's mind was filled with what he had said, and at intervals she and her mother discussed the matter with considerable animation. The thought of joining the community at Zion had not occurred to Clara, though she was stirred by the idea given her of basking in the benignant presence of one whose personality contained all the constituents of divine grace, love and power.

When the hour of ten o'clock came she felt herself impelled by some inexplicable force to put on her hat and walk out. The meeting with the apostle had not occurred to her at any time during the morning, or she might have mentioned it to her mother, and that estimable woman, less susceptible to such influences as had been brought to bear on her daughter, might have deemed it proper to prevent the meeting or at least be present herself. Clara did not realize where she was going.

She only felt that an impulse had seized her which she was not only incapable of resisting but which prevented her apprising others of her intentions. In a moment more she was not even conscious of what she was doing. She quietly put on her hat and, without changing her dress, stole quietly from the house and walked with a brisk but not hurried step to where she felt drawn by an irresistible power of attraction.

A walk of five minutes in any direction was sufficient to take anyone beyond what was, by general consent, the limits of Shelbyville. There were bold cliffs, great, yawning precipices, occasional gentle declivities and dangerous paths that wound their serpentine course in and around and up and down the sides of the cliffs. Mamby had followed one of these paths until he reached a copse. This he entered, and, finding a seat on the decaying stump of what had once been a large forest tree, awaited the arrival of Clara.

He knew she would come, for she could not help herself; and he was therefore not surprised, when he had been seated a few minutes, to hear the cracking of the dead twigs beneath her feet and to see her directly afterward enter the wooded retreat which he had selected to exclude them from the observation of those who might by some mischance follow the path by which she had come.

Though she wore the simple calico in which she had all morning attended to her household duties, and a broad, plain straw hat shaded her fair face from the sun, he thought he never saw anyone more beautiful. Her somnambulistic condition rendered her a trifle paler than was her wont, but the effect of that on one in perfect health is but to enhance the natural charms of person.

The apostle rose to meet her, his gratification plainly visible in his small eyes, which now, instead of being meek, twinkled like twin stars with the inward satisfaction that consumed him. She smiled no greeting as he took her hands, for she experienced neither delight nor regret at the meeting. She did not even appear to know that she was there. She was merely a piece—and a most beautiful piece—of animate clay, subject entirely to the power of his will and totally incapable of resistance. There was a wolfish gleam in his eyes; a lustful longing in his heart. If he had dared! But he did not. There was a power behind him that he feared—a will as much stronger than that he possessed as his will was over that of the helpless lamb in his power.

Schweinfurth was and is averse to such advantage as Mamby may have meditated. The sensibilities of a girl like Clara McCoy would have revolted against his harmless familiarity were she cognizant of what was done. A more serious crime must in time have made itself apparent to even the most innocent and unsophisticated, thus engendering indignation, if nothing more, instead of trust and confidence. She had not yet been advanced to a knowledge of the doctrine of immaculate conception, so firmly believed in by the inmates of the Schweinfurth heaven. Her mind had not been prepared for that. When a dupe has reached that condition any lengths are safe under mesmeric influence, but not before. Mamby understood this and paused in time.

Directly he released her hands and made a few rapid passes before her. She raised her eyes with a startled look and drew back a step or two. Then she said, in a voice which plainly evinced her surprise and fright:

"Why, Mr. Mamby! You here?"

"Yes, my child," he answered, again the paragon of humility.

Then, glancing around with terrified eyes, she asked:

"Where am I? Why I am here?"

"Do not fear, daughter," he gently replied, with his most reassuring smile. "You are not far from home and shall return directly if you desire."

"But why am I here?" cried the still trembling girl.

"God sent you here, sweet sister, to commune with me before I go away to return no more. Our converse will be of holy things, and I believe will be an inspiration to you. If, however, you are not inclined to listen to the voice of the Lord's servant crying in the wilderness. I shall have no more to say, but will permit you to return to your home at once."

"I am willing to harken unto the words of the Lord," replied the girl, still showing some timidity; "but I cannot understand how I came here. A moment ago I was at home by the side of my mother; now I am here."

"No doubt it is very surprising to you; but you must bear in mind the Lord has unlimited power. Time and distance are as naught to him. He can convey you or me to the uttermost ends of the earth in the twinkling of an eye. He has brought you here in a second's time, even without your knowledge. He could take you to where he reigns on earth just as quickly, but the would much prefer to have you go of your own free will. He does not want those near him who are not faithful believers. Were such ones to go he would send them from him. He has seen that your heart is inclined to him. Is it not so?"

"Yes," murmured the girl; "I want to do what is right in the sight of the Lord. But it would be very hard to leave my parents and—"

Here she paused abruptly.

"Yes, yes; I knew whom you mean," replied the wily apostle, with kindness in his tone. "But does not the holy word, with which I am sure you must be familiar, enjoin the faithful to leave father and mother and all else and follow the Lord?"

"Yes, sir."

"Well, now, dear sister, I think you understand, and I am not going to press you. Go back to your home, say nothing to anyone, and carry this matter to the privacy of your room in prayer. The Lord himself will direct you and tell you what you should do. But whether you go or stay, keep him in mind always, and he will be your guide and comfort. Will you promise me to do this?"

Yes, sir; I will promise."

"Well, dear, faithful, holy sister. I will now dismiss you. Take off your hat and receive my blessing."

He placed his hand upon her head, looked down into her eyes a few moments, and again she was in the same condition in which she arrived. She was once more clay in his hands, the subject of his will. As a precautionary measure, and in order to bring her more absolutely under his control, he made a number of experimental magnetic manipulations, first putting her into what would be a normal condition of sleep, and then, by a few additional passes, making her form perfect rigid. Having thoroughly satisfied himself, he reduced the rigidity and brought her back to the state into which he first placed her. He then whispered into her ear:

"Meet me to-night at eleven o'clock."

He now permitted her to return to her home, the meeting in the copse not being of more than ten minutes' duration. Clara started away at a brisk step over the path by which she came.

It will be easy to conclude from the action of Mamby that he was himself directly subject to the will of Schweinfurth and dare not do what he knew would not meet with the approval of the Messiah. He possessed strong passions, that, under the circumstances just described, it would have been impossible for him to curb but for the superior power which held him enthralled. It was for the master alone to decide what disposition should be made of the beautiful victims his apostles brought to him.

When Clara had been gone a few minutes Mamby emerged from his concealment, and sauntered down the winding path to the village inn, where he ordered his horse and carriage and set out for a clearing about six miles distant. There he had spent a day selling books a week or so before, and during his visit had run across an old man and wife

Apostle Mamby arose to meet her.

who were both verging on senility. They had vague ideas of the necessity of embracing some sort of religion before the oil in the lamp of life gave out entirely, and taking advantage of their senescence, Mamby had endeavored to persuade them to dispose of their belongings, add the cash to their accumulated store and pass the remainder of their days in the ineffable tranquility of the new Zion. The unsuspicious old couple were disposed to act upon this advice, and for that reason Mamby wanted to drive over and complete the arrangements, getting back in time to attend to his business in Shelbyville.

There was not much of his time when the faithful apostle was not at work for his master.

Chapter VII
In the Toils

WHEN CLARA LEFT THE apostle she walked back home as briskly as she had gone to meet him, giving no heed to anyone as she went along. As she neared her home Arthur passed her on the opposite side of the street. She did not seem to see him and he wondered at it. He noticed she was walking as though intent on reaching home as quickly as possible, and therefore determined not to accost her; nevertheless, he was surprised that she did not even look in his direction and exchange the customary salutations. He passed on, a trifle nettled, to his destination, and she to her home.

It takes a very small matter sometimes to awaken the suspicious of a lover. It is difficult to eliminate from the purest quality of love every trace of jealousy. The most diminutive spark will oftentimes produce a conflagration in the human breast, searing the heart perhaps beyond the alleviation that the balm of affection should afford. The more Arthur permitted himself to cogitate upon the strange action of Clara in passing him upon the narrow village street without a sign of recognition, the more he became persuaded that something was wrong. Such a thing was unprecedented, and consequently inexplicable. And from the very fact that he could conceive of no reason or motive to prompt or warrant such action, the occurrence soon resolved itself into something of the nature of a mystery, and a mystery where love is concerned soon becomes a torture; and when, shortly after the noon hour, he found his torture becoming unendurable, he resolved to go and see Clara. He could not convince himself that she might merely have been indulging a fit of abstraction—a condition into which all people fall occasionally—and with her mind thus preoccupied had for the nonce permitted her accepted lover to pass within a few feet of her. No; he would have to go and see her—not that he intended to broach this particular circumstance, unless in a jocular way, because, in the event of every thing being just as it should be, he did not want her to fancy for a moment that his confidence in her devotion was anything but unbounded.

Clara had barely reached her home again when she awoke from her mesmeric condition with a start. She glanced quickly and uneasily about the room, uncertain that she was in possession of her faculties or that she was really where she seemed to be. But there could be no mistake. There she was in the home kitchen, where every article upon which her eyes rested was as familiar as the face of her loved mother, whom she heard moving about in an adjoining room. As Clara had gone and returned by the kitchen door, that being nearest the road she felt impelled to take, her short absence from the house was not observed.

"I must have slept miserably indeed last night," said the girl to herself, "when I actually stand here in the kitchen at my work and go to sleep. And such a dream as I had! I thought I was transported as though by magic to a lonely grove where Apostle Mamby was waiting for me. I was terribly frightened at first, and then we had such a pleasant talk on religious matters. I am in favor with the Lord, he said, and he would have me by his side in his terrestrial abode and give me perfect tranquility all my days. And I promised the apostle to pray for direction and guidance, that the Lord might tell me what to do. Dear, such a dream! All the result of that talk we had last night. I will ask for direction in my prayers this evening and perhaps my mind will become clearer. I also promised in my dream to say nothing to any one. I will not speak of it. They would laugh at me—or send for the doctor."

Thus the girl's thoughts ran along all the forenoon, and when Arthur came soon after dinner she felt not only the sensations of joy that usually mark the near approach of the object of one's affections, but believed his presence would divert her thoughts from the groove in which they had been running all day with an effect that was beginning to depress her spirits.

As Arthur drew near she turned to him with the old; happy, innocent look of joyous welcome that can be counterfeited by no other feeling than that of the genuine love that springs spontaneously from the heart. That look was sufficient for Arthur. It dispelled the mists of dread that had chilled his manly heart, and rolled back every cloud of jealousy that for a brief time obscured the ineffable loveliness and purity of the sweet creature he almost worshiped.

"How is my little girl feeling to-day?" he asked, as he went forward and lovingly kissed her willing lips.

"Very well, Arthur dear," she replied; "but hardly as well as usual."

"And what distresses my sweetheart?"

"I think nothing more than that I didn't sleep very well last night."

"I am not surprised," he said, speaking more seriously, "after what you heard from that man. I am not a very devout Christian, I know, and have no right to direct in that particular branch of duty, but if I were a consistent member of our little church over there, or of any other orthodox church, for that matter, I am afraid I should be inclined to pronounce that man—apostle, as he calls himself—either an artful knave or a consummate fool."

"O, Arthur!" she cried, with a look of mingled surprise and pain; "please do not speak like that. I do not believe a man can talk so earnestly and beautifully about holy things without being deeply imbued with religious feeling."

"But, child," argued Arthur, "think for a moment of the very ridiculousness of his preposterous claims, and especially his asseverations in respect to the vainglorious pretensions of this person whom he calls the Messiah. Why, such rodomontade should not be expected to emanate from any one outside of a madhouse."

"Arthur, dear, you should not speak like that. He seemed such a good man; and he talked so intelligently on every subject, and quoted Scripture in support of every proposition he laid down."

"Undoubtedly he did; but the dark-visaged personage with the cloven hoofs is also credited with being able to do the same thing with remarkable facility. I am willing to admit that I found him well informed, instructive and entertaining on all topics outside of this one. Doubtless he is a person of education and acumen, and given to deep meditation on matters of import, and I will be charitable enough to concede that he is honest in his convictions; but on this one question of religion, as you will understand yourself when you turn on the clear light of common sense, he is simply a monomaniac—harmless enough, I apprehend, nevertheless at variance with his wits when in the realm of religion. I hope, dear, you have not let him vex your mind with his hallucinations?"

"I confess I have been deeply impressed by his conversation, and hardly know what to make of it. Father and mother seemed to think much of it as well."

"Perhaps they did. Your father and mother, however, have well grounded religious convictions. They are willing to be entertained by the eloquence of this agent, and may perhaps feel forced to compliment his unwavering devotion and allegiance to his master, but their belief, I opine, is not liable to be influenced by every new light that flits through the neighborhood of Shelbyville, like the luminous flash of a firefly, and is then lost in the darkness of night or paled into insignificance by the reflected light of nineteen centuries ago; and more especially is this true when such improbable doctrines and monstrous pretensions are presented for the serious contemplation of a devout mind. I have no other reasonable theory to advance for this man's belief, allowing him all sincerity, than that I have already given, namely, that he is a monomaniac."

"Maybe you are right, Arthur," said the girl, unable to combat the logic of his remarks.

"I think I am, dear; and I hope you will dismiss him and his absurdities from your mind. Think no more of him henceforth. I saw him leave the village before noon, and you will probably never see or hear of him again. Just take the besom of reason and broom the last vestige of this religious litter from your mind; then, with a good night's sleep, my little sweetheart will be herself again, and, when I see that, you know how pleased I will be."

He patted her cheek affectionately with the closing sentence, and she, looking up into his face with a sweet, trustful smile, replied:

"I am sure you right, Arthur, as you always are, and I will do as you wish."

"Of course you will. My little girl has moral stamina and mental strength as well as grace and sweetness and devotion, and I know her thoughts, like a well-tempered sword blade, will not remain warped when the restraining cause has been removed. I must now go to work," he added, looking at his watch. "I should have postponed my visit until evening, but I wanted to talk to you, and—well, I just couldn't stay away, that's all."

And then he kissed her good-bye and walked away with his mind at rest; and she, too, left materially strengthened by her conversation with her strong, manly, sensible lover. It is true she could not exclude the apostle entirely from her mind, but she was not perplexed and worried as before. Could she have been left free from his baneful influence for a few days, he and his Messiah would have passed out of her mind.

What of the apostle during this time?

Six miles is not much of a drive ordinarily over good roads, though there were no extra good roads around the neighborhood of Shelbyville, the mountainous face of the country being against the people in this particular. Still, the highways were passable, and it was the season of the year when roads are in their best condition, albeit insufferably dusty. However, Mamby soon reached the home of Farmer Whitcomb and his wife, the aged couple whom he expected to make the victims of his avaricious machinations.

It is some satisfaction at least to note that here he met with an unexpected and grievous disappointment. The simple old couple, contrary to Mamby's instructions, had mentioned his plan to a casual visitor; the visitor, in turn, had mentioned it to a distant relative of the old people—who, by the way, had "expectations"—and he, becoming suspicious, at once instituted an inquisition. The result was that the relative, and several of his neighboring friends with whom he discussed the affair, were seriously minded, when the apostle again made his appearance, to make the occasion a memorable one by treating him to a short but interesting excursion, in which the emissary of the Messiah, astride of one of the numerous rails to be found in the neighborhood, would be the most entertaining feature. When Mamby reached the house he found a lusty man present with the aged couple—a sort of bucolic Cerberus upon whom the expenditure of a week of apostolic eloquence would have had no perceptible effect. This individual quickly intimated to Mamby the pleasing prospect before him if he would kindly wait until the men could get together; but the apostle, who, to use a vulgarism, had "been there before," figuratively folded his sacerdotal robes, laid away his Uriah Heap humility, and fairly startled the game along the route as he left the Whitcomb domain behind.

It was not his purpose to go back to Shelbyville until after dark. A number had seen him leave, and he wanted the impression to prevail that he had left for good. He had expected to spend the time with the Whitcombs, but his plans there had woefully miscarried. His only recourse was to drive on to some new field, where he might work advantageously until the shades of night had fallen. He had no fear of being followed, for he knew that all that was wanted by the friends of the old couple was to effectually frighten him from the neighborhood. He was willing to admit they had succeeded in doing that, but perhaps another of the apostles could successfully work the mine he had discovered, to the glory of the word and the material benefit of the heavenly exchequer.

Shortly before eleven o'clock that night a carriage was driven cautiously to a point near the residence of the McCoys. The streets were deserted and every house apparently shrouded in darkness. The pale moon, occasionally emerging from behind the succession of sweeping clouds that passed across the face of the stelliferous vault, afforded the solitary occupant of the vehicle, secreted in the friendly shadow of a building, an opportunity of watching the length of the street in either direction, and he kept no careless vigil.

Presently a slight female figure, clad as though prepared for a journey, came noiselessly toward the carriage. In a moment the occupant had helped her in, arranged the light robes and started quietly away.

There were not, perhaps, three other persons awake in Shelbyville when the apostle and Clara rode down the village street and disappeared in the shadows of the overhanging cliffs and trees that fringed the sinuous roadway.

Chapter VIII
A Stern Chase

WE HAVE ALREADY BEEN informed, in the pathetic tale which the landlady of the tavern on the cliffs related to William Hatfield, of the overwhelming distress that wrung the hearts of the wretched parents when they found the daughter upon whom they doted, the treasure and joy of their household, had gone from them. We have seen, also, that the mystery which enveloped her going had only deepened with the passing years, and that, when every effort to find trace of her had proven futile, they resigned themselves to their grief, firm in the belief, which was shared by the people of the village and neighborhood, that their innocent and unfortunate daughter would come to them no more. Undoubtedly, her sensitive mind affected by brooding upon the exciting religious ideas which the stranger agent inculcated, she had thrown herself into the dark waters of the river and was carried away from their sight forever on earth. It is true nothing was ever found to substantiate this belief; nevertheless it was accepted by the heartbroken parents and sympathizing friends as the only possible explanation.

There was one, however, who questioned this generally accepted theory of Clara's remarkable disappearance. That one was Arthur Fitzroy, her promised husband. He was so nearly crazed by his grief he scarcely knew what he was doing or saying at times; and thus, while all who knew him pitied him and commiserated his distress, they gave little heed to his suggestions during the search for the lovely girl who had a place in all their hearts. His preconception of the character of the apostle led him to believe that person in some way concerned in the terrible affair. Others thought differently, because the agent had been seen to leave the village eight or ten hours before Clara could have gone from her home. Arthur had a wider range of knowledge than most of those around him. The idea of mesmeric influence occurred to him the first day of his sweetheart's disappearance, but he mentioned his thoughts to no one, because he well knew that, when the grief of the community had subsided, he would be made the butt for the gibes of the thoughtless, and heartless were he to advance such an idea. After associating the apostle with the disappearance of Clara for some time, the idea took such complete possession of him that no amount of argument could have convinced him that the one he loved so tenderly had perished in the manner they all believed. Indeed, he felt within himself that the sweet girl had been reserved for a condition worse than death, and he registered a vow that, whatever others might say or think, he would search for her until he secured something more tangible than the unsupported belief that she had taken her life in a moment of mental aberration. He had called Mamby a monomaniac on the subject of religion. His friend, if cognizant of his innermost thoughts, would have similarly characterized him in his adherence to the idea of mesmeric influence.

Nevertheless, in spite of his caution, when he took his departure from Shelbyville, without intimating even to his parents where he was going, it was generally agreed that his mind, too, had become affected by the crushing and unexpected blow which had come to him in the loss of the cherished object of his devotion. In this, perhaps, people were in a measure correct, though knowing nothing of the source of the hope that animated him. When his absence was protracted into years, the wiseacres shook their dignified heads knowingly and said: "I told you so; the poor young man went clear daft over his unfortunate love affair. He will probably wander aimlessly around the world as long as he lives."

Had Arthur not been so deeply concerned himself, or had he started on this mission on some one else's account than his own, so that his mind could have been divorced from the distress which constantly oppressed him and blunted the natural keenness of his perceptions, he would probably have overtaken the object of his search in a short time.

In the cool of the evening one day be quietly stole out of the village, taking the same road covered by the apostle and Clara on the last eventful night the girl's friends had seen her. It was one of the only two carriage roads by which egress could be had from the village. He walked with a long, swinging stride that carried him rapidly over the ground, and in a trifle over three hours he reached the nearest railway station, distant from Selbyville some twelve miles. He found there was no train until two o'clock in the morning, so that there was nothing for him to do but to wait until that time—nearly three hours and a half.

The little station house was deserted by all except the night operator, who did not evince a very strong disposition to be sociable. Most of the time he sat in an arm-chair before the ever-clicking instruments, alternately smoking and dozing. Arthur did not mind the man's taciturnity, for of late he preferred to be alone with the somber thoughts that continually followed him.

After a while, however, a thought occurred to him, and he arose from the hard depot bench upon which he had been partially reclining.

Going over to the window of the little compartment, which was both ticket office and operating room, he said to the silent occupant of the arm-chair:

"By the way. May I inquire which way the two o'clock train goes—east or west?"

The operator leisurely sent several whiffs of blue smoke circling into the air before he deigned to notice the question, and then he turned his head slowly and, looking curiously at the inquirer, replied:

"Both ways."

"How is that? I don't exactly understand what you mean," said Arthur, wondering if he wouldn't better go and sit down until the operator called him to receive his answer.

But the operator, much to his surprise, only waited a moment this time before he replied:

"Number one and number six pass here, one going east and the other going west. Which way do you want to go?"

"I don't know," said Arthur, hesitatingly.

"Well, you better make your mind up on that point. How do you expect me to sell you a ticket if you don't know where you want to go?"

"I have not yet made up my mind," Arthur quietly responded.

"Trying to get away from somebody?" queried the operator, suspiciously.

"No; trying to catch up with some one."

"That's different. Who'd you like to catch?"

"I am in search of a missing young lady, whose friends are very much distressed because of her absence."

"Yes; some of 'em get those streak once in a while, and most of 'em are glad to get back. How long since this girl skipped?"

"She has been missing about three weeks."

"Any one go with her?"

"No one as far as known. Privately, however, I suspect that a man accompanied her."

"Sure thing! She wouldn't go far unless there was a man concerned in it."

This remark of the operator seemed brutal to Arthur in connection with the pure girl he knew Clara to be, but he restrained a rising inclination to answer sharply and quietly said:

"You couldn't give me any information, I suppose, that would aid me in this search?"

"Well, I don't know," replied the other slowly. "Is there anything in it?"

"Is there anything in it?"

"There will certainly be something in it for you," replied Arthur, "if through your instrumentality the whereabouts of the young lady is discovered. I will undertake to see that you are not forgotten. Finding her, or even finding that she is alive, means much more than you have any idea of. If you can aid me, do so."

"Well," drawled the operator, "I've been thinking some since you started talking. It's only once in a while that any one takes the early morning train here either way, so that I don't get mixed on those who do go. You see, these are both limited trains and wouldn't stop here at all, only it's their passing point. When one train or the other is late, and they pass somewhere else, neither of them stops here."

"Yes; I understand."

"Well, along about three weeks ago a man and woman got on here going east—the last passengers I had for either of those trains, unless you are going to be one. He drove up here in buggy along about one o'clock and asked if the train east was on time and would stop here. I told him it would stop, and he said he would drive to the livery barn and leave his rig and be back and get tickets for himself and sister."

"And he came back?" asked Arthur, with growing interest.

"Yes; he and the lady came back in a few minutes and bought tickets through to Kansas City."

"Can you describe either of them?"

"I can't tell anything about the lady, because she wore a veil and I didn't hear her speak during the whole time they were waiting. I took this armchair out for her and she sat down in it and seemed to go to sleep. She was slight built and I should judge a good deal younger than the man."

"And the man; what was he like?"

"He was a kind o' sharp looking chap—appeared as though he might have been a preacher."

"Did he wear a full black beard?"

"Yes; and black felt hat."

"And had small, meek looking eyes and generally subdued deportment?"

"Just what I was going to say. The fellow was as meek as Moses, and had a soft, smooth way of talking, kind o' out of the ordinary, that makes a man noticed."

"How old would you judge him to be?"

"O, 'long about forty on forty-five."

Great beads of perspiration were rolling down Arthur's face, and it was with extreme difficulty he could restrain himself from breaking out in a flood of invective against the villainous agent. He turned from the office window to hide his agitation and immediately began to pace the floor of the waiting room like a caged tiger. The operator rose from his chair, laid down his pipe, and, opening the office door, stood and looked at Arthur for some moments with surprise upon his features. Finally he ventured to remark, without leaving his post at the door:

"Must be you recognize the description?"

"I do," said Arthur, in a hoarse voice, pausing in his walk and attempting to control himself.

"Who was he?" asked the operator, after a moment's hesitation, during which time he sharply scrutinized Arthur's face.

"He was," replied Arthur, with an extraordinary effort to speak calmly. "what he still is—the most consummate and diabolical scoundrel it has ever been my misfortune to meet. I shall have to exercise marvelous power of restriction if I do not kill him when we meet."

The operator drew back, as though he would retreat into his office and bolt the door if there was any hostile demonstration on the part of the other. Arthur, observing that he had startled the man by his vehemence, said:

"There; you needn't be afraid of me. I am not as dangerous as my language would imply. If you were acquainted with the circumstances you would understand my perturbation. I did not know where I wanted to go when I came here, but on the strength of what information you have given me, I, too, will take a ticket for Kansas City."

"All right," said the operator, walking back into his office; "you shall have it. But perhaps this sanctimonious chap was only working a bluff when he bought tickets to Kansas City. He may have changed his route before he got half way there."

"What you say may be true," replied Arthur; "but I can only start as he started and trust to judicious inquiry for further information. Perhaps the conductor or train men will remember these passengers for the same reason that you do and be able to tell me something of their subsequent movements. I am hopeful that I will gain some additional information in this way."

"That's so!" replied the operator.

"Now that I've got my ticket," continued Arthur, as he carefully placed the long slip of paper in his pocket, "perhaps you could find out just how the train east is—if on time or late. I would like to run over to the livery barn and make some further inquiries before I leave."

"I'll ask," replied the operator, whose sympathy with the stranger, coupled with the possibility of there being "something in it," made him quite accommodating.

There was an increased clicking of instruments for a few moments and then the operator arose and said:

"Both trains are reported on time."

Arthur then started for the livery barn with the hope of gleaning something further in that direction. He realized that he would probably have to awaken a sleepy, and therefore grumpy, attendant: but it could not be helped; he must know all he could possibly learn before he left for Kansas City, and the only way to get information was to seek it where it was most likely to be found.

The idea that had invaded his mind the very first day of Clara's absence, and clung to him during the succeeding three weeks, now became a certainty. He was as sure as he was that he lived, since his talk with the operator, that the man and woman who boarded the early morning train three weeks ago for Kansas City were the agent and Clara. And he was just as thoroughly convinced that mesmeric influence had been employed to compass her abduction. Had he confided his misgivings to any ordinarily sensible citizen he would probably have been set down as a fit subject for at least friendly care and restriction; but he felt he was right, and the developments of the night had eliminated the last shred of doubt from his mind.

In a short time he returned to the station from the livery barn, having pursued his inquiries with less difficulty than he anticipated. The visit was not without results. The somnolent attendant, when aroused and brought thoroughly to his senses by means of a silver dollar rubbed carefully on the palm of his hand, recollected perfectly receiving a rig from a man, whose description agreed with that of Mamby, about three weeks before. The man was an agent, and engaged the rig for a week, depositing the requisite security before he took it from the barn. It was returned a day before the stipulated time, the agent stating he had found business unsatisfactory and would try his fortunes in some other part of the country where ready money was more abundant. There was no lady with the agent when be returned the horse and carriage, nor was there any one with him when he engaged the rig. In fact the barn attendant was sure the agent was alone when he left the village on his first arrival, for he saw him, after he procured the carriage, drive to the only hotel in the place, put his supplies in the vehicle, and drive north along the Shelbyville road. If there as a lady with him when he returned the rig, he must have left her at the station or somewhere else, for the attendant had not seen her. As the hotel was not kept open after ten or eleven o'clock at night, Arthur concluded that the apostle had stood his victim in some doorway of the deserted street while he disposed of the horse and carriage and prepared to return to the station.

"Here's a dollar to buy cigars with," said Arthur to the operator on his return. "You have given me very valuable information, and if the young lady for whom I am seeking is found, you will be remembered in a way that will be entirely satisfactory to you."

"All right," said the other, as he pocketed the dollar; "don't be afraid to call on me if I can do anything to help you."

"My name is Arthur Fitzroy, and if you should receive a telegram here from me for anyone in Shelbyville, do you suppose you could get it there?"

"Yes; by hiring a livery rig and some one to drive over with it. That's the way I had to do with a message for Dr. Shannon not long ago."

"Very well; if I send one hasten it to its destination as fast as you can."

"Sure! Here's your train. Good luck to you, and don't forget your most obedient servant, George Brooks."

In a few moments Arthur was speeding along on his way to Kansas City.

Chapter IX
The Lord's Will Be Done

CLARA WAS NOT A little surprised, when she again awoke to consciousness, to find herself amid altogether strange surroundings. Her hat, gloves and other articles had been removed and she was reclining comfortably on an easy couch. A short distance from her sat a woman of perhaps thirty years of age, swaying slowly back and forth in a Sleepy Hollow rocker and engaged in some species of feminine handicraft. The room was neatly but not expensively furnished. There were several pictures, mostly religious, upon the walls. One picture, hung directly opposite where Clara lay, attracted her attention. She recognized in it a reproduction of the face of the Savior, as she had seen it represented time and again, except that the halo that is usually made to surround the face of the "Man of Sorrows" was omitted. She afterwards learned that it was a very correct and fairly well executed painting of the Messiah, George Jacob Schweinfurth. It set her thinking at once, bringing to mind a train of thoughts that embraced the exciting experiences of the last four days. She remembered the dream which made her seem in the grove with the apostle, and his conversation returned with impressive distinctness to her mind: "The Lord can take you into his presence in the twinkling of an eye." Had he brought her here?

Presently she made a movement which attracted the attention of the woman sitting near her, when, seeing she had awakened, went to her couch and kindly said:

"How do you feel, sister? You have had a long and deep sleep. Are you not refreshed?"

Encouraged by kindly tone of the woman, Clara answered:

"I am feeling very well, thank you. But everything is so strange. I do not know where I am, and I cannot imagine how I came to be here. You will tell me, will you not?"

"Yes, sister; you are in the house of the Lord, far away from your home. He has called you to go to him. Are you not pleased to answer the summons?"

"It is not for me to say," replied Clara. "When the Lord calls it is mandatory. I have ever been taught to resign myself to the Lord's will."

"That is very proper instruction. However, you err, sister, in thinking the Lord is disposed to enforce your presence among the pure ones in the holy house of Zion. His mandates, it is true, cannot be evaded. But his call is not always a mandate. He wins by love, not by force. He is calling all the time to all the world to come unto him, his arms extended to receive and welcome the humble and the contrite heart; but how many, O, how many! utterly refuse to hear his pleading voice. Still the stubbornness of the world does not incite his wrath, else he would destroy it, but he is grieved that the fallen creatures to whom he has given life, endued with intelligence and domination over even the forces of nature and endowed with the inspiriting hope of a blest immortality, should set at naught his wholesome laws, violate his divine commands, deride his holy name, and utterly refuse to bend the knee in penitence and receive his blessing. Notwithstanding this, he still knocks without at their hearts, willing to overlook the past if the erring one will but become repentant and tread the path of righteousness. His call to you, dear sister, has been an exceptional one. You are divinely favored. The Lord desires to have you near him, to make you pure and holy and place you beyond the pale of sin even while on earth. The acceptance of this proffered grace remains with yourself."

"But what of my dear parents? What will they think of my absence?"

"You must dismiss them from your mind. They are merely earthly parents. The Lord is your heavenly parent; his love transcends theirs, even as his power and knowledge surpasses that of the puerile creatures whom he could destroy with a breath. Perhaps it may please him to call your parents as well. They are devout people and will be rewarded in the life to come. If he finds they may be made instrumental in advancing his kingdom he will call them, even as he has called you."

"The Lord's will be done!" cried Clara. "Henceforth it will be my delight to be the humble instrument of his will."

"That is right, dear sister; the Lord would not have brought you here had he not known how your heart was inclined. He does not take those to his side who do not love him. Would you like to rise and partake of some refreshment?"

"I believe I would," Clara answered.

At this moment the door opened and a man of perhaps sixty, of dignified demeanor, entered the room, leading by the hand a bright little boy of about three years of age. Clara was introduced to the old man as the head of this branch of the earthly heaven. Apostle Cummings had formerly been a Congregational minister, but the social and religions condition of that denomination did not seem to him akin with the divine spirit. He met the Messiah, was impressed with his earnestness and purity and the divinity that seemed to hedge him around. He soon became a devoted and trusted apostle, finally being placed where we find him, in charge of one of the various branches of the Church Triumphant. The child he led belonged to the woman with whom Clara had been talking. She was only known by her communal name, Amelia. Before becoming a convert to the new faith she was Mary Sandow, the daughter of a prosperous tradesman in a small Minnesota city. She heard Schweinfurth preach several times, became infatuated with him and his religious ideas, and ultimately left her home and friends to follow him through the reminder of her life. For her exceeding faith she was permitted to pass through an ordeal, hereinafter described, that rendered her pure and sinless. Afterward she was honored of the Messiah by being made the mother of the beautiful child which had just entered the room with Apostle Cummings, and the lad having no paternal progenitor or more tangible than the Holy Ghost. Amelia, having been rendered absolutely perfect and sinless, was incapacitated for wrong doing; and this child and other children, ostensibly conceived by the Holy Ghost, differed materially from the born offspring of the world, some of whom were brought to heaven and its branches with their parents in that they were born without sin and were therefore sinless. When children thus conceived reached a certain age they were excluded from association with those conceived in the usual sinful was in wedlock—not that marriage was not sanctioned by the Messiah, for it was regarded by the sect in a purely scriptural light and made binding beyond the possibility of divorce; but it was taught by Schweinfurth, and firmly believed by all his followers, that the material emanations of the holy spirit in the form of innocent and undefiled childhood were far too scared for indiscriminate commingling with the progeny of the flesh.

This peculiar phase of their belief was not imparted to Clara until she had been among the redeemed for upwards of a fortnight; and, in spite of her faith and firm desire to believe fully and do without a murmur all that was required of her, she found this idea unutterably repellent. It is an abhorrent doctrine to the Christian reared in orthodoxy, being even more detestable than the polygamous teaching of the Mormons and some of the religions whose inception was lost in the dust of ages before the Nazarene was born, and which still have multitudes of devotees. Clara had been nurtured in an evangelical church, and every reader who has been similarly reared will have some appreciation of the profundity of faith in the new Messiah required to sweep aside the repugnance which the bare thought of this tenet must engender, and in its stead bring a pertinacious adherence to a diametrically opposite principle taught from childhood's earliest hour of receptive intelligence. When ideas that are rendered inherent can be so perverted to fit such radically opposite dogmas it is no marvel that a faith once established in the divinity of this professed Messiah remains unshaken until the end.

Usually an acknowledgment of firm adherence to this and other peculiarities of the belief of this sect, but of this especially, is a prerequisite to admission to the communal life of these people. In this instance, however, after acquainting Schweinfurth with all the circumstances, it was decided to make an exception; and therefore, after Clara had been at the branch home nearly three weeks, during which time she became acquainted with the dozen or more inmates, all of whom treated her with the greatest consideration and kindness, she was transferred to the central community, or Zion, where the Messiah presided in person, the aged and kindly Apostle Cummings accompanying her. It was believed the benignity and persuasiveness of Schweinfurth would in a short time bring conviction to her heart and make her a valuable member of the household in more than one regard. She interposed no objection; in fact, she was rather flattered by the prospect of being brought face to face with the man without sin, in whose personality reposed the divine attributes she had been taught to venerate and love.

Two days after Clara left Kansas City, Arthur Fitzroy reached there.

He made the journey without mishap, being immeasurably gratified to find the conductor of the train he set out with the same with whom Clara and Mamby rode in their flight from Shelbyville. The conductor remembered the couple, not alone from the unusual circumstances of their having taken the train at the little way station, but because the lady seemed to be strangely indisposed, and was the constant care of her companion. It was necessary to change cars twice during the course of the trip to Kansas City, and the conductor was certain when the two left his train they took the train which would carry them in the direction they appeared to be traveling. Further than that he could not say. Arthur heard nothing more of them after that, but he felt reasonably certain they had gone to the place for which the apostle purchased tickets. Therefore he followed—two days too late. Had he reached the city before Clara was transferred it is possible this recital might have been materially shortened.

Now that he was in Kansas City, what was he going to do? Possibly the wisest course would be to call in the assistance of the authorities. However, it would do no harm to make a few chance inquiries as he went along. Whom had he better accost? Anybody and everybody who looked well enough disposed to strangers to answer questions civilly. He sauntered leisurely along the street, passing a hundred persons before he saw one to whom he cared to address himself. This was a pleasant looking, elderly man, who seemed to be in no particular hurry. Stepping modestly in front of him, Arthur said:

"Good afternoon, sir."

"Good afternoon," responded the stranger, in a kindly tone that at once gave Arthur courage to proceed.

"I am a total stranger, never having been in the city before, and I make bold to ask you, as you do not appear to be hurried, if you will kindly spare me a moment or two for some inquiries?"

Arthur spoke with a grave courtesy that was rather uncommon in Kansas City, and which at once proclaimed him a stranger. The other was attracted to him at once and quickly responded.

"Cheerfully, sir—cheerfully."

"Do you know anything, or have you heard anything, of a new Messiah?"

The man glanced at Arthur critically and slightly changed countenance.

"New what?"

"New Messiah—a person who claims to be Christ risen again from the dead."

"Oh! Why, yes; the country's full of such infernal humbugs—anti-Christs, I call them. I hope you have not had your head turned by such nonsense, my young friend?"

"I am glad to say I have not, but I fear a very dear friend of mine has."

"A young woman, I expect?"

"Yes, sir."

"I knew it, blast them!" said the man, a mighty wrath plainly visible in his face. Calming himself somewhat he continued: "I can probably give you some information, and incidentally some advice, though I doubt if either will benefit you much."

"I shall be thankful for any aid you can give me," said Arthur, with a grateful look.

"Well, I'll give you all I can. Do you know which of these humbugs is responsible for alluring your misguided friend? We did have three such institutions here at one time, but if I am not mistaken there is at least one, if not two, less now. Anyway they were all streams from fountains of iniquity that have their sources elsewhere. I think, in all likelihood, the man you are after is George Jacob Schweinfurth, the king rascal of them all. His headquarters are at Rockford, Illinois, but he has a branch establishment here which I guess he quietly visits once in a while."

"Does he come here at stated times to meet converts, or are the new ones taken directly to his headquarters?"

"I'm not quite sure. My opinion is though, that he doesn't come here very often, and when he does he comes like a thief in the night. Not long ago a number of indignant citizens—I wish I'd been with them—hearing of his presence in the city and knowing something of his infernal work, threatened to mob him, and he had to get out of the city in a hurry. If he comes now he does so surreptitiously. For this reason I think new converts are taken directly to headquarters. I believe only those firm in the faith are assigned to the branches, though I am not just certain how the business is conducted. How long since this person left her home?

"About three weeks."

"Then I presume she is at Rockford instead of here."

"I may inquire at the branch here," suggested Arthur, desiring to leave no stone unturned in his search.

"Yes; you may inquire here and inquire there, and much good will it do you. When this contemptible pretender gets man or woman in his control that's the last of them; he keeps them."

"Is there no legal remedy?"

"There would be if the victims were detained. But he generally fixes them so they want to stay, and there you are. I know something about it, for I have had some experience with these people."

"You!" exclaimed Arthur in wonder.

"Yes, I."

"I am surprised."

"I will tell you, young man. I am a physician—Dr. Wilkie. Two years ago I had a fine practice in a growing city not far from here. My wife got in with this gang of devils, and I was obliged to rent my house, take my children and wife and go into a distant part of the country to get away from them and keep my wife from going to their insane retreat. I had to leave my practice and was gone a whole year. It cost me fifteen hundred dollars, besides the loss of my time. When I returned with my family they stood ready to grab my wife, and she then decided she would not leave them, even though the family went to destruction. Then my wrath was up, and I determined to protect my home and children if it cost me my life, and to save my wife from such a damnable heresy if it lay in my power. I told them to keep away from my house; that if one of them should come within my door I would thrash him within an inch of his life. They simply remarked that they were God's chosen people, and if I laid my hands on one of them, God would paralyze me. I said I

An apostle's warm reception.

would take the chance. So in a few days the king apostle came again. I had no word with him, but simply carried out my promise. I thrashed him thoroughly and threw him out of my house, and to this day I have not seen or heard of him since."

"What was the result?" asked Arthur.

"The result was, my wife's faith was shaken, as I was not paralyzed, and I feel to-day that I am able to thrash a ten acre lot full of the same kind of people, old as I am. On the other hand, if I was paid to-day ten thousand dollars for the loss of time and money expended to save my wife, who is much younger than I am, from destruction, I would not be half paid."

"My dear sir," said Arthur, "let me congratulate you that you got off so well. You at least saved your wife. I am beginning to understand what this business means. I am glad I spoke to you, for you will be able to advise me intelligently."

"As I said before," continued the doctor, "I can give you some advice as well as some information, though I do not know how much either will avail you. If you will do me the honor to walk around to my office we will sit down quietly and talk the thing over. I see my earnest talk is already attracting attention."

"I will be glad to go with you," Arthur answered, and the two started for the doctor's office.

Arthur believed he was making extraordinary progress and would soon succeed in rescuing his darling from the hands of the ruthless abductors and despoilers whose emissary had brought so much sorrow to Shelbyville. But he did not know what he had to contend with. There were many disappointments yet in store for him. However, before the doctor set him on his way to Rockford, he had a much clearer knowledge of the difficulties of the task before him.

Chapter X
The Law Invoked

"HERE WE ARE! TAKE a chair," said Dr. Wilkie, as he and Arthur reached the physician's office. "I've got an excellent brand of cigars here, which we will sample before I begin my talk."

"I do not smoke, thank you," replied Arthur.

"You don't, eh? You're just as well off. I need the soothing influence of a weed when I talk about these disreputable scamps, and if you don't mind the smoke, I will light one."

"I do not object."

"Well," continued the doctor, having lit a cigar and taken a seat, "I do not believe I am much of a Christian; in fact, I know I am not; but I verily believe this man Schweinfurth is the counterpart of the evil one. His actions prove it. I know personally of fifteen families disrupted in the same manner in which he attempted to destroy mine, and they have no remedy at law or otherwise. In my case I think it was money they were after. If they had succeeded in their designs upon my wife she would have gone, perhaps, to one of their communities and all that she had or could possibly squeeze out of me would have gone into the capacious maw of the avaricious demon at the head of affairs. If she remained at home she would be required to pay tithes into the treasury of the Church of the Redeemed, and her share, which would have come out of me, would be no inconsiderable sum. I decidedly object to being assessed to support a harem of that kind, though it has cost me not a little to get out of it. The women he leads into that palatial heaven at Rockford, which he has built with the money of his dupes, serve little if any other purpose than to gratify the base passions of himself and apostles."

"What manner of man is this," asked Arthur, "who can commit these outrages with such impunity? Is there no law that will reach him."

"It seems not. An attempt was made by a lawmaker from this district, State Senator Hunter, to pass a law for his especial benefit, but for some reason it was never done—perhaps because it would have been declared unconstitutional. You see, it is one of the fundamental principles upon which our government is founded that all men shall be guaranteed full religious liberty, and, not only that, but protected in their natural right to worship according to the dictates of their consciences, or not to worship at all, if they feel so disposed. This is an inalienable right. These people put forth the claim of superlative devoutness, and no law can disturb them in their religious observances more than it can interfere with others, repulsive as their doctrines may be to the generality of mankind."

"But, doctor, if they engage in the reprehensible practices mentioned, surely some of the statutes for the preservation of public morals can be made to reach them?"

"Not in a hundred years. If you should swear every man, woman and child within the confines of Zion, on a stack of Bibles as high as that building across the road, they would all make emphatic asseveration that they never saw or heard of an immoral or improper act during their residence in the place."

"And still there must be—"

"Illegitimacy among the children, you mean?"

"Yes."

"Lots of it: but it is all saddled on the Holy Ghost, and that settles it. The mothers would adhere to this declaration were they put to the torture. No one has been found yet willing to give the Lord away who knew anything worth telling. There are varied degrees of felicity in the Schweinfurth heaven, just as there are in the heaven of Mr. Swedenborg, if you have ever read that gentleman's entertaining descriptions of his translation to glory and subsequent return to earth. There is no woman at Zion who has gone through the rigid course leading up to angelic perfection who is willing to impart any knowledge acquired during trying process. It is much like joining the Masons; the degrees will be given to you in their order, and those who want to know what happened to you will have to go through the same experience you did to make the discovery. The women thus honored are called angels; then there are those 'a little lower than the angels,' and so on till you get down to the scullery hands, most of whom have an abiding faith but vanishing beauty."

"This is all very astonishing," said Arthur. "Most of his dupes must come from the ranks of the ignorant and superstitious."

"There you are mistaken again. Most of those among his followers are people of learning and culture."

"How can he hold such people to these preposterous doctrines?"

"I am not prepared to say how he does it; but he does. He certainly has a most unaccountable influence over the minds of those with whom he comes in contact. The man who presides over the branch here is a person of education and excellent parts. He was an orthodox minister not long ago, and is a graduate of Yale College and Andover Theological Seminary."

"It is possible?"

"You now begin to understand, undoubtedly, what I meant when I said my information and advice would be of little avail. The young woman of whom you are in search has made up her mind to embrace their doctrines and become one of them, and if you should succeed in finding and gaining access to her, which latter task will be a matter of some difficulty to begin with, it will only be to find that she is not inclined to return to her home, and that no amount of persuasion will move her. You might have changed her mind before they secured absolute control of her, but now I sadly fear your errand will be a fruitless one."

"I think you are wrong there, Doctor. I do not believe she left her home of her own accord."

"Nonsense, my young friend! It is you who are mistaken. They never force or abduct victims. That would leave them amenable to law—a contingency they always fight shy of. She must have gone of her own volition."

"I still think, Doctor, with all deference to your knowledge of these people, that an extraordinary impellent agency was employed to sprite her away."

"That may be true, in a sense," replied the doctor. "They exert an undue and decidedly unwholesome influence on the minds of their victims when they so far impress them with their pernicious doctrines as to be able to drag them from family and friends. This voluptuary is an Upas tree in the moral vineyard, whose deadly exudations, carried to the four winds of heaven by his satanic branches, ycleped apostles, permeates with a subtle poison the surrounding atmosphere and saps the mental vigor of all who inhale its deadly though aromatic fumes. Of course his is clearly an impellent agency, but one of which the law can take no cognizance."

"I do not believe," said Arthur, in a hesitating way, "that you get my meaning yet."

"Well, what do you mean?"

"To speak plainly, Doctor, I think mesmeric influence was employed."

The doctor opened his eyes a little wider than usual and gave Arthur a quizzical look; but he simply said:

"Why?"

"Because I have known the young woman from childhood and have all along had a clear understanding of her disposition and idiosyncrasies. I have known that she possessed a mind devoutly inclined and was to a degree impressionable. It is true, also, she was influenced in a measure by the eloquence and earnestness with which the apostle who visited our neighborhood presented and maintained the principles enunciated by this sect, barring the feature of immaculate conception, which I am sure was not debated or even mentioned. Understanding this, which seems to me the most unfavorable aspect of the case I can truly present, I cannot reconcile myself to the belief that she was influenced to that extent that she was willing freely to desert her home and parents in the manner she did, leaving them a prey to the deepest agony and distress, and in an uncertainty as to her fate. They and the community have settled down to the belief that she wandered from her home in an unsettled condition of mind and was drowned—"

"Let them continue to believe that," interrupted the doctor. "It is the greatest kindness you can do them."

"I talked with her the day before her disappearance," continued Arthur, "upon these new ideas, and she certainly gave no indication of a purpose or desire to embrace the new faith. She parted from me saying she proposed to dismiss the whole matter from her mind as unworthy of further consideration."

"She may have intended to do this and yet found it impossible. Resolves do not always develop into deeds."

"Very true, Doctor. But I feel very positive in her case."

"Lovers, I suppose?" asked the doctor, succinctly.

"Yes."

"That's the trouble. Love is as blind as a bat in a blaze of sunlight."

"I acknowledge that, too, Doctor. However, I felt from the first day of her disappearance that the agency of mesmerism had been used upon her, though you are the first to whom I have mentioned it; knowing the idea would only bring upon me the ridicule and contumely of the unthinking and heartless. Because of this belief, when it was conceded by all others that the unfortunate girl had found death in the dark waters of the river, I left my home as stealthily as she did, to prosecute my search alone. My investigations have been rewarded by the almost certain discovery that she is not dead, though when I send such information home I will probably be set down as a victim of lunacy, consequent upon the loss of her I love, and be commiserated instead of being believed."

"Don't send it, then," said the doctor. "Let them think her dead. It would be better for her if she were."

"My belief in the power of animal magnetism has had a satisfactory result. Of course I do not expect this influence to be of much further aid to me in this search."

"Well, young man," said the doctor. "I have no desire to wage a discussion with you on the subject of mesmerism. I have given but superficial thought to the phenomena of animal magnetism. It is contrary to medical ethics for a 'regular' to dabble in such things, and I belong to the old school and am perhaps a little hidebound. While I am constrained to admit there is more in this occult power for good or evil than most physicians are willing to admit, I think there is, like the rate of speed of a railroad locomotive, a limit to its exercise. I am skeptical of the power of any man, physician or apostle, to compel, by the pure force of will, exercised at a considerable distance perhaps from the subject, a person to come into his presence in spite of herself, at any hour of the day or night, wherever the mesmerizer may be. It seems too absurd."

"Have you never witnessed the influence of the human will operating upon another?"

"I have seen such exhibitions given by charlatans. I know such a power does exist to a greater or less degree in various individuals; but it is only operative when they come in contact or are placed in juxtaposition—not at great distances apart. This I believe to be impossible. I would as soon expect to send a telegraphic message to Chicago or New York without the aid of a wire. However, we have not time to discuss this hidden science just now. What I wanted to say was this: A person lured from home and friends by this influence would probably not be truly converted, else no such influence would be necessary. If such force were employed the victim, on awakening from the mesmeric sleep, would still remain in the same condition of mind as before the sleep was induced. In that event the victim would be very liable to make trouble at the first opportunity. Of course"—and here the doctor paused a moment to get his thoughts together—"I am free to confess that a person predisposed to these peculiar doctrines, and yet not fully believing, could be hocus-pocused into this confounded heaven with a possibility of enforcing conviction afterward. Really, to obviate controversy if for no other reason, I will say there is practically no limit to the means which these imps of diabolis may employ to ensnare and reduce their victims, male and female."

"I, too, have no disposition for controversy," said Arthur. "I want to act rather than talk."

"What do you want to do?"

"I want first to go to this branch home."

The doctor mused for a moment and then said:

"Well, my young friend, let me assure you that you have my deepest sympathy, and if you are determined to visit this place I will go with you, though I am convinced it will be a wild goose chase."

"We may perhaps discover where she has been taken," suggested Arthur.

"Perhaps," replied the doctor, musingly.

He sat a full minute deliberating upon a proper course of procedure and then abruptly asked:

"Did this young lady take anything away from home that didn't belong to her?"

Arthur felt an indignant flush rising to his cheeks as he replied:

"Certainly not."

"You couldn't swear that she didn't?"

"I do not know what she took," Arthur answered, spiritedly; "but I do know that such an imputation does the young lady a gross injustice, and—"

"There, there, there!" interrupted the doctor, raising his hand to enforce the silence of the other. "You don't seem to understand. Let me tell you. If you and I go to this house as plain citizens in search of information we will not be in the reception-room five minutes before we receive a polite intimation that our room is preferable to our company. Now, if you can swear out a warrant for the arrest of this young woman on some petty charge we can then take an officer with us and search the home for her. Otherwise we may as well stay away. I know what I'm talking about."

A short parley then ensued. Arthur was not insensible of the force and reason of the doctor's argument, but it was no light for a scrupulous, conscientious man like him to make affidavit to a charge of that nature against anyone merely to serve an end, however laudable; but against her who was dearer to him than life itself was like rending his heart-strings. Finally, however, the arguments of the doctor prevailed.

A warrant for larceny of a gold watch and other jewelry was procured, and, accompanied by a grinning and highly amused constable, they started for the branch heaven.

After a while the doctor, irritated by the continued buffoonery of the officer, turned to him and said:

"You seem to be greatly amused by this expedition."

"I am," laughingly replied that worthy.

"I suppose you fancy my friend and myself a brace of precious fools, and that we are liable to have our labor for our pains on this trip."

"Right again; I think it is so much valuable time wasted."

"Well, what do you care, as long as you are paid for your time and trouble?"

"I don't care. In face, I am rather pleased at the prospect of meeting the angels. I'd like to meet them every day under the same circumstances."

"Well, you can amuse yourself all you please," said the doctor, calming down somewhat, "but I want you to make this search thorough. To tell the truth, I'm very much of the same opinion that you are."

"That's all right, Doc. We'll turn heaven inside out while we're at it, and if the girl's there we'll find her."

The party soon reached the auxiliary abode of the saints and obtained admission to the cozy reception-room without difficulty. Directly Amelia, with whom the reader already has a slight acquaintance, came into the room and greeted the visitors pleasantly. The doctor acted as spokesman. He said, speaking as calmly as he could:

"Madam, we are here in search of a young woman who came to this house some three weeks ago. Will you permit us to see her?"

The doctor did not really know that Clara had been there at all. He had hazarded a bold guess. Amelia quietly answered:

"There is no such person here. All the present inmates of the house have been here for months."

"Madam," replied the doctor, with fast rising anger, "we believe that woman to be still here, and we want her; do you understand?"

Amelia was unruffled by the doctor's ebullition of temper. She replied, even more mildly than before:

"I can only reply, sir, there is no such person here."

"Perhaps if I tell you that I do not believe you we will be permitted to look around the house for ourselves."

"It is not my fault, sir," the woman answered, "If you refuse to believe me. I am simply speaking the truth. On the other hand, this house is our home; while I am always desirous of obliging visitors, I cannot recognize the right you demand to invade the privacy of these premises. I fear I am compelled to refuse your request to look the house over."

"Very well, madam," said the now thoroughly aroused doctor; "we will search anyway. The officer here has a warrant for the arrest of this young woman, and if she is here we want her."

During this conversation Arthur stood a silent and somewhat amazed spectator of the proceedings. The constable, now feeling called upon to act, arose and presented the warrant to Amelia, with the remark:

"Perhaps you would like to see the document."

She took it from his hand and glanced at it critically. It was her first experience of the kind, but she was fully equal to the emergency. In a moment she handed it back to the officer and said, with her usual imperturbability:

"We have no wish to traverse the law. You may begin your search at your pleasure."

They did so, going over the house from cellar to garret, much to the astonishment of the several inmates, all of whom were found quietly and industriously engaged at their various avocations in different parts of the house. The whole household seemed to be moving along without the slightest friction, as though regulated by clock-work.

It is perhaps superfluous to say the search for Clara was fruitless. About that time she was making her debut at the main heaven.

Returning to the reception-room, Arthur courteously apologized to Amelia for the inconvenience and indignity to which they had subjected her, and then asked if she could not, for the sake of those who were weeping the loss of one dearer than life, give him an idea of where the young woman might be found. Amelia listened quietly and then replied:

"We, as the chosen people of God, have been subjected to all manner of persecution and abuse, which we have suffered and still suffer in silence, for the Lord's sake. Even now I am assured that this legal document you have presented brings a trumped-up charge against this young woman, made for the purpose of dragging her back into the ways of sin. God did send that young woman here a few days ago, and—"

"The devil sent her, you mean," cried the doctor in an outburst of uncontrollable anger.

"Perhaps so," answered Amelia, with undisturbed equanimity; "but the Lord will care for her. I do not object to telling you that our dear brother, Mr. Cummings, has taken the child to Mr. Schweinfurth, who will defend her from this defamation and preserve her from the enemies of her soul."

"Hell!" ejaculated the doctor, whose face was already purple: "let us get out of this."

He started for the door and the officer followed him. As Arthur turned to go Amelia said to him:

"Perhaps you better take your warrant to Mr. Schweinfurth. He understands these things better than I do."

There was a covert sneer in the woman's quiet remark that was not lost upon Arthur. But he was too astonished to say anything. Every development seemed to come to him in the nature of a revelation.

Directly the three were upon the street again, the constable apparently making an extraordinary effort to restrain himself from a cataclysm of laughter, with but partial success.

In a moment he turned to the doctor and said:

"What would I better do with this warrant, doctor?"

"Tear it up!" was the gruff reply.

Dr. Wilkie took Arthur to his home and kept him until after tea, giving him a great deal of valuable information in relation to the well nigh hopeless mission he had undertaken. Then in the evening he accompanied him to the depot and saw him safely on the train for Rockford.

Chapter XI
In Heaven

IN HEAVEN! WHAT A world of meaning in those two simple words to the zealous Christian who has labored unceasingly to deserve and achieve the promised reward of immortality. The sands of life are fast running out, the confined spirit, eager to wing its flight to an eternal abode, struggles to free itself from its earthly tenement, and the vitreous eyes no longer beam in fond recognition on the weeping friends gathered about the couch of the loved one, whose feet are soon to be laved in Jordan's rolling tide. But if the mortal vision is obscured forever, the penetrating eye of faith discerns the shining spires of the New Jerusalem, and welcomes with ineffable joy the deep, mysterious sleep of death as the vestibule to "mansions not made with hands." Happy the Christian who, falling "asleep in Jesus," is raised on the buoyant wings of victory by the hope of awakening "in heaven."

It is not possible, perhaps, for any but such an one to form a correct conception of the joy with which a Christian hope welcomes the closing period; but if death brings such exultant joy to the faithful, what sensations of exultation must animate the breast of one who can believe in the possibility of reaching the glories of heavenly tranquility without passing through the dark portals of death?

This was the joy to which Clara firmly believed she was destined, as she and Apostle Cummings pursued their journey to Rockford. Had she not believed she would not have gone. She was persuaded in her innermost heart that she had already begun a blissful tour of investigation into elysian fields, where she might wander untiringly along delightful paths to the sound of ravishing melody, and amid the soft perfumes of ten thousand sweet flowers.

Absurd, you say! So it is—amazingly ridiculous and irrational. But, poor girl, she was neither the first nor the last insentient one to nurse this alluring absurdity to her heart until it became an indissoluble part of existence.

The journey from Kansas City would have been more wearisome had not this hope and faith sustained her. She slept all the way when taken to Kansas City by Mamby—a mild mesmeric sleep from which she awoke refreshed and strengthened. Apostle Cummings was unable to exercise any degree of magnetic power had he desired. It was not necessary with Clara now, because she was as ready to go as he was to take her; but if she could have slept again as on the first trip, the long journey would have been relieved of its tedium.

It may be wondered if she felt no solicitude for her parents or lover during this time. Strange as it may appear, she did not. Her mind, filled with the pleasurable anticipation of the blest abode and the joyful associations to which she was fast approaching, had little chance to dwell on the unhappy friends who mourned her as dead. She apparently had no realization of their existence, except in a vague way that carried no uneasiness. Of course she could not be in a normal condition mind, else the natural feelings would have asserted themselves at such intervals as her thoughts recurred to those at home.

Most of us have seen the sensibilities of persons blunted in this way from a variety of causes, and can readily recognize it as one of the multiform phenomena of the human mind.

When the train reached Rockford the heavenly carriage was waiting at the station to receive the apostle and his fair charge. Usually Schweinfurth accompanied the carriage on such errands, bringing with him one of his favorite angels, but on this occasion he did not do so. There was another apostle, Dr. A. M. Brown, with an angel whose communal name was Norma, besides the driver of the carriage, a weak-minded follow named Adolph Smith, who officiated as coachman to the Messiah, and trembled in abject terror at every severe look his master gave him.

The carriage comfortably held four besides the driver. It was an easy riding vehicle, and with a spirited and rapid team of horses the party whirled along the road in magnificent style. Clara thought she had never seen more noble animals than the champing steeds which took them over the road at so invigorating a pace. Her mind reverted to Pegasus, the winged horse of Apollo and the muses, which Bellerophon is said in mythology to have ridden when he charged in the Chimera, and it would not have required a very great stretch of imagination for her to fancy, in her condition of mind, that she was being borne to Zion, behind a pair of just such extraordinary animals. No one in the state has finer horses than Schweinfurth, or more of them.

The home is about six miles from the station, the several routes passing fine, well-cultivated farms, as valuable as can be found in the whole country. The land is gently rolling, so that it presents to the eye at a distance a perspective in fruitful fields of waving grain and farm homes that bespeak wealth and care. One might say after a visit to the neighborhood, that Schweinfurth had located his heaven as nearly in the Garden of Eden as one might reasonably expect to get outside of the realms of imagination or the pages of Boccaccio. And of all the abounding fertile and frugiferous farms that of the Messiah stands unexcelled.

Very soon the party arrived at Mount Zion. The sacred mansion was pointed out to Clara as soon as it came into view amid the tall oak and elm trees with which it is surrounded. A beautiful place indeed it seemed, which her fantastic imagination readily invested with roseate forms and outlines, hardly of the world of reality. An alert attendant swung the large, heavy gate open as carriage approached, and the occupants were driven along the graveled road that wound its serpentine way up the sloping lawn to the house. Clara could not but notice with what scrupulous care the grounds were attended. There was just shrubbery enough on the lawn to make it appear to the best advantage. Each year the house is newly painted. This year the color was maroon, relieved by a medium shade of green. Clara told herself that it was surpassingly inviting, with the pretty porches, the spreading trees, green lawns, and the hedge near the great barns that plainly showed the trimmer's care. But her delight and gratification with the exterior beauty of the house of Zion would probably turn into stupefying astonishment could she contemplate at once the interior glories of the place.

The Savior of mankind said: "The son of man hath not where to lay his head." Schweinfurth, who professes to be the same Lord risen again from the dead, lays his auburn head on a couch that outvies the luxuriousness of the Orient.

Clara was ushered into the reception-room and divested of her traveling apparel by one of the numerous women about the place, who disappeared with the garments. Clara did not see where the other had gone, so quickly and silently did she disappear. But that made little difference. She was in heaven now, and clothing was of little concern. Indeed, although no such thought occurred to her, it was doubtful if she would ever wear them again. It would depend on how close she got to the Lord what indulgences she received in the matter of dress or anything else.

As the female attendant slipped out old Farmer Weldon came in—a venerable, kindly old man, who, before the advent of Schweinfurth, owned and profitably worked those magnificent acres, being assisted by his five lusty and intelligent looking sons, John, Samuel, Peter, Lem and William, and his daughter Mary. All had become converts to the new faith, and had turned their entire possessions over to Schweinfurth, being content to direct the various branches of employment about the house and farm, and to work hard themselves. The wife and mother passed away before the new light came to them.

Old Farmer Weldon was one of those of the household of Zion who called out the sympathy and pity of those who knew him. Not that he felt the need of anything of this kind, for he considered himself one of the most blessed among men, in that he was permitted to give up all to the Lord and bask in the glorious and continued refulgence of his divine presence. But the public looked upon the matter quite differently. They saw in the old, white-haired farmer the marks of senility, and knew he held in reserve no strength of mind to combat the powerful will of the impudent adventurer who had come, under the sacred cloak of religion, to fatten upon his substance. When it became noised about in Rockford that the splendid farm had been deeded in fee simple to the head of the Church Triumphant, a hue and cry was raised that soon impelled the preparation of a second instrument, reconveying the farm to the credulous old man. This action was taken when heaven was a novelty in the neighborhood and the whole institution merely regarded in the light of a sacrilege that of course were better abolished, but not a menace to public morals. This feeling wore away with the growth of the impression that the sect was simply a conglutinate collection of religious simpletons who were as harmless as their methods were ridiculous. They had not then perpetrated the crowning infamy of their belief. When the public mind was disabused of the notion of their harmlessness there were frequent ebullitions of righteous indignation, and the walls of Zion still shelter the greatest pretender of the age.

The reconveyance of the farm to the old man was really a matter of small consequence. Schweinfurth controls the farmer and his family as thoroughly as the juggler his automata, and so regulates the affairs of the farm as effectually as though held in his own name. So crafty is this man that he is never at a loss for safe and efficacious means to circumvent law and justice. Were he sponged from the face of the earth to-day it is likely that someone else, equally bold and unscrupulous, if not as resourceful, would take his place and flourish upon the credulity of human nature.

But we are digressing.

The venerable old man approached Clara and, taking her hand, bade her welcome in a kindly tone.

"Daughter, we have been expecting you. I trust you have fully made up your mind to abandon the follies of the world and lead a pure and holy life. We are a very happy family, and you may be very happy with us if you will."

"O, my Lord!"

"I truly desire to live near the Lord," replied Clara.

"It is well, daughter. May you continue to grow in grace until you attain the divine plane of life that should be the hope and aspiration of all who enter here. Mr. Schweinfurth has been apprised of your arrival and will give you greeting directly. Indeed, he approaches now."

A light footstep was heard on the winding stairway and Clara, glancing in the direction of the sound, saw the descending Messiah. He walked down with a deliberate step, as though he had no need of haste while he had eternity before him. He did not walk slow enough to give his movements the appearance of being affected for the purpose of enhancing the importance and solemnity of his presence, but simply as any great dignitary might walk to whom haste would not seem befitting.

She was peculiarly moved the moment her eyes rested upon him. It was his picture that attracted her at the branch home to which she was first taken. How much like it he looked—how much like what she had always conceived the Savior of the world to look. She thought his features benign, if not gloriously radiant with a coruscating aureola such as she had been accustomed to see pictured as emanating from the divine head. That she was in the presence of one who was more than man she had no doubt.

When he reached the foot of the stairway he stood a full minute and regarded her silently. As he did so the old man disappeared, and the two were alone.

Clara cast her eyes to the floor while he contemplated her. She knew he was watching her, reading her secret thoughts, for she could feel those magnetic eyes burning into her soul. Directly her feelings overcame her. She rose quickly from her chair, ran to the Messiah and threw herself prostrate on the carpet at his feet with the plaintive wail that rose from her heart:

"O, my Lord!"

Chapter XII
A Disappointing Reception

SCHWEINFURTH LET THE PROSTRATED girl remain at his feet a few moments and then, taking her by the hand and raising her from the floor, he said, speaking in quiet, measured tones:

"Rise and resume your seat. It is not required of you to evince your feelings in so demonstrative a manner."

He led her back to her chair, wholly unmoved by the scene he had witnessed or the tears which coursed down her cheeks. Drawing up another chair, he sat directly in front of her and began to question her.

"You have come into the assembly of Mount Zion of your own free will?"

"Yes, my Lord," Clara timidly answered.

"Do not say 'my Lord' in addressing me. Say, Yes, sir, or Yes, Mr. Schweinfurth."

"Yes, sir."

"I believe your name is Clara McCoy?"

"It is, sir."

"Henceforth you will be known in this community as Emeline. When you abandon the world you leave your worldly name with its sins and follies. Our ideal of life is a divine perfection unattainable beyond the pale of the Church Triumphant. We all aim to reach absolute purity of heart and life. When you have attained this beatification you will be as I am, without sin or guile. You can then do no wrong. But this happy condition cannot be reached at a bound. Divine grace seldom comes upon one like a whirlwind. It is a matter of growth and cultivation, sometimes watered with the tears of sorrow and distress. It is possible to fall from the heights of grace into the precipitous cleft of despair in a moment's time, perhaps by some one act of indiscretion, until you have reached a sinless condition, and then you can fall no more. Then you will be loved and venerated by those about you, an example for others, still struggling up the rugged path of faith. You will be filled with the holy spirit."

"I will strive continually to reach the divine plane," said Clara, as the Messiah paused for a moment.

"Have you been made fully aware of what is required of those who become members of this assembly? Do you know the duties that will devolve upon you?"

"I am not sure, Mr. Schweinfurth."

"Very well; if there are any points with which you are not fully conversant, it will give me pleasure to enlighten you. Ask any questions that suggest themselves to you."

"This is your second advent on earth?" was Clara's first hesitating query.

"It is, and I am accomplishing untold good. The time is not far off when I shall make such manifestations of my divinity and power as will startle the world and bring believers to me by thousands and tens of thousands."

"Can you perform miracles? Can you varnish from the flesh and be invisible and pass from one place to another as a spirit?"

"Yes; I have unlimited power. I can come into a room with closed doors or disappear as readily. I can raise the dead, cure disease, and do all the miraculous things which I accomplished when on earth before. I do not do these things often, for I wish to convert the world to the truth without the employment of supernatural power. I want all to see by the light of the truth itself. Physical infirmities are cured by me simply by faith, and I can cure them without even the exercise of faith if I desire."

"Do you expect to live on earth forever?"

"I shall be here many years in the present body, and the world will witness many wonderful sights before I cast it off. But I am incarnate, and when this body goes into the corruption of death my spirit will enter another body and still live on earth. How or when the present body will die has not been revealed of the Father. But in form and substance the body I now possess was that crucified on Calvary. There are many things in the Gospel in relation to my crucifixion that are inaccurate, and I am now occupied in writing a true version of the New Testament, that can be accepted as the perfect and inspired word. When this is given to the world it will create a revolution among those who now consider themselves orthodox believers."

Clara had instinctively turned her eyes to his hands when he spoke of possessing the same body crucified on Calvary. He noticed this and said:

"You were looking with some skepticism for the marks of the nails in my hands."

Clara, startled that he should know exactly what was in her mind, falteringly replied:

"Yes, sir."

"I do not maintain, remember, that the material structure has not changed and put on a new flesh, but my features are not changed; and, though new material substance has covered the imprint of the torturing instruments, in a general sense the same body is now before you that arose from the tomb at my resurrection."

He fixed his keen, penetrative eyes upon the girl's face for a moment and then continued:

"Do you think now you can freely subscribe to the divine doctrines of the Church Triumphant?"

"Yes, sir."

"Without mental reservation on any point?"

"Yes, Mr. Schweinfurth—except that there is one point which I do not understand. It is that in relation to—to—"

Here she paused and cast her eyes to the floor. Her fair face was suffused with the deepest blushes.

"I see," said Schweinfurth, in a tone of disapproval that wrung the heart of the poor girl; "you do not yet fully believe. The taint of the world is yet upon you, for you blush at the thought of the holiest thing that can come to a woman in Zion. You are yet far from the heights of grace, and will need to struggle diligently to overcome the worldly thoughts and inclinations that possess you. All here will aid you. Pure and sinless women, who are mothers in Christ, will minister to your spiritual needs and illumine your mind with a divine afflatus, until by faith and works you have come to realize and acknowledge that the invisible spirit of God, having first clothed you in robes of virgin purity, may come to you as a direct impartation of his will, that you may experience maternity devoid of carnal taint and enjoy and unspeakable measure of blessedness and joy. When you have, by lofty discipline, purged your heart of impure thoughts, all these things will be made plain to you. We will talk again when you have had time to think over what I have told you. I hope you do not regard this as the imposition of an impossible duty?"

"No, sir."

"Those rings you are wearing and what other articles you have about you in the nature of drossy jewelry will be collected by your attendant and brought to me. You do not require such things here. If you find yourself obliged to leave the community these articles will be returned to you on your departure."

"Yes, sir."

"I will send some one to instruct you in regard to your household duties, for there are no drones in the assembly of Zion. Though we may all hope here by faith and devotion to reach a perfectly sinless and blessed condition, we still have our material bodies with us, for the necessities of which provision must constantly be made. For that reason we all have duties assigned to us, and every one is expected to faithfully perform his or her allotted part."

"Yes, Mr. Schweinfurth," answered Clara, apparently in a state of semi-stupefaction.

She was adynamic physically and mentally. A sound sleep of a few hours would have done her a world of good.

Schweinfurth turned and ascended the stairs to his apartments without further remark, leaving her alone with her tumultuous thoughts.

It must be confessed that Clara was far from finding solacement in the interview just closed. Her reception was not what she had looked for. She had read that there is more joy in heaven over the one wanderer the returns to the fold than over the ninety and nine safe within its shelter. There were no demonstrations of joy over her arrival. She was disappointed, as others before and after her have been, though she could formulate no complaint. If there had been no enthusiasm manifested, there had been no indication of an opposite sentiment. She had nothing to complain of—nothing to satisfy her roseate expectations.

She had been forced from her home by the obsequious Mamby aside from the usual avaricious motives which fired his ardor, he having mightily pleased his master in the previous ensnarement of beauty and innocence. It happened that at this time the head of the Church Triumphant was very satisfactorily situated in this respect; therefore, much like ordinary mortals whose appetites are satiated, he looked with indifference on his latest acquisition. It pleased him to exercise neither his repellent nor attractive power. He simply left the girl to the care of those he knew would give her the requisite instruction and retired to his apartments to employ himself as he pleased.

Λ few minutes after he left, a woman, acting of course under divine instructions, came and led Clara to her room, saying as she did so:

"You will now get ready for the evening meal, which will be served in a short time. After that you may rest until Monday, when you will be assigned to your duties. If this room is not entirely what you have allowed yourself to expect, remember that you are starting at the bottom round of the ladder of grace. Your advancement to a higher plane will depend upon yourself. You will soon understand what is required of you."

The woman then left her. Clara found herself in a small, plainly furnished room, that was far from being as comfortable or inviting as the one she left at home. But she reasoned that with her faltering faith and recent contact with the world it was all she was at present entitled to. When she deserved better it would be given to her.

So after tea, being thoroughly fatigued with her long journey, she sought her couch and soon dropped into a deep and dreamless sleep.

The indifference of the Lord of Zion to Clara's personal attractions may properly be more definitely explained. He was not insensible to the charms, linked to a lamb-like innocence, that had so sorely tempted Apostle Mamby in the quiet grove at Shelbyville, for he had a critical eye for feminine beauty; but he had no time or inclination for dalliance with her just then. There were a number of women who, by long residence and devotion, and having passed through the experimental test of faith, had approached sufficiently near to the purity of the Lord to be called angels. It should be remembered that all the women at this heaven are not angels—in any sense probably, but the light in which women are regarded there is what is meant. These holy ones eat with Schweinfurth, taking but two meals a day. The other women, from those a little lower in the heavenly scale down to those whose angelic attributes are still in embryo, like Clara's, are excluded from the Lord's table, eating separately at another house. The men have other quarters for their meals.

Among the most perfect of these superior women was one who, not long before, must have been an exact counterpart of Clara. As she then appeared, she was a pale, dark-eyed lissome creature of twenty-three, not very plump, but willowy and spirituelle, with a far-away, dreamy look in her eyes. Her complexion was wonderful—white as alabaster, her cheeks soft as an infant's. She occupied a special apartment, the most lavishly and richly adorned of any in the house. Her room was very near the Lord's elegant suite on the second floor of the west wing. She was never seen about the house, and was only visible to the favored ones at meal time, when she sat at the Lord's right hand.

Where the fair creature came from very few know. She, too, was one of Apostle Mamby's acquisitions. He met her one day on a train out of Chicago, and, without speaking to her, or ever having seen her before, so influenced her with a glance of his magnetic eyes that when he left the car she accompanied him, until she awoke to find herself within the sacred precincts of Zion.

Schweinfurth was at once attracted to the beauty and determined to make a convert and a favorite of her. It will be remembered there are no favorites there who are not converts, and, more than that, who have not passed through the tests which render their defection the remotest possible contingency. It would not do to introduce those to the inner sanctuary, the holy of holies, who were liable at any time or under any circumstances to read their recantation. The very existence of the Church Triumphant depends upon the most rigid adherence to this rule.

Angelica, the communal name given this girl, proved to be a willing and apt convert and made rapid progress toward the summit of grace and favor of the Lord. This was the more astonishing as she had not inclined to religious thought before her induction as a member of the community. But the Messiah gave her his personal care and attention, and as he found her mind peculiarly receptive it was barely a month before she submitted to the final ordeal, called: "The Garden of Eden Test," and passed the Rubicon of the Church Triumphant. Now the Lord called her "his soul's mate" and most of the time that she did not spend in his apartment he spent in her's. She was the reigning queen of Zion.

Among the others who stood high in the favor of the Messiah was Mrs. H. B. Tuttle, the wife of a clergyman who became insane when she joined the sect, and an exceedingly handsome woman. Notwithstanding she had not seen her husband for three years she had a little daughter but one year of age, a beautiful, lovable child to which Schweinfurth was especially attracted and made much of. She has had others since, all "Children of the Holy Ghost," and of course in purity above and beyond those of the married people in the home.

There is still another especial favorite, Mary Weldon, the only daughter of the venerable farmer to whom reference has already been made. She, too, had reached a pure and sinless condition, although she had not at the time of Clara's coming been blessed with that familiar intercourse with the Holy Ghost which Mrs. Tuttle enjoyed. She nightly prayed that she might thus be filled with the holy spirit, and her faith, firm as adamant, would not permit her to doubt that such fervent, heartfelt prayer as she daily sent up would be ultimately answered.

Mary was about thirty years of age, and was a person who, outside of her fallacious religious notions, would be regarded from her conversation and deportment as a sensible and very well-informed woman. She was much in the rooms of the Messiah, it being her especial and blessed privilege to wait upon him. He needed a good deal of waiting on, and during the heat of the summer she was often called upon to sit by him for hours, bathing his heated brow or placing cracked ice to his throbbing temple, for the egregious mistakes of some of the blundering disciples bothered the Lord so greatly that he frequently suffered with violent headaches. Mary was not less faithful than the Mary of old, and her reward would come in due season.

There were other faithful and sinless women, but none so highly favored as these three, and none of the three so tenderly regarded as Angelica, whose surpassing beauty and willingness to accede to the desires of the Messiah had secured her rapid advancement instead of a long and devoted service. She was not required to attend the Sunday service, unless she felt disposed to sit in an easy chair at the head of the stairs, among the holiest women, where she could see the Lord and hear the sermon without being subjected to the curious gaze of the lower orders of Zion.

Clara's indifferent reception is now accounted for. Perhaps she, too, will be received into high favor and blessed before a great while; or, regaining her wonted good sense, will quit the "sweet fields of Eden" entirely. We must wait and see.

Sunday she was permitted to attend the services, held in the reception room, which began at noon and lasted a little over three hours. The discourse of the Messiah impressed her deeply. She thought his words, as did the others, the language of inspiration. She was especially delighted with the exquisite singing of Schweinfurth and his sister, Marie, another holy woman, and moved by the earnest prayers which he offered to the Father. Anon she watched the busy stenographers, taking down every word the Messiah uttered for transmission to the branches. Indeed, the whole service was a revelation and a delight.

After this she was at liberty to converse with some of the other women until bedtime, and on Monday morning she was informed that she had been selected to assist in the school-room and in the care of the children. The school-room is on the second floor of the main building, where some thirty pupils are daily taught. Not only was she expected to assist in teaching the children, but in caring for them before and after school hours while the mothers were engaged in their several occupations.

But Clara did not mind this. She was fond of children and was sure she would get along with them splendidly, unless it should transpire that the children of heaven are less easily managed than those of the outer world. However, almost all children are susceptible to kindness, and it was not in the nature of Clara to give them anything else.

Now, having introduced her to Zion, and seen her inducted into the duties assigned her, we may leave her for a while to "work out her own salvation."

Chapter XIII
He Couldn't Fool the Messiah

WHEN ARTHUR FITZROY BADE farewell to the kind-hearted, albeit warm-tempered Dr. Wilkie, of Kansas City, and settled himself in his seat for the journey to Rockford, he gave his mind over to an analytical consideration of the vexed question before him. How should he cut the Gordian knot? He was thoroughly convinced from his brief experience with Amelia at the branch home, supplemented by the "pointers" given by the doctor, that the employment of his time and means in legal efforts was "love's labor lost." The physician had prescribed a course of systematic pious dissimulation—that is, he thought the wisest thing Arthur could do was to put on the outer garments of humility, employ what facial effect he was capable of in the cultivation of a meek sanctitude, and enter the community of Zion as a probationary candidate for ultimate translation into the higher glories of the kingdom.

"Put what money and other valuables you have into a bank vault at Rockford," said the doctor, "if you want to see them again. Then put in a day or two practicing deportment and acquiring the feeling and look of a person who has just reached the other side of a sheltering fence two feet ahead of the horns of a mad bull. The nicest way to do this would be to visit your uncle at some of the pawn-shops and inquire what they are willing to let you have on your watch. The looks and answers you will receive will make you feel small enough in a short time to pass through the eye of a needle. If this is not convenient, an attempt to extract information from some of the policemen you meet will answer pretty much the same purpose. Then walk down to Zion. Remember, I say 'walk' and 'down' advisedly. The Scripture says, 'knock and it shall opened unto you'; but you musn't be too sure about it in this case. If you bear the ear-marks of a dejected and perishing soul ahunger and athirst for the waters of life, and have a pretty straight tale of woe to unfold, you may find balm in Gilead. Perhaps you will be taken in—in more than one sense—on probation; otherwise you will stand like Peri gazing in at the gates of Paradise and unable to enter and participate in its glories. If you can succeed in this scheme you may have a chance to see the young woman and labor with her, or spirit her away, or do something to save her from this infernal rascal. I can't tell you just what you should do, more than to exercise great caution and circumspection if you hope to succeed. Above all, don't go off half-cocked and upset the whole thing. This is a general idea of what I conceive to be the most effective method of working. You will have to arrange the details your-self, which, of necessity, will depend upon circumstances."

Though naturally averse to deception, Arthur believed the doctor's plan for more feasible than any other he was able to conjure up as he rode along, and when he reached Rockford he had about determined to be governed by his new-found friend's advice. He might be made acquainted with some more advantageous means perhaps among those residing in the vicinity of the place; if not the doctor's plan would be put into execution as soon as possible with safety.

Arthur found Rockford a city with a "boom," though a remarkably substantial one. He had the appearance of a young man of affairs and means, and had hardly wriggled himself in safety through the variegat-ed aggregation of noisy and importunate hackmen who thronged the station platform when he was beset by another danger—that of being dragged into quarter-sections by "hustling" real-estate dealers, ever on the alert for a customer with cash. The local papers called them "city builders," because they went and sent into the money centers of the country and induced capital to come in and buy their subdivisions and additions and help build factories and big brick buildings; so that what-ever spirit of selfishness or avariciousness may have been the source of the industry and perseverance—untiring as the scissors of the three weird sisters—with which they continually pressed upon the stranger within their gates the golden opportunities for profitable investment, they at the same time helped the city amazingly by accelerating the wheels of industrial effort and extending the unconfined limits of the place by the admission of newly platted additions. Some invested to their regret, as people always do who are influenced by the alluring phantasmagoria and glittering delectations of the real-estate man; but the majority of investors in Rockford turned their money over in a way that gave them no reason to complain, for, as has been said, the "boom" was not of the transitory sort. Nevertheless the person who has had a business transaction with a representative "dealer in dirt," especially in a town with a "boom" auxiliary, is apt to associate the man with the memory of Ananias.

Arthur soon convinced these men that he was not in the city for the purpose of investing, and when assured of this they dropped him incontinently and went each his devious way. He was struck with the spirit of progress on every hand. It was very different from the quiet rural life to which he was accustomed at home. But what afforded him the most impressive food for serious reflection was the succession of church spires which towered skyward. He seemed to be in a veritable city of churches, yet in the immediate vicinity of these striking evidences of Christian zeal rested an abomination of abominations—the community of George Jacob Schweinfurth and his famous zealots.

"How is this?" he said to himself. And then he looked again at the multiplicity of tall smoke-stacks belching out rolling volumes of black smoke, heard the incessant whir of the fast-moving electric cars, the din of the busy vehicles and the hurrying tramp of those whose pursuits called them back and forth upon the streets, he made up his mind that he was in a progressive city indeed, where the people were too eagerly intent upon extending their commercial dominion and laying up individual treasures to stop and storm the citadels of sin oftener than their quasi-social church obligations required of them each recurring Sunday.

Perhaps he was not so far astray.

In pursuance of the suggestion of Dr. Wilkie, he determined to spend a day or so in the city before making his way to Zion. There was a possibility of his learning something that would be of advantage to him. Presently, in walking leisurely about, he found himself in a district that seemed to be devoted entirely to the manufacture of furniture, for he could look in no direction that his vision did not rest on the mammoth outlines of a factory. Being minded to get an idea of the direction in which Zion should be sought he accosted a Swedish teamster near one of the factories:

"Say, my friend, can you tell me which direction I should go to get to Zion?"

The man, who was loading newly-finished chairs on a wagon, paused for a moment to look at him and then resumed his work without answering. He did not understand the question. Seeing this Arthur spoke again.

"Can you tell me where heaven is?"

"A broad grin spread itself over the face of the descendant of the Vikings as he replied:

"Ay daen know; better ask Meester Yohnson."

"Mr. Johnson"?

"Yaw; he baen preacher. Tala Sveroska?"

"I only speak English. But I was not asking you where the heaven of the good Lutheran is. I mean the other heaven near the city somewhere."

"Ay daen know."

"Surely you have heard of him—this man who keeps so many women about him?"

"O, Yesus?"

"Yes; that is the person. Do you know where he lives?"

"Ay tank he baen sax mile thas vaeh," said the man, indicating a southerly direction with his hand, and then launching into an unintelligible jargon that was intended as a disquisition on the general sleekness and superior hoaxing abilities of Schweinfurth.

Arthur heard him through and then walked away in search of someone who had acquired a little better command of English.

During that day and the one following Arthur talked with many people regarding the place to which he was soon to direct his steps. There were none who did not voice pretty much the same opinion as Dr. Wilkie, that any attempt to reach the Messiah by legal methods would be abortive.

"Why," said one lawyer, to whom he talked ten minutes at the very reasonable cost of a dollar, "you might as well try to catch a weasel asleep as to get George into the meshes of the law. We have tried about every scheme we could think of, and he has had the laugh on us every time. A warrant to search the branch heaven was all right, but it wouldn't be worth the paper it was written on here. When Col. Schweinfurth remodeled the building he had the work done by carpenters and others who are members of the community, but it is stated on good authority that there are several secret rooms and alcoves the entrance to which can be found by none but the faithful. Anyone else might hunt for a month of Sundays and never get within a thousand miles of the combination. If he is willing you should see the girl, he will let you see her, if she is there; if he is not a wagon load of search warrants wouldn't help you."

"Have the officers of the law never visited him?" asked Arthur.

"Yes; quite frequently. Deputies have gone there to get goods belonging to those who remained a few days and then lost their religious ardor because of the hard work he set them at. Many people who go to his heaven are disappointed because they have something else to do besides 'lay off' and enjoy the scenery and things."

"Do the officers have trouble?"

"None at all. Jake always appears to be glad to see them, and every bit of property is forthcoming at once."

"Has he never been sued for the recovery of monies?"

"Several times."

"What does he do?"

"Always sends some trusted apostle to effect a settlement before the affair gets into the court. O, he's foxy, is George."

"I presume he is never crowded for means when an affair of this kind comes up?"

"Not often. I guess George has a little treasure laid up in heaven. Of course he spends a good deal, for there is nothing small about the colonel. On one occasion, I think it was just after he remodeled the place, when he had a money settlement to make with some contumacious dupe, he had to put a mortgage on heaven for a little matter of ten thousand dollars. But I think he lifted that very soon afterward. It's a sad thing to have to mortgage heaven, isn't it?" added the lawyer, with a laugh.

"I suppose so," Arthur dubiously replied.

"The papers here made a heap of sport of that mortgage, but I guess it was nothing more than a temporary embarrassment. Schweinfurth well fixed."

"You think, then, there is no use sending an officer after this young woman?"

"Not the slightest. I'll take your case if you like and make the most I can of it; but honestly, speaking as a friend rather than a lawyer, it will only spoil your prospects for the better plan you mentioned a moment ago."

"I am sure I appreciate your kindness," said Arthur.

"O, that's nothing." Answered the lawyer; "we are not all robbers."

"He is certainly a remarkable man," Arthur musingly said, as he rose to take his leave.

"Biggest man in the Messiah business," answered the other.

Arthur left the lawyer's office more firmly convinced than ever that his only course was to follow the suggestions of Dr. Wilkie, and he at once made preparations for doing so. He deposited all his valuables except a few dollars in one of the banks, purchased a cheap second-hand suit of clothes, and put it on, trying at the same time to feel as sinful and as much in need of saving grace as he really was miserable and disheartened, and then set out on foot the forenoon of the next day for the precincts of Zion.

It is not often that persons obtain admission into the community in the way that Arthur expected to enter, for the reason, perhaps, that very few go there in that way. Most converts first pass through apostolic hands, being selected for pecuniary considerations or for the reason that Clara was inveigled, and go to the home at least in part prepared for their reception. Arthur entered the gate, not without observing and admiring the exceeding beauties of nature that environed him, and started toward the imposing mansion. When half the distance from the road had been traversed he saw three or four disciples standing talking in the door of the nearest barn, and, turning, he made his way to where they were. They received him kindly enough, but eyed him very suspiciously. These people were not strangers to imposition; the treachery of those who had come among them professing a belief that was in truth repugnant to them had been a source of repeated persecutions, and therefore the advent of every stranger was regarded with more or less misgiving.

Arthur told the men he wanted to become one of them, but he was poor and had nothing to offer but the labor of his hands, which would be devotedly given were he permitted to remain. He talked with the men for some time, looking over some of the blooded stock in the stables with them and impressing them with his superior knowledge of horseflesh. Gradually, and without apparent intention, he insinuated himself into their good graces, until finally one of the men, Peter Weldon, a son of the venerable old farmer, said there was possibly a place for a man who thoroughly understood the care of horses and volunteered to go to the house himself and speak to Mr. Schweinfurth on behalf of Arthur, which he did in a short time.

Arthur flattered himself he was making good progress as far as the men were concerned, and already he began to indulge a hope that his artifice would be successful. What he had to do now, he thought, was to remember Dr. Wilkie's sensible advice and not "go off half cocked." He would have felt less sanguine had he known that, short a time as it was since he left Kansas City, the legal hunt in which he figured there had been reported in detail to Schweinfurth, with an accurate description of those concerned in it. When his case was presented to the Messiah by young Weldon, the head of the Church Triumphant had a reasonably good idea of who the applicant for admission was, the object that brought him there, and the means he had selected to attain his end.

Still the Messiah had no intention of turning Arthur away. It was not necessary, to begin with; besides, the Lord had a pleasing repute for charity and benevolence to maintain. It was known in the neighborhood that no one, however poor or lowly, was ever spurned from the threshold of Zion. Even shabby mendicants, who made no profession of the faith were cared for sometimes and sent on their way rejoicing and praising the sympathetic kindness of Schweinfurth. No exception need be made in Arthur's case. It was very easy to arrange things so that his presence there would be a matter of small moment so far as Clara was concerned.

Young Weldon was instructed to admit him on probation, and permit him to assist in the stables, and at the same time caution the faithful disciples to keep him constantly under surveillance. Arthur gave the name of John Johnson and was so entered upon the books of Zion kept for that purpose. The Messiah said he would talk with him about his spiritual condition when he found leisure.

Thus Arthur, more easily than he had any hope of, became a member on probation of the Church Triumphant, and began his duties about the stables at once. He worked along until Saturday without seeing the Lord, and had almost made up his mind that august personage had forgotten his existence. Once thing his keenness detected during that time, however—that he was under the espionage of the disciples. At no time, night or day, was he permitted to be alone for any length of time. When the duties of one disciple called him away another quietly took his place, and he rightly guessed that all he said and did was reported to Schweinfurth. He was glad he made this discovery, for, though he had been very careful, he would now exercise still greater circumspection. Saturday Schweinfurth strolled out and looked over the barns and ordered a single carriage hitched up to drive to town. Arthur, who towered a head above the pretender, was compelled to confess himself in the presence of a wonderful man—a man whose mild yet piercing eyes and magnetic presence were powerfully felt the moment he drew near.

He talked with Arthur for a few minutes, seemingly finding the answers to his queries satisfactory. Then he gave him a few words of praise for the manner in which he had discharged his duties, made some suggestions as to the means for attaining the higher walks of life and returned to the house.

No mention was made of Clara by either one, it being no part of Arthur's purpose to have it known why he was there; and it had not pleased the Messiah to give any intimation of her presence at Zion. Indeed, so far as Arthur was concerned, he was not even certain that she was there, though he presumed she was. He confidently expected that at the Sunday service, when the whole household was supposed to gather, he would at least see her, though he did not expect to speak with her. After awaiting with feverish anxiety for this hour to come he was cast down by the keenest disappointment. He could not discern her sweet, well-known features in the motley congregation, for the sufficient reason that she was not there. She was present the first Sunday she passed in the house, but very many Sundays came and went before she was seen there again.

Arthur continued to play what he conceived to be a clever deception upon the members of the Church Triumphant, but the Messiah, who knew exactly what he was doing, smiled at his futile efforts.

Serving Christ.

Chapter XIV
Prosperous, Beautiful Zion

A CARDINAL IDEA OF THE Christian heaven is perfect tranquility. Schweinfurth would have this condition obtain in his sublunary heaven were it possible, which is not always the case. All the members of the community cannot be made absolutely sinless and holy, thus eliminating the promptings of envy, jealousy, unbelief and cognate frailties of degenerate humanity. If this could be done Zion would be heaven indeed. Sometimes, however, the members of the Church Triumphant pursue the even tenor of their way for considerable periods undisturbed by these incitant motives. Then, again, there comes a season of unrest. Some disturbing element stimulates the latent worldly passions beyond the control of the powerful will at the head of affairs, and an uproar ensues. As troubles seldom come singly, there is generally a surprising increase in the quantity of cracked ice and tender offices required in the sanctified apartments on the second floor. While, even in the domestic economy of Zion, such *contretemps* cannot be entirely obviated, they are generally subverted in a way that resounds to the glory and honor of the Messiah.

It is a year now since Clara and Arthur became inmates of the home, and it has been a year of gratifying quiet. They have not seen each other in all this time. Clara has been rigorously excluded from the body of the congregation at the Sunday services, the only place where there was any probability of his seeing her. Occasionally she was permitted to sit in the spacious hall at the head of the stairs, where she could hear the sermon and look upon the divine features and yet remain concealed from those below. She had no knowledge of the presence of Arthur at the place, and, as far as holding communication with her was concerned, he might as well have been at home at Shelbyville.

He had, in reality, no more positive knowledge of her being there than the day he came, though some of those better versed in the affairs of the mansion told him there were several young women there who came from Kentucky, but none of them had attained the higher plane of life and were consequently not in favor with the Lord. This was all so far Arthur had to encourage him, for he knew that as long as they kept themselves separated from a condition of perfect holiness their honor was safe. When at night he repaired to his unattractive quarters, over one of the barns about which he spent most of his time, he breathed a fervent hope that this state of affairs might remain undisturbed until an opportunity came to him and rewarded his patient waiting.

Clara still performed her unchanging daily round of duties in the school-room and among the children, and no fault could be found with her in this respect. She remained in much the same condition of mind as when she entered the home. The Messiah had many talks with her, in which he praised the unremitting care she gave the children. But she was in possession of a peculiar phase of unbelief that effectually precluded her spiritual advancement. This, of course, was provoking to Schweinfurth; still he treated her with a degree of consideration he let her feel she did not deserve, because he knew she was earnestly striving to overcome her unbelief. It was his policy to avoid any semblance of harshness unless absolutely essential to maintain the discipline of the home.

Clara only thought of her parents in a vague way. The memory of them seemed more a dream than a reality. She did not seem to realize the possibility of anyone in the outer world mourning her absence.

In a material way the year past had been a very satisfactory one for Schweinfurth. His crops had been abundant and brought good figures; his stock had multiplied; the new converts had been unprecedentedly tractable; everything, in short, tended to a great increase of his mundane possessions and the upbuilding the Church Triumphant.

He had gained ground as well during this year of prosperous peace in the estimation of his more immediate neighbors, and nothing had transpired to call down the further opprobrium of the people of the neighboring city of Rockford. The adjacent farmers said they never had a better neighbor. Belated in securing their crops, any of them, he sent men and teams to their aid, positively refusing to accept remuneration. Was there an accident to man, beast or implement, aid was tendered from Zion without waiting for a request. Did sickness overtake a member of a neighboring family, the skill of the heavenly physician, Dr. Brown, and his well-stocked pharmacy were their's free of cost. Sometimes the Messiah would go himself to minister to a sick child—he seemed to be so fond of children—and often, without the aid of drugs, seemed to draw the suffering one back from the very jaws of death.

Several instances of this sort are often spoken of by the people of the neighborhood. One case was that of a child six years of age, who was seized with a severe cold and remittent fever. The disease soon increased, with great heat on the head, the tongue coated and very dry, with great thirst and copious vomiting. Schweinfurth heard of the illness of the child and personally called to see him before measures had been taken to summon a physician. In two minutes he put the lad to sleep. He then placed his hands upon the child's stomach and in less than five minutes he awoke and was relieved. The following day the boy was up and had only the usual feelings of excessive weakness. Ever after that when sick he would refuse to take physic, but invariably asked to be taken to Mr. Schweinfurth and put to sleep. And in no instance did the Lord fail to make him well in a few minutes.

On another occasion he went to see a child who was suffering with paralysis of the hip downward on one side, which the parents said came on while he was cutting his teeth. Schweinfurth put the child into a deep mesmeric sleep, and when he awoke he walked across the room, exclaiming to his mother:

"Oh, mamma! my leg is well. See; I can walk on it."

There are many reputable persons who are willing to vouch for these and similar instances of his magnetic power.

The Messiah seldom employed this remarkable power except for healing purposes, and in many cases he found it far more efficacious than all the medicaments of the pharmacopoeia. Indifferent and trivial cases among the children of Zion he let Dr. Brown attend to, concerning himself only with those likely to conduce to his divine repute. A surgical operation of course, would have to go into the hands of the doctor, for Schweinfurth was a physician only in the intelligent application of animal magnetism, though posing before his people as "the great physician."

Between the two, Dr. Brown, being really a man of much skill, there was during the year just passed, or at any time previous for that matter, very little sickness among the members of the community.

It would be a little hard for the ordinary observer to tell why Dr. Brown found himself at Zion. Notwithstanding his professions of unwavering faith in the divinity of Schweinfurth, he was not at heart a true believer. He had not been a successful practitioner in the outer world—not that he knew less than the generality of physicians. To tell the truth, he probably knew more than the majority of reputable men in the profession. But he seemed to have started out under an evil star. Bad luck continually dogged his footsteps. He lost case after case that a man with half his ability might have saved. Every physician who has practiced any length of time knows what this means, and any honest one will acknowledge how much of an element of success or failure a run of good or bad fortune may be. A man will get a succession of cases that he loses, while his brother practitioner whose office is "over the way," and who is no more skillful or careful, will perhaps not lose a case within a year. This is something neither patients nor the public take into consideration, but at once set down the lucky doctor as a man of surpassing skill and ability, and the unlucky one as a medical sciolist.

Dr. Brown, leaving college with the brightest prospects, experienced a series of just such misfortunes at the outset of his career, the whole culminating in a suit for malpractice by a revengeful patient upon whom he performed a delicate operation, and from whose person he failed to extract a piece of needle he had broken while using. The man obtained judgment for a considerable sum, and the doctor, finding his purse depleted and his professional reputation sadly tarnished, became disheartened and no longer sought to acquire a legitimate practice. When an opportunity was offered him of prescribing for the saints in the Church Triumphant he gave up all—which was not a great deal—to devote himself to the service of Schweinfurth. Apart from his skill, it my be stated, he was a man of divers quirks and crochets, as will appear in a subsequent chapter; but he was a most useful member of the community and was given greater latitude in the home than any other apostle. However, if he did not believe in the divinity of Schweinfurth, he admired the magnificent, unblushing effrontery with which he proclaimed himself and the extraordinary executive ability with which he maintained his analogous position.

The doctor knew little or nothing of the power of animal magnetism when he became an inmate of the home. Being an allopathic doctor he did not feel himself at liberty to consider with any seriousness the patient philosophical researches of such minds as the Baron von Reichenbach or Dr. Ashburner, unless he was willing to cast aside medical ethics. But when he left the world and its multiplying disappointments and reverses to feel the pulses and look at the tongues of the angelic host and their progeny he was free to explore and field of science that promised to reward his investigations.

The first thing that drew his earnest attention to the mesmeric power of Schweinfurth was when a small, slight built woman belonging to the home fell down in an epileptic fit. The doctor believed that her epilepsy was dependent upon a severe form of hysteria, and he treated her for two months with iron and valerian. In spite of his utmost efforts her fits remained as severe as ever. Schweinfurth took the case in hand himself finally, and put the woman into a heavy mesmeric sleep. During the next month she exhibited no phenomena more remarkable than a common deep unconscious sleep, never having a return of her fits.

The mesmeric treatment was continued at intervals, with the result of eventually bringing the woman back to health and strength.

Thus the doctor from first being a skeptic, became an enthusiast in this undeveloped science. He soon discovered that he possessed extraordinary magnetic power, and in a short time exceeded in successful experiments anything the Messiah would have attempted or believed possible.

There was only one case at Zion during the year that these men felt themselves incapable of treating successfully. It was that of a woman in the last stages of consumption. She was beyond the power of medicinal skill, magnetic or otherwise, and Schweinfurth knew that no divine interposition of which he was capable could long keep the brittle thread of life from snapping. Both knew this, and each knew that the other knew it. But it was not the purpose of the Messiah to have anything transpire in the home that would cast doubt upon his supernatural power. A death would have that tendency, inasmuch as his followers firmly believed he could not only heal the sick in all stages of disease, by simply willing that dissolution should not take place, but could raise the dead as well. It was therefore given out that the unfortunate woman, not being firmly grounded in her belief, desired to be removed to the hospital at Rockford, where she was soon afterward taken. Of course she died, but it is doubtful if anyone at the home besides the doctor and the Messiah knew what became of her; and as she had been an inmate but a short time, and so sick during that time that she formed no attachments, no one thought to inquire what followed her removal to the hospital.

Thus quietly passed the first year which Clara and Arthur spent at Zion. If Schweinfurth had cast his divine horoscope he might have discovered more troublous times ahead.

Chapter XV
The First Death in Heaven

SCHWEINFURTH WAS INDEED SORELY troubled. Had it been the unfortunate woman so unceremoniously dispatched to the hospital three months before it would have been a much less serious matter. He could have found some pretext for permitting the worn and emaciated form to rest undisturbed in the silence of the tomb. But this was a beautiful and amiable child that had passed away—a little daughter of William Weldon and granddaughter of the venerable owner of the farm. She was a child deeply loved by all within the home. With the announcement of the little one's death it seemed as though an irreparable calamity had overtaken the people of Zion. It was a sudden call for the Messiah to stop and think, and the more he thought the more perplexed he became. However, he kept his thoughts to himself and disclosed to no one the feelings of uneasiness that agitated his mind.

Some time before the child had been ill—very ill—but by the exercise of his healing magnetic power he brought her back to health and strength. Subsequently the child was wounded by the accidental discharge of a revolver in the hands of the father, from the effects of which death soon ensued, despite the well-directed efforts of Dr. Brown, who employed in vain all the means at his command to stay the fast-ebbing tide of life. And when the last flickering spark flew upward and expired he wondered what the outcome would be.

The funeral was invested with more than ordinary solemnity. There were about a hundred sorrowing friends in attendance, including a number of the neighbors. The casket was placed in the reception-room where the Sunday services were held. It was covered with flowers and adorned with beautiful floral designs, the gifts of sympathizing friends in the neighborhood. In the funeral sermon Schweinfurth had little to say about the future of the child, the entire discourse being in the nature of an apology for his inability to raise the dead to life. He felt the gathering expected to see him restore the child to its anguished parents, and his remarks, therefore, were along the line of an explanation of the impossibility of such an act. He pointed out the fact that John the Baptist was beheaded and that the Lord was unable to interpose in his behalf; and he then expressed the belief that the Father, in his wisdom, had called the little one to empyrean joys, as a flower too sweet and beautiful for earth.

The address was a miserable disjunction of incoherent sentences, but one idea advanced may be worthy of preservation:

"Those who believe in worldly pleasures—pleasures of sight, taste, touch, smell and feeling—will suffer untold agony in the world to come. With death there comes a taking away of those senses, and the consequent taking away of the only pleasures which the dead person is capable of enjoying."

He referred feelingly to the time when the dead child was ill—the emotions that played upon his soul. God had then permitted him to restore her to health and the enjoyment of life. From that time he had loved the child—loved her with an intensity heightened by her near approach to the grave. He was glad the bereaved father and mother felt like saying, "Thy will be done"—glad that the sun of light had risen so high that its golden rays were not obscured from mortal vision.

At the conclusion of his address the friends of the family were given an opportunity of viewing the remains. The corpse was remarkably life like, and the sight of the beautiful features, now forever locked in the calm embrace of death, brought tears to the eyes of many of the spectators.

A pathetic incident occurred while the friends were taking their last look at the sweet features of the child in the coffin. Stepping forward to the casket, and raising his hands high above his head, his voice meanwhile trembling with suppressed emotion, the father of the dead girl proclaimed his unshaken belief in the claim of Schweinfurth as Christ manifest in the flesh, and voiced his desire to bow submissively to the will of the Father, who gave and who also took away.

Then, after a hymn by Schweinfurth and his sister Marie, the remains were conveyed to a point northeast of the house and temporarily interred, the intention of the Messiah being to select a more appropriate private resting place at an early day.

Apart from the parents of the dead child there was probably no one who mourned her death more sincerely and deeply than Clara, under whose especial care the little one had been for more than a year. She had formed a strong attachment for the child, which was fully reciprocated, and when the last sad observances were finished she relieved the poignancy of her grief in a flood of bitter tears. Her deep distress was not of long duration, however, for she soon felt she had no right to murmur because it was not the will of the Father to restore the beautiful and tender bud of affection to the arms of her agonized parents and others of the household who loved her almost as well. She would cease her repining. Still a question as to the divine power of the Messiah did not enter her mind. Doubtless there were all-sufficient reasons why the child should not be called back to earth that were beyond her feeble comprehension.

Arthur, impressed by the genuine sorrow of those around him, mourned with the others the death of the little one; but he did not say much, for it was hard for him to restrain the feelings of indignation which moved him as he listened to the hypocritical discourse of Schweinfurth at the funeral.

When the solemn services were ended, Schweinfurth issued a variety of orders to the faithful and retired to his apartments. He intended to remain in seclusion two or three days, unless some untoward circumstance called for his personal attention. He did not believe that anything awkward would grow out of the mournful occasion, but he wanted to be alone for a time and think. It was reasonably certain that the pure and holy women to whom he devoted so much of his time, even Angelica, his soul's mate, would be shut out from his gracious presence for the time being. However satisfied with his reasons for not bringing back to life the lovable child the members of the household might be, he was not satisfied himself. His postulate was readily accepted, but he wanted to contrive some way to give it still more effect. There must be no murmur of grief or woe within the confines of Zion.

Schweinfurth had been in his apartments but a few minutes when there was a quiet tap at the door of the outer room. At first he paid no attention to this, but directly afterward, when he heard the well-known voice of Dr. Brown softly calling to him, he arose and opened the door.

"Ah, Doctor! is that you?" he said. "I was thinking of you a short time ago and wondering why I did not see you at the grave. Come in and take a seat."

The doctor did so, and Schweinfurth continued:

"I suppose my people feel keenly the loss of this dear child."

"They can hardly feel otherwise, Mr. Schweinfurth," replied the doctor. "She was such a truly affectionate and delightful child."

"So she was; and my heart is moved with sorrow because the stricken friends cannot comprehend the purposes of the Father. He would have her with him in the higher heaven. I would have restored her to the sorrowing friends had it been in my power."

"I am sure you would, Mr. Schweinfurth."

"Do they murmur because of God's will?"

"I have heard no voice of complaint, but I suspect some of the less faithful may feel in their hearts that your power has been curtailed, though I sincerely hope I am mistaken."

"I have said to the Father, "Thy will, not mine, be done.""

"Beyond dubitation," replied the doctor. "But I came to make a suggestion, or rather to beg the privilege of an experiment I have in mind."

"That were hardly necessary, doctor; I have never interfered with your experiments."

"That is true, Mr. Schweinfurth; but the experiment I have in view is no ordinary one. In truth I do not regard it as an experiment, for I am as certain of its accomplishment as that I am here. It is something as well that may be made to redound to your credit."

"I can have no part in any imposition upon my people," returned Schweinfurth, with a significant look at the doctor.

"I would not dare to ask you, sir, to be a party to any imposition," said the wily doctor, understanding thoroughly what was in the Messiah's mind.

"Very well; you may state the nature of the experiment you propose to perform."

"You understand the peculiar mental and physical condition of Mrs. Bruce?"

"I believe you told me she has been in a trance condition closely resembling death on several occasions."

"I did. Notwithstanding this there is no probability of the woman's dying a natural death at present."

"You do not propose to dispose of her summarily, I hope? I have had enough of death for the present."

"No; not exactly dispose of her at all—only temporarily."

"Make yourself clearer, doctor."

"I will. Mrs. Bruce, as you are aware, spent many years of her life as the exponent of the phenomena of spiritualism. She was one of the best of mediums until her mental powers succumbed to the continual strain which she imposed and left her with woefully impaired faculties. She came here, indeed, firm in the belief that you are a powerful agent of the spirit world—a medium greater than any other."

"I am aware of that, and because I realize her deplorable mental condition I have humored her whims. Argument would be wasted upon her."

"It would of a surety; but that is not the point. Her peculiar organization enabled her to throw herself into a trance at will, which she always did preceding a manifestation. From continually subjecting herself to this condition by the power of her will she has finally reached such a stage that, in the present enfeebled state of her mind, these trance spells come upon her involuntarily and are of much longer duration

A conference on resurrection.

than when induced by her own will. My investigations into the science of animal magnetism have shown me that so-called spiritual manifestations are nothing more than another form of the same magnetic agency which you and I have so often employed in mesmerism."

"I had not thought of that," said Schweinfurth.

"The ancients worshiped human spirits," continued the doctor, "and it is contended by some writers, Hugh Farmer for one, that heathen mythology took its origin from these manifestations. I can trace the analogy of these phenomena to the operation of magnetic currents. I have thoroughly convinced myself that the trance condition into which Mrs. Bruce, had been accustomed to force herself, and which now comes involuntarily, without the faculty of clairvoyant reading, my be as readily induced by the will power of another person—by my power—and may be made of such duration as I please."

Schweinfurth inclined his head in approval, and the doctor continued:

"On several occasions of late I have put this woman into a trance condition, all animation apparently suspended and the respiratory apertures hermetically closed, and left her in this state for a period of eighteen hours."

"I have no doubt of the possibility of this, Doctor. It is only another form of magnetic sleep. The natural functions are not entirely suspended, although they may appear to be."

"Well, what I want to get at is this: If life can be maintained for a considerable time in this way in her room, it can be just as easily done in a coffin under ground."

The Messiah started, but said nothing, and the doctor went on.

"If the body is inhumed care must be had to prevent the escape and absorption by the earth of the heat of the body. Should it become cold and the blood congest, death would ensue, for, although the subject is to all intents and purposes dead, the vital organs still perform their functions. The blood circulates and the process of digestion continues, but in such a immeasurably low degree as to be beyond detection by ordinary methods; and the body might be left under ground for a month with perfect safety if the animal heat is retained."

"And you want to perform this experiment with Mrs. Bruce?"

"I do."

"When?"

"At once—to-day. I have everything in readiness. The woman has been in a trance since early this morning and will remain in that condition until about four o'clock to-morrow afternoon."

"And if she should die?"

"She is presumed to be dead before she is buried. If she really does die she will have to remain dead. But she will come up out of the earth again none the worse for her night's sleep below ground."

"Are you sure?"

"I am quite positive."

"This is an unheard of performance."

"No, it is not, Mr. Schweinfurth. I have myself seen it done three times in India—at Allahabad, Delhi and Benares. The medical profession has long recognized that a certain East Indian caste calling themselves Adepts possess the power of practically suspending the vital functions for an indefinite length of time while they perform these burials and resurrections. The secrets that make this possible have been handed down through numberless generations and are believed to be unknown outside this religious sect. In the course of thousands of years these Adepts have gained a vast amount of occult knowledge, and many of the feats they are able to perform seem to practical westerners a little short of being miraculous. It is the belief of the medical profession that the feat is performed by means of a drug which reduces respiration and the action of the heart to a condition that can only be detected by the most rigid tests. With a supply of food and water on the stomach, life may be maintained for a considerable time. I have assured myself that no drugs are necessary, and I do not believe any are employed by these Adepts. The will power of certain individuals is strong enough to enable them to put themselves into a state of asphyxia, or this power may come from another, as it will in this instance."

"Well," said the Messiah, musingly, "I understand what you mean. You have my consent, *sub rosa*, to perform this delicate test in the interest of the science to which you are so heartily devoted. But it must be understood that I am not a party to this death and resurrection. I cannot consent to practice a deception upon my people, however much the success of the experiment may accrue to my advantage."

"Certainly not, Mr. Schweinfurth. But I do not propose to make an explanation to any others of the nature of this test, and if you are not present and the belief should become general in the home that you have called the dead one back from the grave, it will not be my fault."

"I will hold you responsible for nothing for which you are not to blame," replied the Messiah.

The doctor rose to take his leave. As he was about to do so Schweinfurth added the parting injunction:

"Doctor, I trust you will proceed in this affair with extreme caution. I believe you understand what you are about or I would not give you permission to do this thing. You must see to it that you allow yourself to have no unfortunate or embarrassing accidents."

"I will use every possible precaution against mishap," replied the doctor, and then he hastened to his apartments to make his final preparations for this astonishing undertaking.

Shortly after, he caused the announcement to be made that Mrs. Bruce had been found dead in her room, and that she had probably been dead since early morning.

Meanwhile Schweinfurth locked his door and resumed his cogitations.

Chapter XVI
The Doctor Disappointed

IT MAY BE WONDERED why this remarkable physician was not tempted to supplant the Messiah in the government of Mount Zion. It would be a very natural desire for many men similarly situated. Perhaps the doctor, if he thought of such a thing at all, called to mind the story of Lucifer, who "would rather rule in hell than serve in heaven," and, as is universally understood throughout Christendom, was given the opportunity to do so. Lucifer fell to rise no more. The doctor did not care to incur any such risk. He appreciated the Messiah's extraordinary executive ability and the cohesive power he was able to exercise among the diverse elements of the Church Triumphant, and was content to remain first in the confidence of the Lord instead of usurping the throne of grace and attempting to carry on a work for which he felt himself ill-fitted. He would never make a successful head of the church, but he made an astonishingly successful and useful auxiliary to the head.

There was great consternation in the home when the death of Mrs. Bruce was announced. Two deaths in such rapid succession had a paralyzing effect on the inmates, and some of the more timid ones stood around as though petrified with fear. Then it became whispered about that it was the purpose of the Lord in this case to raise the woman from the dead. No one seemed to know on whose authority this statement was made, but it was generally believed and expected the miracle would be performed, and very soon every member of the community was a prey to the liveliest sensations of eager expectancy. Even Arthur Fitzroy awaited the outcome with an unusual degree of interest.

Where was the Messiah during this time? Still closeted in his chamber; and the impression prevailed that, like Christ in the Garden of Gethsemane, he was lifting up his voice to the supernal throne for power to preserve the chosen people of God from the ruthless assaults of the grim King of Terrors. His followers had faith to believe in the efficacy of his direct intercession.

Meanwhile a grave was prepared in a portion of the grounds apart from where the child was buried, the doctor himself preparing the body for interment.

He would have preferred to have her remain under ground several days before being resurrected, but, in truth, he did not consider her a good subject for the experiment and was willing to take no hazard. She was thin and feeble at the best, with not too large a reserve of vitality. However, having this test in view, he had fed her for several days previous on oleaginous foods, thus producing an excess of caloric to maintain warmth in the body during burial and keep the blood from becoming congealed. The first thing he did when he carried her rigid form to his apartments to complete his final preparations was to fill the lungs to the utmost with pure air. The tongue was then turned back in the mouth and pushed down the thorax in such a way as to close the aperture to the lungs and stop respiration. The mouth, nose, ears and eyes were then hermetically sealed with wax. The next operation was to completely coat the entire body with a preparation of paraffin, in order to close the pores, thus preventing exudation or infiltration. The whole body except the face was then swathed tightly in flannels, a fillet being reserved to cover the face just before the body was lowered into the tomb. The purpose of this was to retain the caloric while the body was in the ground. These being covered by the shroud, the "remains" were ready for the coffin.

The casket differed from that ordinarily used, in that it was much larger than the body it was intended to hold. This casket was to rest inside of a rough box, much large again than the coffin, and both were perforated here and there on the sides. The perforating was merely a precautionary measure. It was not expected there would be any poisonous gaseous discharges during the short time the body would remain buried, but if there should be the perforated boxes would permit of their escaping and being absorbed by the soil. A clay soil was selected, that being impervious to water in the event of rain.

The perforated sides of the casket were concealed by appropriate drapery, and with the aid of two disciples the body was placed in this peculiar receptacle and left in the doctor's apartments to await the hour set for burial at dusk that evening.

There was little discussion of the death, every mind being intent on the coming resurrection which they all felt sure the Lord would bring to pass. Most of the disciples believed he would prevent the remains being inhumed and call the sister back to life at the grave. It was certainly an important epoch in the history of the Church Triumphant.

In the meantime the doctor had another faithful apostle select suitable pall-bearers, those being selected who were least intimate with the woman during her short but rather eventful life at the home.

It was also given out that there would be no burial service, the expectation in regard to the woman rendering such offices unnecessary.

At the appointed hour the faithful gathered at the grave only a few of the members of the community being absent. It was announced the Messiah would not put in an appearance. There was a visible feeling of disquietude among the saints because of this, but it found no more forcible expression than was given in the anxious and furtive glances of the apprehensive men and women assembled there.

There was no one beside Dr. Brown to whom the faithful could address their anxious inquiries, and he was so busy it seemed impossible for him to stop and answer questions. Still, as he moved about, more concerned as to the success of this experiment than anything else, he was occasionally stopped with such inquiries as these:

"Will the Messiah be present?"

or—

"Will Mr. Schweinfurth raise the sister up at the grave?"

To all these eager questions he gave but one answer:

"Have faith. The sister will be with you again in life before another day has gone."

Then Apostle Scott, one of the select among the men of Zion, stepped forward and made some remarks:

"Dear brothers and sisters: It is not for us to inquire what the purpose of the Lord is at this time. We have had the blessed assurance that the dead sister will be wrested from the power of death. That is enough. It is not necessary the Lord should be here in person. Even now he is in the seclusion of his chamber holding communion with the Father, to the end that more fruitful blessings may be vouchsafed to the people he loves by the beneficent hand of omnipotence. What matters it if he be here or there, or if the cold earth clods cover the body of her we love. She will rise again triumphant over the sting of death and the corruption of the grave."

Despite an exoteric indication of unbelief there was really nothing of the kind to speak of. Their faith was ample, but the two succeeding deaths had imbued them with a feeling of fear and dread that the simple presence of the Messiah for even a brief moment would have dispelled.

The doctor, followed by the pall-bearers, was on the way to his apartments when a messenger handed him a note from the Messiah. Hastily glancing at it, he saw it was an imperative order to proceed no further with the burial operations. Fearful of the outcome, Schweinfurth had determined at the last moment to forbid the test, being assured that if the woman was reported dead and should yet be restored to her friends on the following day, it would serve the same purpose without incurring the risk involved in interment.

The doctor was sorely disappointed at the unexpected decision of the Messiah. He had set his heart on the performance of this test, feeling sure of its successful accomplishment, and disliked to give it up. However, there was nothing to do but obey the orders of Schweinfurth. These could not be disregarded by even so favored an apostle as Dr. Brown. So he went reluctantly back to the grave and announced that the Lord did not desire the sister to be buried, from which it was only to be inferred that he did not intend she should pass from among them forever.

There was much joy among the faithful when this announcement was made. None of them wanted to see the grave close over the narrow tenement, and as they dispersed they loudly expressed their gratitude that the Lord had decided to prevent this.

It was stated the next morning by the doctor that the dead sister would probably be restored to life about the middle of the afternoon. To some of the inmates of the home, impatient to witness the promised evidence of the Messiah's divine power, the day dragged along very slowly, as would be the case with most of us under similar circumstances.

Early in the afternoon the doctor took the body in hand. The bandages were removed and the wax taken from the various sealed apertures. Then the body was briskly rubbed with a warm solution intended to open the pores. It had retained its warmth, though no signs of returning animation were yet apparent.

Half an hour before the time set for the woman to come from her trance her limbs began to twitch. These movements continued with increased force for perhaps twenty minutes, when the patient opened her eyes and looked calmly around, as though she had all the time been perfectly aware of what was taking place.

"How do you feel?" asked the doctor.

"Much better, thank you," was the calm reply. "I have had a long and refreshing sleep."

"That's good. I will now leave you to get yourself into shape to see company."

The doctor then withdrew and caused to be spread the gratifying intelligence that Mrs. Bruce was again of them and with them, and could not remember when she felt so well.

To the faithful in Zion, who had so eagerly watched for a manifestation of the supernatural power of their deific head, the restoration of Mrs. Bruce was nothing short of a miracle. The Messiah had not even gone near the dead woman. He had not seen her in the embrace of death except through the eye of omnipotence and this made her restoration to them the more impressive.

It was announced that the Lord would not appear until the Sunday service, and when, at that time, the assembled members of the Church Triumphant saw him take his place in the pulpit, they looked upon his calm face with a deep reverential love that absorbed the whole being. There were few present who would not have felt in an ecstasy of joy to lay down their lives in the service of the Messiah.

Schweinfurth made no allusion to either of an important events of the last few days, but preached a long, powerful and affecting sermon, in which he expatiated at length upon the supreme duty of unquestioning submission to the decrees of the Father.

After that the affairs of Zion again resumed the even tenor of their way.

Chapter XVII
A Vain Woman's Blighted Life

THE SECOND YEAR OF Clara and Arthur's connection with the Church Triumphant was drawing to a close when the peaceful life of the members was again disturbed by the obstreperous actions of a recalcitrant convert, followed by the persecutions of the unhallowed world.

Clara still cared for the children of Zion—except those born without sin—in a very satisfactory manner, only that her lack of faith still kept her in a secondary place, for, to imbue the minds of the scholars with the doctrines of the new dispensation, required the exercise of authority by one wholly converted. However, the Lord had lately promised her that she would soon have an awakening from her spiritual lethargy and attain a condition of purity and holiness of which she now had no conception. She did not know the nature of the change in store for her, though she felt sure the Lord would keep his promise and she would soon be abundantly blessed.

Arthur still filled his position of equerry to the prince of light in a way that frequently called words of praise from that gracious personage. The Messiah gave himself no concern as to what advancement Arthur was making spiritually. He knew very well he was making none and probably never would; but if he performed his arduous duties satisfactorily, asked for no remuneration and made no disturbance he might go along till the "crack o'doom," or until he was worn out.

Strange as it may seem, Arthur and Clara had not yet seen each other, not even at the evening concerts and entertainments which were sometimes held, and which will be hereafter described. While Clara remained in ignorance of Arthur's presence, he now felt assured from what he had been able to learn, that she was in the house and had not yet rid herself of the phase of unbelief that kept her from advancing to a higher plane of life.

Among the newer converts was a pretty, vain and very foolish little woman—Mrs. Medora Miller Kinehan—who was a source of vexatious care to the Messiah. Previous to becoming a member of the community, nearly a year before, she had resided with her husband, an industrious mechanic, in Rockford. She was considered a consistent and earnest member of the Presbyterian church of which Dr. Conde was then pastor; but she fell into the hands of the emissaries of Schweinfurth and in a short time became a convert to the new faith. The result was the disruption of another family. She declared her purpose of going to heaven to live, and her husband left her, their little son and the city, and never returned. In a short time Mrs. Kinehan carried out her resolution of going to Zion. She moved her household effects down to the farm, where they were stored in the loft of one of the barns, and she and her little son were admitted to the community.

Under the influence of Schweinfurth this woman exhibited peculiarities that would be laughable were they not overcast with such somber shadows. She had been flattered by being told that she was a pretty woman, and she was. Her beauty had the effect of making her exceedingly vain. She therefore conceived the idea that when she went to Zion the Messiah would at once install her in a comfortable place, where her duties, if she had any to speak of, would be light and pleasant. In this, of course, she was disappointed. It has already been seen that things are not done that way in Zion. Instead of being agreeably situated, with merely nominal duties, she was informed she would have to start at the bottom, advancing as she grew in grace. This, being altogether something else than she anticipated, was harrowing to her vanity, and the seeds of rebellion were lodged in her heart from the beginning.

It was while she was in one of these rebellious moods that Schweinfurth called her before him and held her spellbound for two hours. When she entered the room she made a flippant and angry remark, but before she could let loose the floodgate of her wrath he transfixed her with a glance and the single word, "Medora!" He kept those eyes of his fixed upon her for two hours, and when he got up and left the room she fell to the floor in a faint.

Mrs. Kinehan had frequent talks with Clara, and it is likely that, in sowing the seeds of unbelief, she did much to keep the latter from progressing spiritually.

Finally one day when the Messiah was absent, Mrs. Kinehan stole away from heaven. Throwing the bag over her shoulder which she had filled with a number of smaller articles belonging to her, and clasping her little boy firmly by the hand, she sallied forth from the gates of Zion, bravely trudging along in the heat and dust until a friendly farmer came along and gave them a "lift" into the city.

It soon became noised about in Rockford that an angel had deserted heaven, and the pretty, misguided little woman became an object of exceeding interest to the representatives of the various local papers. She was interviewed by nearly all of them in succession, and, being in a vindictive frame of mind, did not hesitate to impart all she knew of the

An angel stole away from heaven.

workings of Zion. She stopped temporarily with a lady friend, a member of the church to which she had belonged before her infatuation for Schweinfurth, and there Mr. Williams, the reporter for the "Times," found her. After a few preliminary remarks she said, in response to a query if she had left the home and the Messiah for all time:

"I have had an experience that will last me a lifetime. Schweinfurth is Satan in sheep's clothing. I am convinced his relations with other women are of the most unholy nature, and that, while the rest are deceived, he is a villain, a fraud and an immoral reprobate."

"What are your reasons for thinking so?" asked Williams.

"Because I have seen Miss Mary Weldon, the daughter of the old gentleman, go into his chamber when he retired and remain there until morning."

"How do you know she remained there?"

"Of course I am not positive as to that, but I have seen her come out again in the morning as I went to my work."

"Did no one ever say anything about this?"

"I spoke to the Lord once about it and he said he was suffering from a severe headache and his head was so heated he could not sleep, so she attended him, administering cracked ice and cold clothes. I remarked that if he was the Lord he ought to be able to dispel his head trouble without the aid of Miss Weldon, but he said his disciples gave him too much trouble."

"What else did he do that seemed to be out of the line of propriety?"

"When he was tired in the daytime he used to go into Mrs. Tuttle's room instead of his own. I thought it very odd, but he used to explain it by saying he wanted to get away from the noise."

"What else have you observed?"

"A short time ago I discovered that Miss Weldon was in a delicate condition. I told Mr. Schweinfurth what I had found and asked him how he accounted for it. He looked at me a moment and then said: 'It is true. It is the work of the Holy Ghost. If you were entirely redeemed and sanctified you would understand it. There can be no sin in her.'"

"Did you believe him?"

"I must confess I did not. I tried to believe it, but couldn't. If she had a natural protector like the Virgin Mary it might not seem so strange, but I don't see how God can expose a girl that way."

"They do not deny the girl's condition at the home?"

"Of course not. Do we not all have eyes? The child is liable to be born at any moment. When I saw her yesterday she was reclining in an easy chair in the front parlor, hourly looking for the coming event."

"Happy, was she?"

"Supremely so. Her eyes fairly sparkled with the satisfaction she felt at being permitted to bring a sinless child into the world."

"Are there other children of the Holy Ghost there?"

"Yes, several. Mrs. Tuttle has two, and there are others."

"This will be news to the people of Rockford, Mrs. Kinehan."

"I guess it will. Dr. Brown attends to all these things, so that they never have to call a city doctor or let people outside know what is going on."

"Did you ever speak to Mrs. Tuttle about her children?"

"Yes; I told her once such things were beyond my limit of faith, and she said to me, 'O, hush! When such wicked doubts enter your mind you must not give way to them. Believe and trust; it is all you can do.'"

"Did Schweinfurth ever say any thing improper to you?"

"No; he knew better. He is a very sharp man and he knew he had not won my soul fully. Don't you suppose Satan knows whether he has got a soul fully delivered to him. Schweinfurth knows, for I verily believe he is the evil one himself."

"Do you remember anything he said to you recently?"

"Not long ago he said I had reached the time when I must give up my life, my soul, my all, to him; when I must have no thought of my own, no will of my own, no aspirations—when I must become fully redeemed and live only to execute his will and obey his pleasure."

"Then what?"

"My eyes were opened at last and I was disgusted and disheartened. I decided to leave the place and its infamy and if possible get back to my husband and live again a life of devotion to my home."

"How were you treated then? What about your work and your food?"

"If ever there was a set of devoted, uncompromising white slaves, they are the people who live at heaven.

He teaches absolutely that there is no other God on earth by himself—that his word is the law. All the women and men, except those who have reached the dignity of angels, have their task assigned them, and they work hard and constantly. My work was cooking, and I was kept in the kitchen all the time, with scarcely any rest often from seven o'clock in the morning until ten at night. When I went there I was told I must give up everything to the Lord. I gave him my watch and chain, my rings and all my jewelry. They were tithes to the church, and he has them yet. The others gave up everything. I have no idea what money and valuables he has, but he must have a lot. We were given vegetables and bread for food. He always had meat, but told us it was not good for us, and that we should deny ourselves. He gave no butter and no coffee. The food was hardly nourishing enough for the fatiguing work we had to do. Very often we were faint and worn out and during his long sermons would fall asleep from exhaustion. That used to make him terribly angry. One day he preached a sermon in which he said he would summon thunderbolts and strike those who went to sleep during the service. After that we just propped our eyes open and forced ourselves awake. We were afraid he would call a stroke from heaven and destroy us. But I noticed it didn't bother Mrs. Tuttle any. She used to go to sleep as she pleased, but no thunderbolts ever struck her."

"What does the venerable Father Weldon think about his daughter and the Holy Ghost?"

"O, he is awfully pleased. He has perfect faith in Schweinfurth and worships him devoutly. The other day he stood up before a lot of us and solemnly said: 'What God has done once he can do again, and do as often as the pleases.'"

"Did you anticipate if you remained much longer the Holy Ghost claim would be used to your injury?"

"I can't say what might have followed. I saw enough and learned enough to be satisfied that with all his smoothness and pretense he is a consummate impostor, and I left. I think when I lost my belief in him there was no other extreme to which he could lead me."

After a few more questions and answers of an unimportant nature, Mr. Williams took his leave and hastened to his office to write his interview. He knew, though Mrs. Kinehan did not, that her disclosures were certain to awaken the indignation of the community, and it would be surprising if vigorous measures were not taken to put a stop to the infamous proceedings at the Weldon home.

It will be observed in all of Mrs. Kinehan's answers to the questions of the interviewer that she was able to state very little with positiveness beyond and fact of Miss Weldon's condition and the treatment accorded herself and others not in favor with the Messiah. It was enough to awaken the righteous wrath of the respectable people of Rockford, but it was not enough upon which to base legal proceedings, as the sequel will show. For the next few days the papers teemed with sensational and highly colored accounts of life at the hot-bed of infamy so near their doors, but except in one or two instances the reports were altogether inaccurate.

It was generally conceded that Mrs. Kinehan was a disappointed woman, and very many people were uncharitable enough to say that had she reached the exalted place she expected at the outset, she would have yet been a shining light in Zion.

The next day she secured the services of a lawyer, and in a short time a wagon and an officer were sent to heaven for the household goods she had stored there. They were readily given up and carted to Rockford, and again stored at the home of a friend. Meanwhile her husband was communicated with by her former pastor and an attempt made at reconciliation. The effort was futile. He firmly refused to have any further intercourse with the misguided woman, and the correspondence ceased.

It is surprising into what a peculiar condition of mind Schweinfurth succeeds in bringing those who are brought into daily contact with him. This woman, notwithstanding she had pronounced him "a fraud and an immoral reprobate," besides several other things in a day or two left the home of her protector and, with her little boy, walked back to the door of heaven, threw herself at the feet of the Messiah, humbly sued for pardon and pleaded to be taken back into the fold.

Did the Lord lend ear to her obsecrations?

Not he, indeed. He spurned her from his presence as though she were the most loathsome thing on earth; and she, driven from even that poor refuge, with a heart torn with anguish turned her face once more toward the city, and with tears of bitterness streaming from her eyes led her little boy along the hot and dusty road.

Now what? The next day she found the lawyer she had employed to recover her effects from Schweinfurth had, on learning of her proposed return to Zion, attached the goods for his services and was unwilling to make any concession, expressing the belief that whatever he might do in that direction would eventually inure to Schweinfurth. He had some consideration for the erring woman but none for the blasphemer at Zion.

Again her friends came to the rescue. The claims of the lawyer and the costs of the justice were satisfied and her goods packed and shipped to the home of her mother in Kentucky. In a few days she and her child followed, a broken-spirited woman with blighted life and frosted hopes, without a ray of sunshine to brighten the pathway of the future.

But she had attained this distinction, if it could be made of any advantage to her: She was the first woman to desert heaven.

Chapter XVIII
A Certificate of Moral Character

THE DAY AFTER MRS. Kinehan's interview with the newspaper representatives of Rockford Miss Weldon's child was born. It was a gala day in heaven, and the rejoicings indulged in exceeded anything ever known there before but once, and that was when the Messiah returned after an absence of a fortnight at the branch homes. Both occasions were made memorable in the annals of Zion.

On the first occasion his angels had sorely missed him and the apostles had yearned for his return, and when they received definite information that he was on the homeward journey Mrs. Tuttle resolved to make his return no less illustrious than the entrance of Christ into Jerusalem. Two days before he was due all ordinary labor was suspended and every one went to work on the grand reception and feast which were to signalize his home-coming. Details scoured the woods for wild flowers and the flower beds around heaven were stripped of every blossom; and not only that, but the florists of Rockford were called upon for many elaborate floral designs.

The morning of his coming dawned bright and fair, and one hour before he was expected the prettiest damsels, decked in gala attire, literally carpeted the road for a mile with the flowers. The entire heavenly host met him nearly two miles from the house, where they unhitched the horses from the carriage that bore his sacred person, and, attaching a long rope covered with evergreen, hauled him to the abode that had been so lonely while he was away. Cheers rent the air as the procession moved over the flower-strewn road, and the vociferous applause that went up when the house was reached was something those present will remember as long as they live.

Old Father Weldon was standing on the front step, and while he waved one hand vigorously kept the other behind his back. As soon as a halt was called he advanced with stately step to the carriage, and then all saw what he had been hiding. It was a big gilt-paper crown, and as he placed it over the Messiah's pompadour he made a low bow and stentoriously shouted:

"Hail, thou mighty King—thou the Almighty God!"

Then revelry and rejoicing began. All the handsome girls wore short dresses—some of them exceedingly short ones—and danced until they could dance no longer. Fiddlers fiddled, harpers harped, paeans of thanksgiving went up, and in every possible way the poor dupes evinced their devotion to the prodigal Messiah. The evening was spent in dancing, singing, and a series of tableaux, and the welcome home ended in a grand feast, at which wine flowed like water—for Schweinfurth and his favorites—while the others had to be satisfied with something just a little better than their usual homely fare.

The birth of Miss Weldon's child was not made so munificent an occasion, but it was made memorable by the mirth and hilarity which prevailed during the day and evening. A good deal of time had been spent getting ready for the great event, the work being done under the direction of Mrs. Tuttle. There were passages selected for each member of the community to recite, except a few, among whom was Arthur, who were not permitted to have any part in the festivities.

Although celebrating the advent of the child, and the passages were selected eulogistic of Schweinfurth and some of the poor people had a hard time committing their speeches to memory.

In the evening they all met in the parlor, where all except the musicians and the dancing girls in abbreviated skirts formed in line and awaited the blowing of the horn which should announce the approach of the Messiah. Directly he came in, leaning on the arm of Mrs. Tuttle. She led him to a large arm-chair decorated with flags and flowers and placed the gilt-paper crown on his head. Then the music began and the faithful marched and counter-marched until they were thoroughly tired. Then the prepared speeches were directed at the benign individual who sat there smiling on his faithful people. When the oratorical outburst subsided the marchers stepped aside and the short-skirted girls danced and capered until out of breath. And it is only fair to say that in the matter of high and lofty kicking some of the young women elevated their pedal appendages in a way that would have done credit to professionals.

The child, which is called Myrtle, is as like the Lord as it is possible for man and child to be. Schweinfurth has sandy hair, "kinky" and wavy, and so has the child. The eyes of both are identically the same hue of hazel, and nose and mouth are strikingly similar. The Messiah has exhibited a marked fondness for the child since the day of its birth.

Indeed, he is very fond of all the children of heaven born into the world without sin. The day of Myrtle's birth a thoroughbred Jersey cow was set apart for her exclusive use and a maid was appointed to wait upon the mother. It is needless to say the luckless young woman who officiated in this capacity was kept busy late and early.

There was rather an unpleasant sequel to the birthday festivities when the papers were brought from the city, the next day. They contained Mrs. Kinehan's expose with comments on the birth of Miss Weldon's child that were anything but complimentary to the professed Lord of the universe. There was an intimation, also, that the grand jury, then in session, would take cognizance of this sink of iniquity, as one paper described the place. Schweinfurth was unconcerned as to what the grand jury did, for he knew it could not go far without evidence which it was impossible for it to obtain; but his serious apprehensions were aroused by the announcement that a number of indignant citizens were earnestly debating the advisability of taking the law into their own hands and mobbing the libertine blasphemer. When he saw this he called the household together and made a lengthy address on the want of obedience on the part of some of them. He said there was no telling what God would allow to happen if they did not render obedience. If a violent mob laid hands on heaven it would be directly due to their disobedience. He so worked on the feelings of his dupes that some of them cried bitterly, and one disciple, more earnest than the rest, burst out with these words:

"O, Lord, I love you with all my heart, my mind, my soul. I will never disobey a single command. I will willingly lay down my life for you and do anything you command, even if I am burned at the stake for it."

That night and for some time after a picket guard of ten men went on duty every evening and remained until daylight, when another guard of five men took their place during the day. The house was put in shape to give any visiting mob a warm reception.

There was one person in the community who secretly wished a mob, and a strong one, would come. That person was Arthur Fitzroy. He believed such a visitation would mean the success of the long deferred project which brought him there.

That afternoon Schweinfurth prepared the following manifesto, to which he caused to be attached the signature of a considerable number of the members of the community and then procured its publication in several of the local papers:

To the People of Rockford and Vicinity:—

We, the undersigned members of this family or assembly of Mount Zion, desire to bear unto you a word of testimony in solemn truth and verity, as to the relation that exists and has ever existed here between the opposite sexes.

Mr. Schweinfurth has, from the very beginning of the history of the Church Triumphant, taught us that to rise to the divine plane of living, it is absolutely necessary for the married people to all practice continency and the unmarried chastity; both in the strictest sense of the word. In this matter there is ever uniformly observed the greatest rigor on the part of us all.

We are a family. The deportment of the men is such as it would be if all the women and young ladies about them were mothers and sisters. No looseness or impropriety would here be tolerated for one single instant. We are all of the same mind on this, as well as all other subjects. The men, by noble endeavor and lofty discipline, have banished from the mind the idea of sex and sexual love. The love existing between the sexes is purely platonic, or more properly expressed, Christadelphian—a Christly brotherhood and sisterhood in the family of God.

The closest proximity of male and female in meeting or parting, or associating, is manifested in the shaking of hands. Nor is there aught here of the nature of unpleasant constraint or restraint. We delight thus to live.

There has by us, for the time being, been laid aside the idea of marrying and giving in marriage. Nor do we feel that in so doing we have jeopardized the morals of our church and society.

Our church is established upon the foundation of absolute and divine purity of heart and life. Our society is inside the church. The church has erected her walls and boulevards of chastity and virtue around her society. Thus is safety insured unto her charge and foster child, which her society is.

We, as a church, believe that Jesus of Nazareth was conceived by the Holy Spirit of God; that the Virgin Mary did not bear the seed of man, but that the new life was a direct impartation from God, the Invisible Spirit. We also believe that this same God still lives and that when He had clothed souls in robes of Virgin white He blessed some of them in precisely the same manner in which He blessed the Holy Virgin of yore. We, with one voice, solemnly declare before God and man that inside the Church Triumphant or in this family there has been no compromise of virtue and no traversing of the civil law of this fair country nor this our magnificent commonwealth. It is as far from us as is vice from virtue to foster or practice or tolerate aught that is condemned in our civil statutes.

Herein have we ever exercised ourselves to have always a conscience void of offense toward God and toward man. We are most assuredly in the closest friendship with law and order. We are in our private lives just what we desire you to believe us to be.

Witness our hands and seals:

S. S. Weldon,
Mrs. A. Weldon,
Mary L. Weldon,
John E. Weldon,
Samuel Weldon,
Peter Weldon,
Wm. G. Weldon,
Lem S. Weldon
Marguerita Weldon,
Geo. J. Schweinfurth,
A. Marie Schweinfurth,
Walter M. Johnson,
Abram M. Brown, M.D.
Geo. Eddy,
Mrs. Myra S. Eddy,
Laura Scott,
Mrs. Eva L. Welch,
Thos. McGinty,
Mrs. S. E. Paynter,
Melissa Collins,
Mrs. A. J. Tuttle,

Paul T. Bartlett,
Geo. B. Morgan,
Miss S. S. Freeman,
M. Lucile Barr,
Geo. F. Ostrander,
Miss H. R. Lines,
Ruth B. Chase,
Leicester A. Bartlett,
Lily A. Raymond,
Mary Scott,
Wm. H. Barnes,
Sara Armour,
W. H. Armour,
Elmer G. Furbish,
Bertha I. Olson,
Mary E. Remsen,
Archibald Fraser,
Mrs. Amelia Frazer,
Norma Condrey,
J. Chester Whitney.

It will be observed that the names of Arthur and Clara are not appended to this document. It contains only the names of the trusted ones.

The following evening a meeting of citizens was called at Rockford, which was largely attended. The former pastor of Mrs. Kinehan, Dr. Conde, presided, and in announcing the object of the meeting he said:

"As American citizens we should never allow such an imposition on our community. If there is no law that can reach Schweinfurth it is time there was one. It was never contemplated by our forefathers when they made our laws that such fallacies as this should be permitted within the borders of our liberty-loving country. A short time ago this man dared not proclaim what he is now proclaiming. We are gathered to-night to devise some measure to suppress this daring impostor. I do not advocate violent measures, but I want a committee to wait on him and express the united sentiment of our citizens. Why, this man is ten times worse than Brigham Young, and there is no law to reach him. Now, let us act together in this important matter and at least show the outside world that we do not and will not sanction such infamy."

The tendency of the remarks made by others indicated that no violence would be employed, but he was to be calmly and determinedly informed that his presence was objectionable. If he did not accept the invitation to go, legal measures would be employed. A committee of representative citizens was appointed to wait upon him, but the members never seemed to be able to get together afterward to make the visit, and the meeting was thus shorn of practical results.

When Schweinfurth read in the papers of next day what had been done he smiled to himself and then reduced his guard. He cared nothing for any legal measures that might be taken, for he knew that in that respect he was impregnable. But he was afraid of mob violence. The day of this meeting a mysterious stranger procured a license authorizing the marriage of George Jacob Schweinfurth and Mary Weldon. Afterward the members of the home denied that such a marriage was ever contemplated, and the Messiah himself declared the license was secured through the agency of some of the newspaper people for the purpose of creating a sensation.

A few days afterward the birth of Mary Weldon's child was made a subject of inquiry by the Grand Jury. The plea of Holy Ghost paternity was there made with such earnestness and apparent innocence by the inmates of Zion as to call forth the following remarkable document, which is described by a local attorney as "a certificate of moral character:"

> To the Hon. James. H. Cartwright,
> Presiding Judge of the Circuit Court,
> Of Winnebago Country
> State of Illinois.
>
> We, the Grand Jury, would respectfully report to your honor:
>
> That at the suggestion of the State's Attorney, in his charge to us, and upon the formal complaint of one of our body, we have made a thorough investigation of the alleged immoral practices of George Jacob Schweinfurth and his followers who live at the Weldon farm in the Town of Winnebago, this county.
>
> That we have taken the testimony of all persons whom we had reason to believe would be cognizant of any facts in the case, including nearly all those who live on the Weldon farm, and their nearest neighbors, and that we find absolutely no proof whatever upon which to base any criminal prosecution.
>
> With the exception of the fact of the birth there of one illegitimate child (whose paternity cannot be ascertained; the mother, Mary Weldon, making a preposterous claim in relation thereto) no fact has

come to our knowledge, that in any manner bears against any of these people, so far as the morality of their lives is concerned.

LUCIEN WILLIAMS,
Foreman of the Grand Jury.
Filed October 11, 1890.

LEWIS F. LAKE, Circuit Clerk.
Office of Clerk of the Circuit Court.
STATE OF ILLINOIS,
WINNEBAGO COUNTY.
} SS.

I, LEWIS F. LAKE, Clerk of the Circuit Court and Keeper of the Seal thereof, and custodian of the Records and Files of said Court, in and for the County of Winnebago, in the state of Illinois, do hereby certify that I have carefully examined the foregoing and hereto annexed Transcript .... with the original now on file and of record in this office, and that the same is a true and correct copy of the original record of the report of the Grand Jury in regard to the investigation of the alleged immoral practices of George Jacob Schweinfurth and followers.

{ Seal } In witness thereof, I have here unto set my hand and affixed the seal of said Court, at my office in Rockford, this 11th day of December, A.D. 1893.

LEWIS F. LAKE, Clerk.

The indignation which the birth of little Myrtle aroused very soon subsided, at least so far as any further public demonstration was concerned. Some of the members of the committee went so far as to consult legal experts, but they were told there was no legal means of reaching the wily pretender, and from that day to this he has remained unmolested by the law.

Chapter XIX
Another Holy Ghost Child

THERE WAS A LONG season of peace in the home after the exciting events recorded in the preceding chapters. A Sunday or two after, however, in one of his sermons, the Messiah said:

"There is no question but Mrs. Kinehan was possessed of an evil spirit, which will eventually lead her to everlasting destruction and punishment. Time and again, as some of you know, she has averred her firm belief in the doctrine of immaculate conception and expressed the hope that the Lord would some day select her as an instrument of his will. That she was controlled by the powers of darkness is evident from the fact that she was frequently seen walking through the dormitory of the apostles after midnight, to their great chagrin and displeasure. Therefore there was nothing for me to do but to rid my blessed family of so disturbing and dangerous a person. She came here of her own accord, and departed in the same way. It is not the fault of the church if we could not make our views coincide with her whims. She brought down upon us by her false and wicked stories the minions of the law, and we were made the victims of cruel persecutions and unmerited obloquy because of her deviation from the line of moral rectitude. It is my purpose to eliminate every element of discord, to the end that the chosen people of the Almighty may not be disturbed in their onward an upward march to a divine perfection of life. Let her fall, into the pit of everlasting darkness and despair, incite you to renewed efforts for a better and purer life. It should remind you also of the imperative necessity for implicit obedience to my every mandate, and a shutting out from your hearts of all desires, inclinations and motives that are the outgrowth of wicked and wordly thoughts. It is a lesson that all may, and I hope all will, take to heart and profit by."

Thus Mrs. Kinehan was formally and publicly excluded from further connection with the Church Triumphant.

In the meantime there was another diminutive arrival at the home. Angelica, the "soul's mate" of the Messiah, was the woman to whom the blessing came this time. It was a beautiful little girl, and, like all the children of the Holy Ghost, was made much of by Schweinfurth, and placed high above those who had entered the world less auspiciously. It seemed to be a delicate child, yet Dr. Brown expressed the opinion that it would outgrow this tendency and in time become strong and robust.

The advent of this little one was kept from the knowledge of the public, though, as usual on such occasions, there was much rejoicing in Zion. This time the festivities did not begin until nine o'clock in the evening, because of the pressure of work about the place. Then charades, tableaux, and dancing occupied the evening. There are two organs, a piano and a variety of wind and string instruments in heaven, and people who know how to play them, so that pleasure may be had whenever the Lord feels disposed. On this occasion he sang a sacred solo, after which Miss Test and Norma Candrey represented statues, having little upon them to disabuse the mind of the thought that they were chiseled from marble. William Weldon, the one who lost his child, and who usually took the heroic rôles, represented Moses cursing the golden calf, and the same evening he showed his versatility by a spirited personation of Diabolis. The night ended with some terpsichorean revelries, in which Schweinfurth demonstrated that, however efficient as a Messiah, he was a miserable failure as a dancer.

Angelica herself seemed to fail after the birth of her little girl. She never was strong—always pale faced and fragile as a delicate house plant. A careful examination by Dr. Brown failed to disclose a diseased condition, more than that her lungs were weak and she showed a predisposition to bronchial trouble. The greatest care, he said, would have to be taken of her health. After that she was taken to the city very often with the Messiah and permitted to be in the open air when the weather was suitable as much as she pleased. There is no doubt her moderate and continued outdoor exercise did her good, and for a time at least her health was improved.

It has already been remarked that at one time she bore a striking resemblance to Clara. She did, yet only that she was so much more pale and delicate. But one who had not seen Clara for upwards of three years, and who knew that people in heaven, under the effects of incessant toil, confinement and insufficient food, are liable to great physical as well as mental deterioration, might easily mistake Angelica for the other.

She was walking leisurely about the lawn one pleasant day when Arthur Fitzroy caught sight of her white face and slight figure. His heart seemed to leap into his throat. Now, for the first time since the incarceration of his loved one within the detested walls of Zion, he would have an opportunity to speak to her. For he was sure it was she, notwithstanding the astounding change she appeared to have undergone. Certainly Schweinfurth was a severe and unrelenting taskmaster, destroying the fairest among his dupes without the slightest compunction; and it seemed to Arthur, as he contemplated the unnatural color of the face turned toward him, that both mental and physical faculties had been sadly impaired.

He must accost her at once. Looking stealthily about to see that he was not observed, he walked forward to meet her. When within a few feet of her he said, in a voice that was husky and uncertain:

"Clara!"

She heard him speak and turned her great, luminous eyes toward him; but there was no sign of recognition. She was about to pass on without replying when he again asked:

"Do you not know me, Clara? I am Arthur Fitzroy from Shelbyville. I came here just after you did. I have been looking and waiting for you ever since."

The young woman looked at him strangely, apparently not understanding what he was talking about.

"Speak to me, Clara!" he continued, in tones of anguish. "Tell me, for God's sake, that you know me!"

"My name is not Clara," she replied, in a soft, sweet, calm voice, with a look of pitying tenderness, "and I do not know you. You have mistaken me for someone else."

"No! no!" cried Arthur, his voice choking with emotion. "I am not mistaken. You are Clara—Clara McCoy. Tell me that I have not passed entirely from your mind."

"How can I say that when I certainly have no recollection of ever seeing you before?"

"Are you not from Kentucky?" persisted Arthur, the tears springing to his eyes in spite of himself.

"Yes; I am from Kentucky. But what makes you look and act so strangely? Are you unhappy?"

"I am very unhappy, Clara."

"Do not call me Clara, please," she insisted, though in a kindly voice. "I am Angelica, chosen of the Lord, and divinely blessed, and placed among the holiest women by the loving Father."

Arthur's eyes were fairly starting from his head. As soon as he was able to articulate he gasped:

"Have you a child?"

"A pure and holy child," she answered, with a smile of ineffable joy. "A sweet and beautiful daughter, born into the world without sin or carnal knowledge."

"My God!" cried the anguished man. "Have you, too, come to this?"

"Tell me, for God's sake, that you know me!"

"Blessed be the name of the Lord!" she answered. "His righteousness endureth forever. Are you enrolled among the fully redeemed?"

Arthur cast one despairing look at the calm, white face before him, and then, his own features distorted and his heart filled with unutterable woe, he turned and walked toward the barn where he spent his comfortless nights. He went directly to his room, where he sat motionless for an hour, his face buried in his two hands and his mind a prey to torturing thoughts.

In the evening when a room-mate entered the cheerless chamber he found Arthur stretched upon the floor insensible.

After lingering for three years among associations altogether repugnant to him, nursing a hope that he could not relinquish, the sudden and unexpected discovery that the object of his unwavering devotion had surrendered body, mind and soul to the arch-plotter at the head of the unholy brotherhood, was more than his mind, already shaken by repeated distresses, could withstand, and he sank beneath the cruel stroke.

Schweinfurth was promptly informed of his condition and Dr. Brown was directed to go and see what could be done for him. The Messiah well knew what had affected the unhappy man so deeply, for he had watched the interview with Angelica from behind the sheltering blinds of a convenient window, and was very well satisfied to let stand the false impression he knew Arthur had received. Perhaps now that the lamp of hope no longer burned the man would want to go away. Very well; he could be spared, although he had been intelligent, diligent and faithful in the performance of his allotted tasks, which was all the Messiah ever expected of him.

The doctor found him threatened with brain fever, which disease subsequently developed. The result was that Arthur lay for a long time hovering between life and death. His strong constitution triumphed in the end, and after a time he was able to be upon his feet again. But the saddest phase of his illness was that the disease—at least that's what the doctor said it was—had left his mind greatly impaired. He stared vacantly at those who spoke to him, sometimes without answering, and again would give replies altogether irrelevant to the questions asked. His mind seemed to improve some after he was able to be out and around again, but the cloud did not pass entirely away. Any attempt to concentrate his thoughts was invariably a failure, and he seemed to have lost the faculty of placing events in any consecutive order, so that he could not tell when he came to Zion, or whether he was an inmate once or a dozen times.

Of course in this feeble mental condition Arthur was no longer able to fill the responsible position he held about the stables before his illness. There had never been so efficient a man at Zion for the duties which he performed. Now he was only capable of the meanest drudgery under the supervision and direction of someone else. However, the Messiah did not turn him adrift, as he thought of doing when the poor man was first able to be about again, or, rather, of making him a county charge, for he was incapable of caring for himself. Schweinfurth had a pronounced opposition to running what he termed a private lunatic asylum, though no one probably ever saw so many disposed to idiocy gathered together before, outside of an asylum for the insane.

"What do you think about this man Johnson?" asked the Messiah of the doctor one day. "Do you believe his mind will ever be clear again?"

It will be remembered that Johnson was the name by which Arthur was registered at Zion.

"I hardly know," answered the doctor. "There's no accounting for the vagaries of the brain. Sometimes in cases such as his the patient recovers his reason in a moment, the light of intelligence coming as swift as an electric flash, which it really is. The cloud that obscured the illuminating rays of reason seems to be swept aside with a stroke and the light floods in. Others regain their reason gradually, some only partially, and others remain about the same to the end. I am inclined to the belief that Johnson's reason will return to him by imperceptibly slow stages. Mesmeric treatment, I think, would help him, even to a greater extent than it would one whose mind was filled with strange hallucinations. His brain is in a stunned, lethargic condition, from which it must recuperate much as a person would recover from a severe blow on the head. Of course drugs are of little or no avail. But he has a most vigorous constitution, and that is greatly in favor of his full and complete recovery in course of time. He is a person of fine sensibilities, and I do not think he ever had much faith in the truths of the Church Triumphant."

"I do not believe he had any," replied Schweinfurth. "Indeed, I am quite certain he came and remained here for no other purpose than to sprite Emeline away if the opportunity was ever afforded him."

"He must have thought a good deal of the girl to seek her rescue with such remarkable patience."

"Her what?"

"Beg pardon, Mr. Schweinfurth," said the doctor, with the faintest symptom of a smile that found no encouragement in the look of the Messiah. "That was a *lapsus lingua*. I intended to say that he exhibited remarkable pertinacity in remaining here for the length of time he has, in order to secure possession of this young woman and drag her back into the follies of the world."

"He will not care for her now?"

"Certainly not in his present condition."

"Do you fancy, Doctor, that if his reason were to return at once he would develop an ungovernable disposition—that he would be a dangerous person to have about the home?"

The Messiah was thinking of the consuming anger that would be liable to take possession of the outraged man with returning reason.

"I hardly know what his disposition was," returned the doctor; "but it seems to me he was not an irascible person. Of course a man who will quietly pursue a plan with such unwavering persistency as he exhibited, is liable to have a dogged will somewhere back of his placidity that might make him ugly to handle when he took hold for the final struggle. Quiet, determined men are the most to be feared, and he was not here, as you say, for his spiritual uplifting. But I think there is no liability of our being able to say that 'Richard is himself again' for a long time to come. If he regains his reason it will come by slow degrees. I will keep an eye on him and let you know from time to time how he is progressing."

"I wish you would, Doctor. Watch him closely. I do not like to send him away; at the same time I am fearful that he may just get sense enough before long to make him troublesome."

"I'll watch him, Mr. Schweinfurth. By the way, if I may be permitted to change the subject, have you noticed another proposition to put an act through the legislature aimed directly against the perpetuity of the Church Triumphant?"

"I have."

"What will you do if it is passed?"

"Just what I have always done. The story of the Savior's birth will be my only defense, the Bible my only plea. Is that not enough?"

"It is," replied the doctor, as the two walked toward the house from the shade of the spreading elm beneath which they had been talking. "But, between you and I, Mr. Schweinfurth, I do not believe the measure will ever become a law."

"Nor do I," replied the other.

Chapter XX
Out of Bondage

MATTERS RAN ALONG IN the usual quiet groove for a few months after this, and Schweinfurth began to think it was time Clara had acquired the requisite degree of faith to entitle her to a condition of holiness. There could be no fault found with her work. No case of inattention or dereliction had been reported against her that was not soon shown to be groundless, and the children loved her as deeply as she loved them. But the Lord was growing impatient of her perversity. She expressed a firm belief in his divine attributes, as all his poor victims accepted his magnetic fascination for supreme power, but recoiled with undisguised horror from the repeated suggestion that she might become blessed through the avenue of immaculate maternity if she but desired. Schweinfurth had said little of this to her himself, but his women had repeatedly done so for him. Their efforts were fruitless; she could not be made to reconcile herself to it. Therefore Schweinfurth, having cast his lascivious eyes toward her very often of late, resolved to take her in hand himself.

She was surprised one afternoon to receive a summons to wait upon him in his private sitting-room. A premonitory feeling of dread took possession of her when she received this order. She could not think of any sin of commission or omission except the one, grave enough, it is true, that she could not acquiesce in the doctrine of immaculate conception. However, she did not dare hesitate to obey the imperative call of the Messiah, and in a few minutes she found herself tapping timorously at the door of his room, the palpitations of her terrorized heart being almost as distinct to her ears as her timid rap upon the door.

Schweinfurth admitted her, and as he bade her enter he gave her a reassuring smile that had the effect of putting her more at her ease. He took her hand and led her to a seat on the sofa, and then he drew up a rocking chair and seated himself immediately in front of her.

"I have called you here, Emeline," he said, "to talk with you of your unbelief. I am exceedingly distressed to know that now, after a residence of nearly four years among God's favored and accepted people, you are still unwilling to accept in full the mandates of the Most High—to acknowledge the honor conferred only upon those whose faith has borne them upward beyond the possibility of sin."

As he talked he kept his gaze fastened on Clara's face until the room seemed to swim before her and the chairs to be going through the measures of a minute. Everything grew dark before her eyes, and for a moment or two she could see nothing. Then his face emerged out of the cloud of darkness, with the basilisk eyes still fastened upon her. Clara made a powerful effort to concentrate her will forces and bravely combated in spirit the snake-like fascination of his eyes. She succeeded, but when he withdrew his gaze she was so weak and exhausted that she could not have risen to her feet had she tried.

"You must know, Emeline, there is no clause I teach, or anything in the principles of the Church Triumphant in opposition either in letter or spirit to the Scriptures. Our religion is the only one in existence in strict accordance with every word of the Gospel.

Were you not a student of the Scriptures before you came here?"

"I cannot remember the time," answered Clara, "when I did not read my chapter at night. I was brought up to revere the Bible as the best of books."

"That is quite right; every word of it is pure gold and should be studied carefully."

"I am sure of that, Mr. Schweinfurth."

"But it is greatly distorted nowadays by the theologians. One would scarcely recognize it, so masked and misshapen a thing have they made of it. Repeat some of your favorite passages."

Clara did as requested, and the Messiah let her go on for some time without interruption until she reached a verse especially dear: "For I am persuaded that neither life nor death shall be able to separate me from the love of God."

"That is in entire accord with my teachings," he said. "I love with a love unending, as true as the love of God, my Father, all who obey my mandates."

He then permitted Clara to recite nearly half of the fourteenth chapter of John, one dear to her since childhood, when he said:

"Yes; but you have a wrong idea of its meaning. The mansions mentioned are not a collection of houses in the skies. Jesus meant the body of man. I teach that heaven can be established in our own bodies. You are the temple for the indwelling of the Spirit. I believe that an ideal society such as we have here is as much heaven as can be found after death. Why, what would you think of a God who would make an earth and then go off up in the skies, leaving his poor creatures groping blindly for an invisible God. No; he sent me to be the truth, living and incarnate, to show men how to bring heaven down from the skies.

The site of the temple of glory is here on earth. The higher heaven is reserved for the supremely blessed."

"But," suggested Clara, "if the spires are in the heavens who would remain in the basement?"

"You may be assured of plenty of fresh air even in the basement, and the fires of Gehenna are near to destroy the offal."

"Is the temple itself not liable to destruction with such a sandy foundation?" she asked.

"The Lord is my refuge and my strength—my high tower into which I may run and be safe. Here we are away from the world and its snares. We live perfectly sinless and are therefore happy and safe."

Clara did not reply. At times during the conversation the could scarcely resist the powerful will he exercised upon her. Finally she felt that she was losing her control.

He had overcome her with his hypnotic influence and she was under his sway. He then went and sat down upon the sofa beside her and took her hand. She made no resistance—she could not.

"Pure and holy and beyond the power of sin,"—he spoke in a low, mellifluent voice—"you will conceive of no wrong in anything that you or I may do, for I am absolutely without sin. Even now you can feel no sense of wrong when I place my hand upon you in such a way as would be deemed improper by those in sin."

Clara felt a strange sensation thrill her whole being as he placed his hand upon her, but she was compelled to admit to him in spite of herself that she could see no wrong in it. Like others who came under his magnetic power she was forced to speak a belief in his words to which her whole nature was antagonistic.

When he had made her confess her belief and future adherence to the doctrine of immaculate conception, he said:

"At three o'clock to-morrow afternoon you will present yourself here, and an attendant—a pure and sinless woman such as you may become—will prepare you for the final rites that will seal you forever to the Lord. This is called, as you are already aware, 'The Garden of Eden Test.' It is necessary that you should pass through the ordeal in an absolute state of nudity in my presence. But, if you are free from sin, even thus unattired, you will be purity itself. If you have any feeling of wrong-doing while undergoing this test you will be compelled to return to your present sinful condition and remain without the pale of divine purity until your faith lifts you up."

He then permitted the poor girl to return to her duties. As soon as she passed beyond his baneful influence and had an opportunity to think, she began to realize the dreadful prospect before her. She ran to her room, closed the door and burst into tears. For the first time since she had been in heaven she longed for the security of her home at Shelbyville. Presently she dried her tears and sat down to think, and in a few minutes she had formed a resolution: She would run away and thus escape the fate which awaited her. She would go that very night, as soon as it was dark enough to enable her to get away without being seen. Having made up her mind to this, she returned to her duties in an easier frame of mind.

Running away from heaven was not as easy a matter as might be supposed. In the first place she had learned to love the children with whom she had been so long associated, and she knew they loved her and would grieve keenly for her when she came among them no more. It wrung her heart to tear herself away from them. Physical force was never used against anyone who desired to leave, but a much stronger power was employed. Clara, in common with all the others, had been taught all manner of evil would befall her if she should venture to withdraw from Zion—that the outside world would heap insult and rebuff upon her. She had seen others ask for money to get away and they had always met with refusal. These things, strengthened by the unfortunate condition of a mind for years under the destructive influence of the cunning teachings of Schweinfurth, was enough to hold almost anyone captive. Every attempt to throw off the yoke invariably subjected the unfortunate offender to a long period of humiliation, the punishment being supplemented with lengthy extracts from Schweinfurth's "revised" bible committed to memory when the victim should be resting. The sister of the Lord looked after this branch of the business, and she took a keen delight in seeing that the allotted tasks were righteously performed.

Notwithstanding her foreboding, Clara did not relinquish her purpose of leaving Zion. She informed no one of her intention, but as soon as it was dark put on her hat—it was the same one she brought with her—stole out into the night, and hastily left the place. She did not know what road to take to reach the city; but that did not matter so much, if she could only get away among strangers and escape the contempt she had been taught to expect. She sincerely hoped she would not meet anyone belonging to the place, for she knew they would use all manner of entreaties and arguments to persuade her to return, and, failing in that, would hasten to inform Schweinfurth of her desertion. He would speedily overtake her, and if he did and asked her to return she knew she had not the power of will to disobey him.

She walked steadily and rapidly for about an hour, when she began to feel fatigued, not being accustomed to that sort of exercise. Then, observing a light in what seemed to be quite a large house standing a little distance back from the road, she made her way to the door, not without much trepidation, for she feared a cruel rebuke the moment she announced where she came from. But, though the night was warm, she was too timid to remain alone out of doors all night. She had already been frightened several times by shadows she unexpectedly met in her path, and she felt herself becoming more nervous every moment. She could better stand the taunts of those with whom she came in contact than remain longer alone amid the silence and the shadows that so excited her fears.

To her surprise, instead of being despised and treated coldly she found kind treatment and sympathy. The house was that of a comfortable farmer named Simpson. They heard her story with many expressions of indignation, and told Clara, for whom the whole household felt truly sorry, that she could make her home there as long as she liked, or until she found some place that suited her better, and commended heartily the spirit that prompted her to make her escape from the machinations of the bold, unscrupulous impostor. The family knew all about him and his blasphemy, and had on more than one occasion refused his proffered assistance in busy seasons.

"That man," said Mr. Simpson to Clara, "is a wily, scheming villain, and sharp to a preternatural degree. You are extremely fortunate in getting out of his clutches. I believe he is an adept at mind-reading. The secret of his power is probably in his hypnotic influence over minds not steeled against the strength of his will."

"I am sure of it, sir," Clara replied.

"Well, you do not want to come in contact with him again. I think the most sensible thing for you to do would be to go back to your parents as soon as you feel able to make the journey."

"Do you suppose he will follow me there?" Clara asked, with a frightened look in her eyes.

"I can't tell," responded the farmer; "but if your parents are anything like I am he wouldn't follow you there but once. Are you afraid of him?"

"Yes, sir."

"Well, you'd better go to bed and have a good rest. You are certainly worn out. We can talk about what is best to do to morrow. You needn't be afraid of his coming here after you, for nothing would give me greater pleasure in the world than to stand the scamp on his head in the middle of the road out there and then start him back to his infernal

She made her way to the door.

harem with the aid of this good right foot," and as the angry farmer spoke he involuntarily raised and projected forward a pedal appendage that looked as though it might accomplish considerable in the direction he suggested.

"Would you like a cup of tea before you retire?" asked the kindly Mrs. Simpson.

"I am afraid it would put you to too much trouble," Clara replied timidly.

"Not a bit of it. Sit right still."

The good-hearted woman hurried away to procure the cheering beverage, and while she was gone her husband indulged in a few more remarks.

"He of Calvary had no place to lay His head, but this dude Savior— this dandified fop who struts the streets dangling a cane, with a glossy silk hat on his golden locks, attired as a gilded youth of fashion, or riding behind a coachman who draws the reins over the best pair of prancing steeds the country affords—is served as an Oriental potentate by a band of deluded followers. There in his harem he enjoys ease and indolence, subsisting on the ill-gotten gains of his scheming brain while the real possessors of his wealth toil in the fields."

Mrs. Simpson now came in with a steaming cup of tea, which Clara eagerly drank and was at once shown to her room.

Chapter XXI
A Ghost of The Past

CLARA AWOKE THE NEXT morning greatly refreshed. James Simpson had been called to the city and would not be back until evening. He was a man of superior intelligence and broad reading for one whose life had been spent upon a farm, where hard work a good part of the year is the portion of those who would succeed. His industry, thrift and good management had rewarded him with a competence, and there was no need of his working so hard now unless he felt disposed. He was a man of acute perceptive faculties and strong convictions, and his neighbors generally respected his opinions and sought his advice in matters of public and private import. At present he was a member of the county board, a special meeting of which he had been called to attend at Rockford. His son Charlie, who had just reached his majority, accompanied him to attend to some business matters, thus leaving Clara with Mrs. Simpson and the two younger members of the family, George, a boy of sixteen, and Florence, a bright, pretty girl of fourteen. Mrs. Simpson was a kind, motherly woman, who sympathized deeply with Clara in her unfortunate and humiliating condition, and she and the children did all in their power to make the poor young woman from Zion comfortable and draw her thoughts away from the accursed place. That, however, was not so easy of accomplishment. Clara found her mind continually reverting to the dear children she had learned to love, and she knew there were many pairs of eyes, which had sparkled with delight at her approach, now dim with tears because she did not come to them.

"Yes, dear," said Mrs. Simpson, to whom she confided her feelings, "those poor children will undoubtedly miss you, but that cannot be helped. Those little ones are innocent of wrong-doing, and it is a pity they cannot be rescued from the miserable fate in store for them. Their loves and affections are, of course, as strong as those of any other children; but you have this thought to console you—children soon forget their troubles. You will soon pass out of their minds and hearts, and some other unfortunate woman will take your place. Thank the good God above you that you have escaped from the power and influence of that monster of iniquity, and let your mind rest as little as possible on those you love whom you have left behind. Pray that they, at the first opportunity, may follow your example and escape."

"I am trying not to think of the home or its people," Clara replied. "That is right."

But, try as she would, it was impossible to drive the place from her thoughts for any length of time.

It seemed as though the powerful mesmeric influence of the Messiah was operating upon her even where she was, and the frightened glances she cast toward the road from time to time indicated a fear that she might see him approaching at any moment.

During the day the two women had frequent talks about the place, for Clara, in truth, could talk of little else, in the condition of mind in which the influence of Schweinfurth had left her. Indeed, during the entire day the poor girl experienced a tumult of emotions—sometimes of joy at her escape, again a fear that her refuge would be discovered, then a yearning to be back among the sisters and children she loved, while at times the sensations she experienced were entirely beyond the possibility of definition.

Late in the afternoon Mr. Simpson and Charles returned, and after tea, in the presence of the gathered family, he and Clara had another talk—he doing most of the talking and using the most emphatic expletives that a family conclave of Christian people would admit of. With his keen perception and knowledge of the methods of Schweinfurth he had not failed to diagnose the condition of Clara's mind, and he did his best to impress upon her the unfathomable depths of infamy of which the man was capable.

"You are familiar, Miss McCoy," he said, only with what has come under the limited range of your vision since you have been an inmate of the place. People outside know things that you would perhaps never hear of if you lived there all your life. You know, I suppose, how this sect originated?"

"I believe Mrs. Beekman was before the Messiah," answered Clara. "I have never been told any particulars."

"Well, I will tell you something that may be the means of helping you out of the miserable rut in which the influence of this man has forced you. If he ever indulges in reflection, which I doubt, he ought to spend some unpleasant moments, even in heaven surrounded with his adoring angels."

"I am sure I shall be glad to hear more about him," said Clara, in a tone of humility.

"It is true," resumed the farmer, "that his spiritualistic boom, so to speak, was received from Mrs. Beekman. Her first intimation that she had been entrusted with the task of building up a new spiritual kingdom resulted from what seemed to her a deliberate slight put upon her occult powers by the ladies of her husband's parish. It was said this indignity was in some way connected with the leadership of the weekly prayer-meetings; but, as Mr. Kipling would observe, that is another story.

"There is a long train of miserable events for which Schweinfurth is directly responsible that might furnish him food for thought when his mind is free from the case attendant upon his state, were he not utterly without compunction. Just how many homes he has broken up no one but himself can tell; nor can anyone else tell how many women to whom he has been the cause, direct or indirect, of ruin, or how many men's lives he has blasted. I will only speak at present, however, of the family of Mrs. Beekman herself, whose members are now scattered far and wide. The affairs of this family ought to weigh heavily upon his seared conscience, for the reason that it was the first into which he carried disaster.

"In the Beekman family there were two daughters, Lily and Rose, one a beautiful girl just growing into womanhood at the time their mother's connection with Schweinfurth began to be notorious, and the other a child too young to realize what the so-called spiritual union portended. Lily Beekman is variously described by those who knew her at that time as 'beautiful,' 'brilliant,' 'winning,' 'accomplished.' She was all of these, and more. The photographs taken when she was eighteen, shortly after she graduated from the Rockford seminary, show a delicate, sensitive face, with perfect features, clear cut and expressive, crowned by a mass of dark hair, breaking into curling waves over her forehead. Her eyes were brown, her teeth white and even and her complexion exquisite. 'She had a flower-like face,' said a prominent Chicago woman who was deeply interested in her, 'so beautiful that I never tired looking at her.' She is also described as unusually bright, devouring every book she could get hold of and studying eagerly and persistently. She played and painted, conversed well always, and at times even brilliantly. In short, she was a most interesting and lovable girl.

"It is no wonder that, possessed of so sensitive, refined and nervous a temperament, she felt keenly the miserable effects of the friendship her mother felt for Schweinfurth, or that she was acutely hurt by the unpleasant comments it aroused. Confronted daily by the evil wrought by perverted religion, all things religious became a nightmare to her. 'Don't talk to me about God,' she said to a gentle women with whom she boarded during a short time at a medical college. 'I have heard all I want to hear on that subject at home—and a good deal more, too!' Nothing would induce her to enter a church, and her views on Christianity, when she did express them, shocked those about her by her bitter cynicism. Schweinfurth she loathed, regarding him as the cause of her blighted home life and blank prospects. 'He is everything that is hateful to me,' she said at one time, 'but he has a curious sort of influence over me. If he should will me to take any step, no matter how abhorrent it might be to me, I am afraid I should do it.'

"The fact that Mrs. Beekman was very anxious for her daughter to accept her teaching and that of Schweinfurth and that she frequently alluded to her as 'set aside' for him, whatever that might mean, did not help matters much. All the circumstances of her daily life were such as would naturally fret and wear upon her almost to madness. Existence at home was an impossibility. She had no money and could only depend upon her untrained efforts for her daily bread. She was young and beautiful. What happened finally was only what her friends had feared, and what she herself had occasionally alluded to as a possibility.

When she left the medical college in Chicago at the end of her term, she visited some friends of her father in Oregon, Illinois, giving music lessons and teaching painting there for a short time. There the impulse to cut loose from the notoriety that followed her as Mrs. Beekman's daughter and the ward of Schweinfurth overcame every other scruple. She went away, saying she was going to hunt up a woman on the faculty of the medical college who had been particularly kind to her during her connection with that institution. That woman never saw her from that day to this—never heard from her, never knew, close friends as they had been, what had become of her until she was located by a newspaper man at Romeo, a little town in Michigan. The woman did see the Messiah, however, who, suave and self-possessed, went to her office looking after his straying lamb. She sent him away with ears that should have burned, though they probably didn't. Afterward she received letters from various of the apostles implying that she was party to Lily's disappearance, which of course was not true. The letters she invariably answered as courteously as she could.

"For several years her people heard nothing of the girl and had begun to fear that she was dead, when, shortly after her mother's death, she reappeared for a short time among her father's friends at Oregon, dropping out of sight at the end of three weeks as suddenly and as mysteriously as before. She is still at the little Michigan town where she was discovered, living with a relative and giving painting lessons. Her sister Rose, who has grown up with one of her aunts, is the only member of the family she ever sees.

"Recent photographs of Lily Beekman show many of the characteristics that were her's years ago. She is still delicately pretty, but her eyes have great shadows under them that not even the photographer's art can conceal. She looks worn and weary, and there are traces of illness and care in her face. It is the photograph of a woman who has lost out of her life all the brightness, sweetness and happiness that its beginning promised her. It is a face that, could this scoundrel see it, might well seem to him a ghost of his own dark past come back to haunt him."

When he paused and looked at Clara, tears were streaming down her cheeks.

"These are solemn facts, Miss McCoy," he added, "and susceptible of the clearest proof."

He paused for a moment, and when she did not answer he continued:

"I will not inflict you with anything further of the doings of this wretch to-night. You will hear enough of him now that you are away from him. But, I may say, while I have no desire to hurry you away from my house, that I do not think this is the safest place for you to remain; for we are not very far away from Zion, and there is no telling when, in an unguarded moment, he may find an opportunity to bring his blighting influence to bear upon you again. I have therefore made arrangements with a friend of mine in the city to care for you for the time being. His wife, who is not very strong, needs someone to help her in the care of her children, and is willing to give you a trial and a home, for the present at least. If the care of children is not irksome to you, you will find the duties light, and your work will bring you some remuneration as well. You will be able to save in a little while enough to take you home, without being dependent upon the sympathetic charity of those who may be inclined to befriend you. Do you think you would like to go?"

"O, Mr. Simpson!" Clara eagerly replied; "I shall be so glad to have such a place, and I will do my very best. You are all too good to me."

The poor, grateful girl's tears began to flow afresh.

"There, never mind," said the farmer, kindly. "You shall have another good night's rest and in the morning I will take you to the city."

"He will not find me there," she said, her face brightening.

"He will not be very likely to," replied the farmer. "I think you will be perfectly safe from the further prospect of becoming pure and sinless. He will undoubtedly make an effort to find you, for the Messiah has an eye for the beautiful, and—I may say it without awakening a feeling of vanity, I hope—you are an exceptionally good-looking young woman. Good looks may be akin to piety; they often are; but it has been observed that young women not blessed with fair forms and figures rarely attain a state of redemption at Zion. Handsome women, however, have little trouble in rapidly losing the worldly taint that envelopes unbelievers and becoming members of the select circle. You are an exception to the most of them, but I presume it is owing to your own obstinacy. By the way, have you ever seen any of these flesh-colored tights in use that he is charged with making some of the girls wear on festive occasions?"

"Yes, sir."

"You have, eh? Well, I didn't quite believe that part of the story, for I know that when the local papers get a little short of sensations, and can find nothing fresh about the Messiah, they put on their thinking caps and invent some new wrinkle for him. How often are these variety stage appliances brought into use?"

"Every week—sometimes twice a week," replied Clara.

"Are they worn by the angels or just by the common women?"

"Both, sir—whoever Mrs. Tuttle selects to take part in the tableaux."

"What characters do they take?"

"Some are biblical, other historical. A favorite theme is that of Moses reading the Ten Commandments. Mr. Schweinfurth never takes any part."

"Yes; the whole thing must be typical of the sacrilegious mockery of his entire career. I can fancy the children of Israel decked out in pink, yellow, mauve and purple tights."

"James," said Mrs. Simpson, "I do not think we should discuss these things before Florence."

"I guess you're right, wife," the husband replied. "We will drop the whole infamous business—for to-night at least. Let Miss McCoy retire early. She probably needs all the rest she can get."

Chapter XXII
Music, Tights and Tableaux

IN THE MORNING CLARA awoke as the first dawn of young Aurora's blush tinged the eastern horizon. She was the first one up and about, though all were early risers at the Simpson farm. Not for a long time had she felt such a buoyancy of spirits; certainly not since her girlhood days on the old homestead at Shelbyville. A sense of freedom, an exuberant feeling of glorious liberty, had taken possession of her, lifting her above the trials and tribulations of earth, and bearing her away, on the wings of the morning, it seemed far beyond the possibilities that confronted her at Zion, and out of reach of the rebuffs she had feared might be offered her because of her connection with the place, which the outside world held in such detestation. This was an unusual emotion for the girl to experience, bound down as she had been for years by the narrow, selfish, dwarfing teachings of Schweinfurth, and was undoubtedly the outcome of the counter-influence exercised upon her mind by the astounding revelations of Mr. Simpson. The distressing stories of the Messiah's flagitious methods and perfidy were as new to her as though she had never been an inmate of the home. She had for two nights breathed the pure air of freedom which invigorated her with a intensity in ratio to her previous enervated and depressed condition.

When the family arose they were surprised to find her moving around; moreover, they were all extremely gratified to find her in such exaltation of spirits and so improved in appearance. If she was beautiful plunged in an ocean of tearful grief and despair, she was four-fold more so when the inspiriting, joyous touch of renewed hope mantled her fair cheeks with the bloom of the rose and her luminous eyes sparkled and danced with the expectancy of full freedom from the influence that had long held her in thralldom. The soaring morning lark that winged its way upward toward the blue ethereal dome of heaven felt no more truly the rapturous thrill of regenerating life than she did.

Of course this superabundance of spirits could not be expected to continue indefinitely. Presently she would descend from the Olympian heights of ecstasy to the hard realities of mundane existence, and again her mind would go back to the detested place from which she so lately made her escape and contemplate possibilities of a renewal of her miserable life there.

However, to the very great gratification of the members of the Simpson family, her elevation of spirits continued until breakfast was over and preparations had been made to start for Rockford. Then came a revulsion of feeling. She was about to quite those who had treated her with so much consideration—whose brave words had imbued her with a courageous feeling to which she had long been a stranger and stirred into activity her womanly aspirations. Now, when the moment came to bid these kind friends farewell, she broke down entirely, and her grief was pitiful to see.

Farmer Simpson, having a variety of matters to attend to at home, had deputed Charles to drive her to the city, which he could do as well as his father, for all the preliminaries had been arranged with the family to whom she was going. Charles was far from being averse to this plan, for he was already more than half in love with the beautiful, shrinking girl. He was a young man of excellent parts, respected by all his acquaintances for his good sense and sterling qualities; yet his heart was turned topsy-turvey with love for the fair creature his family had succored.

Clara had no thought of anything of this kind. Love, under the influence of Schweinfurth had been as far removed from her mind as the antipodes from where she stood. She had no thought even for Arthur Fitzroy, who certainly would have been first in her affections had the sentiment of love been given exercise. She had no thought for aught else except the scope of her freedom, now obscured for the moment by the gloomy apprehensions that took possession of her mind as she was about to separate from those who had done so much for her during the short time she had been with them.

When the carriage that was to bear her away drew up to the door the poor girl burst into tears, and there were other eyes that exhibited a suspicion of moisture as well. She shook hands heartily with George and then kissed Florence and Mrs. Simpson with many demonstrations of affection. Then she ran to Mr. Simpson, and, dropping on her knees before him, grasped his hand and pressed it to her lips before he could anticipate her purpose. When he gently withdrew his hand to raise her to her feet it was wet with tears.

He led her to the carriage and assisted her in. Then, taking the reins in his hand, he bade Charles follow her, and when all was ready he clasped her hand warmly and encouraged her with cheering words. As the vehicle drove off and he and the family walked back into the house there was a peculiar feeling of dread at his heart—a premonition that her troubles were not yet ended. But he said nothing of this, for he saw the family were all deeply affected.

Charles and Clara rode on for some time before either of them spoke. Then he requested her to lean back so she would not be seen, as they were about to pass the house of Zion. She needed no second bidding, for she was again overcome with fear the moment she knew she was near the place. Charles assured her there was really no danger, as he felt himself equal to a contest with a field full of disciples and apostles; but if it would be better if she were not seen, for they might be followed and the place to which she was going discovered to Schweinfurth. She then made the discovery that when she escaped from Zion she had taken a course leading from instead of to the city.

But in spite of all precaution she was seen. Half a mile beyond the house they passed an apostle whom she well knew. Although she drew back within the cover of the carriage as far as possible their eyes met for just a moment, but long enough for the man to recognize her. She spoke to Charles about it, and he hurried his horse along to the city, assuring her in the tenderest tones of his protection in any event.

"Never," he said, "be afraid to let me know when you are in need of help. I or some of my family will respond at once; and if you should be forced back to that abominable place and I go after you I will tear down the whole house but I will find you."

Reassured by the earnestness of the young man, she made the rest of the journey in a comparatively comfortable frame of mind.

Meanwhile the apostle who had detected her presence in the carriage hastened to Zion and reported to Schweinfurth. He was at once started after the carriage on a fleet horse and directed to spare no effort to discover the destination of Clara. The order was faithfully carried out. When the man returned to the home he was able to tell the waiting Messiah just where his runaway could be found when he wanted her.

The story of Clara's liberty can be very briefly told. She went into the family of John Belyea, a prosperous merchant of Rockford, and found her duties light and pleasant. The children given to her care were amiable and easy to manage, and Mrs. Belyea proved to be a kind and considerate mistress. Clara was very happy with these people, and grew to love the children and esteem the parents in a very short time. They regarded her as of rather feeble intellect, for in her meek, quiet devotion to her duties she gave no indication of the sparkling brilliancy that had characterized her as a girl at home. They did not take into consideration the fact that her mind, influenced as it had been by the teachings and surroundings of the home, and debarred for years from contact with the outside world, had fallen into a lethargic state that would require months in which to recuperate and resume a normal condition.

Clara had been three months with the Belyeas, and was improving in health and spirits and growing in favor every day. She was accustomed, when her duties were through and the children off her hands for a while, to walk down to the city, where her mind was given to pleasant diversion in looking at the attractive displays in the store windows and mingling with the busy throng upon the streets. The city, though containing a population of not more than thirty-five thousand, was a constant revelation to the poor girl, who had never before had the freedom of a place larger than her native Shelbyville with a population of a few hundred slow going citizens and a half dozen little general stores.

One fateful afternoon she took her accustomed walk down town and entered one of the elegant stores to purchase some trifling article of which she was in need. As she emerged from the place she found herself face to face with Apostle Mamby, whom she could recollect having seen but once since she met him at her own dear home at Shelbyville. She did not know that he had been lying in wait for her for weeks or she probably would not have ventured from her home.

His small eyes were at once fastened upon her. Her heart felt as though it were being pressed in a vice; her eyes became blurred; she was helpless. He had thrown his diabolical magnetic toils around her, and she could not even struggle for release.

"I am glad to meet you, Emeline," he said, in his smooth, insinuating tones. "You do not know how much they have all missed you at the home since you went from among them. The dear children, who loved you so well, have wept for you as though their hearts would break, and have refused to be comforted by anyone else; and the sisters, with whom you fraternized so long, have been altogether inconsolable. It would give them joy unspeakable if you were among them again for but a single day."

"I am sure I would like to see them all," Clara faltered.

"Get into the buggy, Emeline," pleaded the apostle, "and I will drive you home. We can talk as we ride along."

Clara, being powerless to refuse, did as he requested, and the result was that in a few minutes they were driving along the quiet country road toward heaven, she completely under the influence of his mesmeric spell, and he gloating over the achievement of leading the helpless lamb back to the den of the relentless wolf.

She found herself face to face with Apostle Mamby.

When Clara did not return at the usual hour Mr. Belyea was notified by telephone, and he in turn at once directed the police to institute a vigorous search for her. The fact was soon developed that Apostle Mamby, who was well known in the city, had been seen driving in the direction of Zion with a handsome young woman, and the friends of the luckless girl had no longer any doubt of what had happened. The officers were unwilling to undertake a rescue in which they knew they would be worsted by the cunning of Schweinfurth, and so nothing was done. The Belyea home was a gloomy one that night, for the children, and the parents, too, missed the gentle, lovable girl who had quietly grown into their hearts. They at once sent a messenger with their own carriage to inform Mr. Simpson of what had taken place, having a vague hope that perhaps there was something he could do or suggest. In this, however, they were disappointed. He was no less helpless than they. The members of the family were all together when the messenger brought the sorrowful news. Mr. Simpson sprang angrily to his feet with the exclamation:

"Damn that scoundrel!"

"James," said his wife, horrified at his profane outburst, "you forget that you are with your family, and also that you are a member and an officer of the church."

"I don't care if I am," was the reckless and angry response. "I am almost willing to go to hell just for the satisfaction of seeing that damnable villain get his just deserts."

In the meantime there was far greater joy in heaven over Clara's return than when she first made her appearance there. Every member of the household, except poor Arthur of course, hastened to welcome her back as she alighted from the carriage. The sisters embraced and kissed her over and over again, and the children hung to her skirts and shouted for joy at having her once more among them. The poor girl's heart was moved, and for a few moment she regretted she had ever left the home. It was indeed a pleasure, after her absence of three months, to be among her old associates once more.

Schweinfurth, contrary to her expectations, received her without reproof. He patted her on the head and said he was overjoyed to see her back in the fold. He hoped her contact with the world had done her no harm. All had mourned her absence and prayed for her, and he hoped she would never again separate herself from those who loved her so dearly.

The Messiah had a bifarious purpose in procuring the return of Clara. He first wanted her for the reason that he wanted all beautiful dupes, feeling quite assured that with a little more earnest effort on his own part, he would bring her to a full acceptance of his doctrines. In the second place, he had heard of nothing she had said to the outside world against himself or his people, and he wanted her again under his control before her presence outside was discovered by the irrepressible newspaper reporters and she was induced to talk. He had succeeded in his desires and was therefore correspondingly happy. In proof of this he at once issued orders that a celebration should be held that evening in honor of her return. Then he told her she might enjoy herself among the happy children and her sisters during the rest of the day.

In the evening they were gathered, nearly all the household of Zion, in the spacious reception-room, where they had music, dancing and spectacular productions. Angels, so-called, and other women paraded before the admiring and exultant gaze of the pretender and his presumably passionless apostles. Tableaux gave ample opportunity for a display of the female form that would delight the eye of the proverbial front-row baldhead. Then two well-developed girls did a turn at dancing to the unapproachable music of Disciple William Hicks' violin. Hicks, by the way, was one of the old-fashioned Indiana fiddlers who are well nigh extinct. How he ever came under the influence of Schweinfurth is a mystery to this day, for he belonged to a guild that had not, since the embryonic days of the Republic, exhibited very startling evidences of having strong ideas of sanctity. Most of his selections were lively, old-time airs that can be learned from none of the modern books and instructors. For Miss Test, the first fair dancer to make her appearance on the platform, he played "The Rye Straw." This is an air that can only be properly played with a reel, or round-bow, movement, in which the bow at the point where it is held by the player seems to describe a continual circle. It is a method of bowing which modern instructors are unable to master, much less teach; and the air is said to have been a favorite with "Mad Anthony" Wayne and Little Hatchet, the invincible Miami chief, in the frontier days when Indiana and Ohio were a part of the great Northwest, both of whom, it is also claimed, were able to play the air with the regular reel bow. It is further maintained that "the father of his country" abjured the violin for the fiddle in his boyhood days and learned to play "The Rye Straw" and other lively airs from those whose progeny are fiddling to this day on every prairie and in every woodland from the lakes to the gulf.

When Miss Test had danced herself out of breath Miss Eva Welch took her place on the platform. No other music but that of Hicks would answer. They wanted something full of fire and life. So the old man turned the strings of his fiddle down to what is known as a rebeck tuning and set going the inspiring strains of an air that has been known among old Indiana fiddlers for more than a hundred years as "Hell on the Wabash." Miss Welch was gifted with remarkable pedal and "limbic" agility, which faculty had been assiduously cultivated. The enlivening music seemed to give added power to her muscles and she gave the admiring congregation of Zion a dance the like of which the patrons of the professional stage are seldom able to witness.

When Miss Welch retired the Messiah arose and said:

"The performance this evening has pleased me greatly and reflects much credit upon all the participants. I hope the others present have been as agreeably entertained. Before dismissing Miss Collins will preside at the organ while we all join in singing that familiar and beautiful hymn—'I am so glad that Jesus loves me.'"

Chapter XXIII
Humiliation

THE FOLLOWING AFTERNOON CLARA was called before Schwein-furth for reprimand. It would not do to let her desertion pass unno-ticed and without adequate punishment; it would have a bad effect on some of the others who, not so thoroughly grounded in the faith as they should be, were often disposed to attempt an escape. The Messiah, in his reprimands, "tempered the wind to the shorn lamb;" that is, were the offender a victim more fully under his control the reproof would be a severe one, in which dire threats of thunderbolts, paralytic strokes and similar calamities were freely made; but if the deserter was one of those of an inquiring turn of mind, and disposed to exercise his or her own thinking faculties or prove recalcitrant, milder methods and paralogy were brought to bear.

The Messiah was not quite positive what course he should take with Clara. She was one of the most tractable beings in the world, as long as she was not forced to an unwilling acceptance of the one abhorrent doctrine upon which the perpetuity of a sinless race was based; but that was the very thing to which he most desired her to give adherence. However, it was plain her faith must be a matter of cultivation and growth; it would not do to force her, under magnetic influence, into an acknowledgment, with what it implied, which she was very liable to repudiate at another time. This would be a procedure that night result in making him amenable to law, and that was something he had not yet done and had no intention of doing.

Clara was inclined to show some spirit during the interview. She was content to remain and work, ambitionless as the life there seemed to her in her reasoning moments, and was willing to make an effort to accept the full faith, though she certainly could not do so now. She would regard and respect all the communal rules, and would attempt to dissuade no one from believing even were she never able to do so her-self. She would like to be called by her own name instead of Emeline, because there were a number of others in the home who were permit-ted to retain the names which had always belonged to them. And she would prefer to go back to her former duties among the children. If these things were granted her she gave her solemn promise never to attempt to leave the place again.

The Messiah was surprised and chagrined at the spirit and independence she exhibited. Another two months of freedom and intercourse with the world would have made it well nigh impossible to do anything further with her.

Still, she had asked for much more than he was pleased to grant. He at once launched out on a doctrinal tractate that did more to mystify than enlighten her, closing with these words:

"I am afraid I cannot put you back in the schoolroom, at least not at present. That department of the work is managed excellently now, both the young women employed there being firm in the faith and capable of imparting to the youth in their care the principles of our belief—a highly essential qualification. Though you were long permitted to perform a portion of these duties before absenting yourself from the community, it was because of your faculty of managing children rather than your fitness to guide their spiritual footsteps."

"I was always careful," persisted Clara, "to give them the prescribed lessons."

"I do not question that; but you must remember that you have sadly impaired your usefulness in every direction by your recent conduct, and you must begin anew again in a more humble capacity. You will be promoted as your spiritual advancement merits. I have decided to place you as an assistant in my private kitchen for the present."

"I would rather go back and work for Mrs. Belyea," said Clara, determinedly. "They invariably treated me with kindness, and I did not find that I was despised because I had been here."

"Of course you are at liberty to go out from among us if you choose," said the Messiah, though he had no thought of allowing her to go. "You shall not be constrained to remain here against your inclinations. But let me tell you, when you speak of the kindness of these people, you have simply mistaken a spirit of hatred for the very commendable feeling of which you speak. The people to whom you first went are bitter enemies of mine and of my people. They took you to the city and placed you among those who are no less bitterly disposed toward me. You know nothing of outside feeling beyond what you found in these two families. Had they treated you else than kindly they well knew it would have a tendency to influence your return here. When you had been thoroughly weaned of any desire in this direction, or more likely induced to do something which would make your return impossible, you would then have been cast out as a creature whose very presence shed an atmosphere of unwholesomeness, and thus subjected to the obloquy of a cruel and contumacious world. Unceasing contumely would have been your portion."

Clara could not help shuddering at the dismal prospect thus presented.

"Let me illustrate," he continued, "in a way in which you will find more easy of comprehension. There are a great many people in this country who are constantly crying out against the injustice and indignities heaped upon their fellow-citizens of African descent by those in certain portions of the land. Notwithstanding their constant commiseration of the woes of these people, when brought in contact they absolutely decline to mingle among them; and not only do they refuse to accord the dusky brother social recognition, but he is even debarred from equal opportunities with others of earning a livelihood, and is except in rare and notable instances, relegated to the meaner and less remunerative occupations. So it is with those of God's people who, falling from the heights of divine grace, essay to mingle again with the world. Such a condition of utter hopelessness cannot be one that you can contemplate with any measure of satisfaction. Is it not far better to serve God here with gratefulness and devotion than to be miserable and despised in the service of the evil one?"

"Yes, sir."

"Even your parents, Emeline, who undoubtedly loved you with all the strength and earnestness of which wordly love is capable, are no longer willing to accept you as their child, and have caused it to be understood in the community that you have passed from earth. If you were to present yourself there now you would be denounced as an impostor and turned from their door."

"O, sir," faltered Clara, with tears in her eyes.

It was quite evident the words of Schweinfurth had deeply affected the poor girl. She was utterly cast down and humiliated; and although she knew she was going to have a hard time of it, for a while at least, she signified her willingness to accept the work to which he had intimated his intention of assigning her.

Having now impressed her mind with the hopelessness of disinterested sympathy outside, the next thing was to make her feel of how little importance she was among the blessed and redeemed.

"Nor can I permit you to resume your worldly name," he went on, when he had paused long enough to satisfy himself of the effect of his words. "These are various reasons which you cannot now understand why you should continue to be called Emeline by your associates here. If I do not change the names of some of the sisters it is because I think those they bear are as good as I can give. There are a great many things you will comprehend more clearly when you have become fully redeemed. I will dismiss you now. You may go at once to your new duties, and I hope I shall hear none but the best reports of your conduct from this time on."

Clara arose and left the room with the air of one in the deepest dejection.

After her return the affairs of the community went on without further disturbance for some time. Then came a series of events which required the Messiah's closest personal attention and her presence was partially lost sight of.

One day Schweinfurth announced a couple of recent redemptions. Sometimes he announced these in person at the Sunday service and sometimes by letter. All such announcements, like the sermons, were read the following Sunday at the branches. The members of the community were made acquainted with the two redemptions in question by letter.

The redeemed ones were Mary Scott and Lizzie Weldon, the latter a niece of the owner of the farm, who had been brought up in the family, both her parents having died while she was yet an infant. Miss Scott was the daughter of a woman who had been a member of the community from the start, having taken her young daughter and left her husband when Schweinfurth first discovered his divine exaltation. The two girls were fast friends, and both, realizing the fate that awaited them in continued communal life, had made frequent attempts to escape. They had nowhere to go and no idea of anything more than to get away from Schweinfurth. The result was that each desertion was followed by their return to heaven not later than the following day, these occurrences being invariably followed by a longer or shorter period of humiliating penance, in which they committed to memory the greater part of the Messiah's revised scriptures. Both girls had been for a long time under the especial instruction of a woman named Mrs Eddy. Little attention was given to their regular education, the woman merely seeking to inculcate the doctrine of her master's divinity and the utterly lost condition of all who opposed or differed from him in word, thought, or deed. Once a week Schweinfurth would present himself to see what progress they were making. Now they had both grown into rare specimens of beautiful young womanhood and had relinquished all thought of any other existence than that which they intuitively felt in their girlhood days would be theirs if they remained at Zion.

Both were separately called one day into the presence of the Messiah and closely questioned as to their condition of heart. Their responses were those of every helpless victim. They were willing to undergo the final test that would ensure them for all time holy and sinless lives, and no time was lost in putting them through the ordeal. Then they were taken away from the duties which had hitherto occupied their time and given rooms in the immediate vicinity of the apartments of Schweinfurth, to which he had access at all hours of the day and night. However, neither of these young women, as far as anyone outside is aware at least, has yet presented palpable evidence of having been blessed by the holy spirit, though they are both looking forward expectantly, if not joyfully, to the customary manifestation of divine grace vouchsafed to those in Zion who have been fully redeemed.

The redemption, so-called, of these girls was inevitable, for there was nothing to retard their progress toward an absolutely sinless condition, unless Schweinfurth might have been cut down in the zenith of his usefulness, which has not happened. But their degradation was Clara's gain, inasmuch as the Messiah, having these girls and others to whom he could turn for cracked ice and tender solacement when his brain was overworked in the direction of the affairs of heaven, was content to let her alone to grow into a full belief gradually and quietly.

There was one thing connected with her presence there that gave him some annoyance. Shortly after her return he received with his other mail matter a brief missive which contained only these words:

"Mr. Schweinfurth:—If you harm a hair of Miss McCoy's head I will kill you.
                                                    "ONE OF HER FRIENDS."

He had no idea from whom this threat came, and perhaps it was because he did not know that he allowed it to worry him. After a long consultation with Dr. Brown it was agreed that it could not have been the work of Arthur, because he was in no condition of mind to have a clear perception of any evil that might menace her. He was too deeply shrouded in the gloom of mental darkness to be able to form a conception of retaliation for any real or fancied injury to himself or friends.

But somebody sent the threat; that was certain enough; and the Messiah was not content to rest without making an effort to discover who it was that was willing to resort to so desperate a method of revenge for the sake of Emeline. To make this discovery the customary machinery of heaven was set in motion.

Chapter XXIV
An Astonished Detective

IT WAS NOT LONG before Schweinfurth had a succession of new troubles to keep his mind engaged, and Clara, who seemed hopelessly incapable of making further advancement in faith, was allowed to continue her drudgery in the Lord's private kitchen without molestation.

Old Deacon Weldon, to whom the reader has been introduced as one of the earliest and most devoted of converts, conceived in his weakened brain the supremely ridiculous idea of going into the Messiah business on his own account. He therefore announced that he was the only real Christ and that Schweinfurth was a devil. All the members of his family took side against the old man, though he was not without his adherents in the community. Of course he could not be turned out, for he was still the legal owner of the farm, and for a period extending over six months the contest between the two was warmly waged. However, the odds were against the old man, and the struggle ended in favor of Schweinfurth, he proving conclusively to the community that it was the silver-haired, rebellious deacon who should be decorated with horns and tail. Beaten and humiliated, his head bowed in deep contrition, the poor, misguided old man acknowledged himself in the wrong, humbly sued for pardon, which was granted, and once more fell back into the ranks, where he served with more abject devotion than ever before. From that day to this, despite his age and feebleness, he has taken his place among those assigned to the more arduous work of the farm and toiled on uncomplainingly.

During the progress of this contest there was a relaxation of the hitherto vigorous discipline of Zion, and some of the passionless apostles sought the solacing presence of those of the opposite sex from whom they had previously been kept apart. This was especially vexing to the Messiah, and as soon as he resumed full sway he announced his intention of promulgating a new phase of divine doctrine, which was nothing less than that all apostles should be eunuchs. But he never did this. There was at once such unmistakable and alarming symptoms of a general apostolic uprising, which would be much more serious and far-reaching in its results than the recent unsuccessful rebellion of the old man, that the Messiah was compelled to admit that this was not a prerequisite of redemption. He did, however, contrive some new rules in regard to these delicate matters, that had the effect of restraining such inclinations on the part of the apostles as were calculated to infringe his peculiar prerogatives or weaken the heavenly discipline.

He soon conceived another idea, which he did put in practice, although it took some time to get it in thorough working order. Each member of the community was requested to make confession every day to Schweinfurth of every thought or deed as to the propriety of which there was any doubt. These confessions might be put in writing and handed in each evening, unless the individual was required for any reason to make oral confession. When this practice was thoroughly established the Messiah found it of very material advantage, for if any inmate said something he should not say in the presence of another it was invariably reported, and the angel who officiated as secretary and read these confessions never failed finding anything of this nature. After a while most of the inmates seemed to find it a source of satisfaction to unburden themselves in this way; but very many of the confessions were practically the same, day in and day out, and the gist of them might be stated in the following words, an accurate copy of one confession now in the hands of the writer:

"I have thought of the Lord and of his goodness all day, and I am so thankful that I have found him and that I am permitted to dwell with him in heaven. I realize what a wonderful thing it is to have heaven here on earth. By every act in my power I am going to show my appreciation of the Lord's goodness. I am determined to show my faith and following my devotion to him, and I will forever cleave to him through life and death."

This the poor dupe signed and left in the letter-box at the Messiah's door. Of course those so unfortunately situated as poor Arthur was at that time were not required to make confession, but if any of the ordinary inmates missed for a day or two the word would go round:

"Look out for him! He is going to run away, for he hasn't confessed for two days."

One thing that worried the Lord not a little was the advent of a female detective in the guise of a convert. Some friends of an inmate of Zion employed a clever woman to put on the outer garments of humiliation, visit heaven, and discover whatever she could that might be legally used against the Messiah. This young woman, Miss Ama Howard, went about her task in a very systematic manner, and, although she failed of the object she had in view, succeeded in giving Schweinfurth a good deal of trouble, at the same time making a discovery that subsequently proved of much importance to Clara and her friends.

She first presented herself for admission to the sacred precincts of a branch office at one of larger cities, on the plea that she desired to become more fully conversant with the new faith, about which she had heard a great deal. Like all others who present themselves in the same way she was at first an object of suspicion, but, to her great gratification, was permitted to hear one of the sermons read by the leading apostle in charge the very first Sunday she attended. After the meeting the men and women present talked with her for a long time about their beautiful religion, and Miss Howard agreed to attend again on the following Sunday.

She kept her promise and was much more cordially received than before. This time she was put through a severe cross-questioning as to her motives, her condition in life, occupation and many other matters. Her answers seemed to be very satisfactory and she was invited to come to the branch through the week as well as on Sunday. The result was that Miss Howard continued her visits to the branch until by a bold stroke of diplomacy—some might call it deception—she got a note of introduction to Schweinfurth and permission to visit him at the Rockford heaven.

The Messiah was at once notified of the intended visit of Miss Howard and made his preparations to receive her, though he was not apprised of what day she would be there.

It was a raw March day when she set out for Rockford. She was now on her way to beard the lion in his heavenly den.

At Rockford she visited a livery, procured a double seated carriage, a driver and a team of strong horses, for at that time of the year the roads were in a horribly muddy condition, and with this outfit set out for the drive of six miles to heaven.

Her driver was one of the loquacious sort and voluble in his accounts of Schweinfurth and how the people regarded him. She made up her mind before they had gone far that neither the driver nor the citizens of Rockford had much reverence for the so-called redeemer.

"Are you one of the new converts?" asked the driver.

"Not yet," Miss Howard replied, evasively.

"S'pose you will be before night," said the man, with a broad grin. "He is powerful fond of ladies. Always brings one of his angels to town with him when he comes. He always buys the best of every thing, too, and dresses in the height of style."

"Indeed!"

"He's just too smart to leave the smallest hole for people to get at him. Don't know whether you'll find him up yet," he added, after a pause.

"Why, it's nearly ten o'clock," said Miss Howard.

"Yes, but"—with a facetious grin—"ye see, he don't have to get up till he wants to. He can have one of the angels to minister to him with coffee, bread and honey, and such spirtool delights."

He further expressed something to the effect that it was a pity a young woman like the person addressed should get into the clutches of Schweinfurth. Then after a few moments of thought he suddenly turned to Miss Howard and said:

"I'd like to know if it's a heavenly arrangement to make some o' the women work and 'nigger' while them that's mothers o' Holy Ghost children are allowed to sit all day in the hammocks in summer and read or at other times drive all over the country behind blooded horses?"

Miss Howard made no response, and after waiting a moment or two he went on:

"Crowds go to hear him in the summer time, but there ain't very many Rockford people who believe in him."

"A prophet has no honor in his own country," said his companion.

"No," he said, with a hard laugh, "for Rockford people know him too well. How do you account for those children born there?"

"One of his ladies says that to doubt the possibility of their heavenly parentage is to doubt the divinity of Christ," was the reply.

"The devil!" he ejaculated, under his breath.

"I beg your pardon," said the detective, innocently.

"Nothin'," he replied, shortly, and relapsed into silence.

After a while he asked:

"What do you think of their religion now?"

"O, I suppose in the end I will be one of his converts."

"He'll be glad enough to get you, even if you haven't very much money, though he generally wants his converts to have money, or else they have to be pretty nice looking. I think you'll suit him all right."

With this adroit compliment the driver again retired behind a cloak of silence, leaving his passenger feeling as flattered as though she had just been informed that she had made a conquest on the king of the South Sea Islands.

Directly they reached the house and Miss Howard dismissed the carriage. She was admitted by a nicely dressed and comely woman, to whom she delivered her letter of introduction.

"Be seated, please," said the woman, and then she disappeared.

After an absence of perhaps five minutes, during which time Miss Howard devoted herself to a critical inspection of the furniture of the room, the woman again made her appearance, with the information that Mr. Schweinfurth would be down in a few moments. Directly she said:

"You must have had a cold ride. Won't you sit by the register until Mr. Schweinfurth comes?"

The prospective convert said she would and did so. She had hardly taken her place there before the Messiah made his appearance.

The two shook hands cordially and Miss Howard said:

"I am glad to behold you at last."

The Messiah looked at her searchingly and replied:

"I hope I will be glad to know you."

He drew up a chair and bade her to be seated. Then he said:

"How long have you been attending the meetings at the branch house?"

"A little over a month," she replied; "but you know there are times in which we seem to live eternities."

"Yes," he smiled, reminiscently. "What first attracted you?"

"Curiosity. But I went away greatly impressed with the teachings set forth in the sermon, and also by the seeming earnestness and fervor of your followers. I went again, and have been much troubled since, having always dreamed of an ideal society and wondered if the time was near at hand when I should have my heart's desire."

"What impressed you most at the meetings?" was the next question.

"The wonderful power of the sermons," answered Miss Howard. "Wonderful words! Remarkable!" she continued meditatively. "Then, too, your people seemed to be so happy, and I have sought so long to be perfectly happy."

"You should seek more after righteousness than happiness," the Messiah said, reprovingly though he seemed to have swallowed the flattery of the other.

"O, but you know," she answered naively, "if I have found righteousness and know that I am in a state of life and society of perfect righteousness, then I shall be happy. That was what I wanted."

The Messiah nodded approvingly and then launched into an account of his own early peculiarities. Theses, however, the reader is already familiar with. When he had finished this he said:

"You are sure, Miss Howard, you are seeking for the truth and righteousness?" transfixing her meanwhile with his eyes.

The lady detective.

She could not then have removed her eyes from his face had her life depended on it, but she was not thrown off her guard. She summoned all the forces of her will to resist the evident effort he was making to mesmerize her and get her in subjection to his will. She met his gaze unflinchingly and replied, with evident earnestness and conviction:

"I came on that mission, Mr. Schweinfurth. I would risk my life for a conviction or a principle. I have had dreams and seen visions of a time when all that is divine in man should crush out and triumph over that which is evil, and he be less the beast he is and more the god he should be."

Here she fancied he flinched, but it may have been only fancy. He replied, quickly and kindly:

"If you are really searching after truth and righteousness we want you; we want all such. But all who follow me must be thoroughly tested before they abide with me. Those who are to be angels of the Lord must be pure and perfect in heart and mind and obey his will in all things. I will now turn you over to some of the sisters, who will take care of you, and to-morrow or the day after we will talk again."

Schweinfurth then left the room and ascended to his own apartments, and Miss Howard was left to her own reflections for a few minutes once more. He was not entirely satisfied with her, in spite of her letter of introduction and clever answers to his questions. He never was entirely satisfied with those of too inquiring a turn of mind. Before he reached the head of the stairs he had determined upon what course to pursue. He would leave her alone that day and the next and in the meantime have her every movement watched.

Directly after a pleasant appearing woman, whom she afterward learned was Mrs. Tuttle, came and showed Miss Howard to her room.

We are aware the presumed convert was at Zion in the capacity of a detective, who expected to gain all the information she could in the shortest possible time and then take her departure. In order to accomplish this she would require to be continually alert and to ask a great many questions of those with whom she came in contact. While she was busy in the work of detection, the faithful and argus-eyed angels of the household were industriously engaged in detecting her. Her movements and the questions she propounded to the inmates were all promptly reported to Schweinfurth, the result being that his suspicions were still further increased and the espionage upon her movements made more rigorous.

In her intercourse with the women of the community she met and talked both with Clara and Angelica, discovering something, as has been already intimate, that was subsequently of immense advantage to Miss McCoy and Arthur Fitzroy.

Dr. Brown was called into consultation with the Messiah, and the decision reached was that Miss Howard should be taken in hand by the doctor, mesmerized, and then made to tell, while in that condition, just what her purpose in Zion was. The doctor found her a difficult subject, and it was not without considerable effort that he subjugated her will. He was rather amused when, having got her under perfect control, she quietly related the object of her visit to the home and told him who had engaged her. Her progress toward righteousness was stopped then and there. In a few minutes a single rig was driven to the door and the doctor and Miss Howard entered the carriage. When she awoke to consciousness again she found herself in a private room at one of the Rockford hotels. She could not explain how she got there, but she understood enough to know there was no room for her in heaven. The next outgoing train carried one woman passenger who was willing to acknowledge that in certain lines of detective work there were possibly those who might do better than she could.

Chapter XXV
Diabolism

THE UNUSUAL EVENTS RECORDED in the preceding chapters, while not taking long to relate, covered a considerable period of time. Of course there were many other occurrences that would indubitably be of much interest, but being irrelevant to the sad story of the fair, unfortunate girl, the unhappy portion of whose history it is the province of the writer to trace, they have been passed over in silence. Those briefly described had the very satisfactory effect of so completely absorbing the attention of Schweinfurth that Clara was permitted to toil on in reasonable content, without being further agitated and distressed by the operation of the divine will. This continued until nearly five and a half years had expired from the time of her first arrival within the sacred precincts of heaven.

It will be remembered that when Arthur was prostrated by the attack of brain fever, after his affecting interview with Angelica, that young woman seemed to be experiencing some improvement from her pleasant exercise in the open air, and the doctor, not finding her in a diseased condition, entertained the hope that she would gradually recruit her strength. Possibly this hope would have been realized had she not permitted herself to contract a severe cold, which at once fastened itself upon her and speedily developed into quick consumption. After that she failed rapidly, and it hardly needed the experienced professional eye of Dr. Brown to see that it would be but a short time at the best before she disappeared forever from mortal ken. Neither the medical skill of the physician, nor the powerful auxiliary of magnetism so frequently and successfully employed there, could avail her now.

As she was one of the blessed and sinless ones—the "soul's mate" of the Messiah, at least until her babe was born—he was not disposed to have her pass from earth while yet an inmate of Zion. Some means must be devised to prevent another such unpropitious occurrence as the death of the beloved little one of William Weldon; and, as the case of Angelica had already passed beyond the prophylactic power of him or the doctor, some action must be taken at once. The Messiah was prolific of resource; he soon found a plan and began to put it into execution. Soon there was another lengthy consultation between the doctor of medicine and the professed doctor of divine law, and the determination that Angelica and her little girl should be transferred to one of the branches, where she would pass a few days in a course of mesmeric treatment under the care of Apostle Mamby, who should be directed to repair to that particular branch for that purpose at once. Mamby was to remain with Angelica until she was effectually disposed of as far as the Lord and his people were concerned.

The mesmeric treatment to be given this poor young woman, already at the threshold of eternity, was not such as was intended to benefit her mentally or physically. It was the very opposite, and was to be given her in pursuance of the cruel and heartless purpose which the Messiah had planned and already put under way some time before he called the doctor into consultation. In truth the interview with the doctor was but for the purpose of elaborating the plan, and when all was in readiness it was followed to the end without the slightest compunction of conscience, a feeling, truly, of which Schweinfurth seemed incapable.

In a day or two word was passed around that the fair, fragile Angelica, who moved about more like a spirit than a sublunary being, would lend her angelic presence to one of the branches for a time, where there was a work of the master to which she was peculiarly adapted; and within the week she and her sweet little daughter Marcia left the confines of heaven, forever. Her former associates at Zion never saw her more, and one day when the Messiah was spoken to anent her fragility he said her body would never take on corruption. If the Father desired her presence in a sphere beyond this she would be translated to regions supernal even as Elijah was caught up by God, and should never experience the pangs of earthly dissolution. It will transpire later on that these representations were but the part of a plan as cunning in its inception as it was diabolical.

In the meantime Arthur, as Dr. Brown predicted, was gradually recovering his mental equilibrium. There were times when he appeared to be perfectly rational, although his mind was not strong and clear. Again the obscuring cloud would become dense and copious. But a gradual and sure improvement was easily discernible, and it was only a question of time when the past would recur to him with all the vividness in which he had witnessed the lamentable condition of Clara previous to his illness. Even now his thoughts often reverted to the happy days at Shelbyville—to his early and lost love—and the pangs of grief were again laid upon him. The occurrences immediately preceding his illness were happily excluded from his thoughts except in a vague, indefinite way, so that in his more lucent moments of ratiocination he was not stirred to any demonstrative action that might have called more critical attention to him. The habit of reserve and silence that had grown upon him since his connection with the place, kept him from imparting his thoughts to his associates, and therefore none of them had any definite knowledge of how much clearer his mind really was. It was known to the Messiah and the doctor, however, that he was materially improved and his mind daily growing stronger.

It has been seen that Schweinfurth feared the consequences of the complete return of Arthur's mental powers, and as soon as he became convinced that this was not only possible but extremely probable within a short time, he bethought him of the danger of any revengeful inclination that might be engendered with the return of the illuminating light of reason and wondered how it might best be averted. The Messiah was equal to the occasion.

Shortly after the departure of Angelica for the branch home Schweinfurth caused the information to be carried to Arthur by one of his associates that Clara McCoy was no longer an inmate of Zion. He was quite able to comprehend what this meant, and at the first opportunity appealed to the doctor for verification of the story. The cunning medico told him the report was quite true. Miss McCoy had been gone for nearly a month.

"What made her go?" Arthur innocently asked, unable to understand why such unusual permission had been given.

"Why," replied the doctor, "there were several reasons. The principal one was that her health is not very good and it was thought a change would help her."

"When will she come back?" was the next very rational question.

"I do not think she will ever come back," replied the doctor.

"Never?" said Arthur, musingly.

"Never!"

Arthur was silent for a few moments, and then he said:

"My own health is not very good. I wonder if Mr. Schweinfurth would left me go away for a while?"

"Where do you want to go?"

"I think I would like to sail around the lakes for two or tree weeks, until I get a little stronger, and then go home and visit my people."

"You have no money. How are you going to sail around the lakes?"

"I could work my way on some of the boats."

"That's so," replied the doctor, rather surprised at the clearness of the other's reasoning. "I will speak to Mr. Schweinfurth and let you know at once."

"Thank you, sir," said Arthur, humbly.

When the Messiah and the doctor talked the matter over a few minutes later it was quickly resolved that Arthur should be permitted to start upon his contemplated trip at once if he pleased—the sooner the better. Schweinfurth, contrary to his almost invariable rule, even intimated his willingness to give the man something in the way of pecuniary aid. The doctor agreed that it would be the part of wisdom to do so, seeing that up to the date of his illness he had been a valuable and faithful worker and had received no remuneration beyond the bare necessaries of life.

Accordingly, Arthur was at once summoned into the reception-room, a place that, for obvious reasons, he had seen little of during his protracted stay at the home. Schweinfurth questioned him closely in regard to the proposed trip—how long he expected to remain away, what he was going to do, and if he was sure he would return when he got better? In reply to the last question Arthur innocently asked:

"Do you want me to come back?"

For a moment, but only for a moment, the Messiah was nonplussed. Then he replied:

"I do not want you to come back until you are fully recovered. To show you that I am desirous of helping you on the road to health, as I want to help all my people who are faithful, I will give you twenty-five dollars, about which you must say nothing to any of your associates, however. That amount will give you a nice lake trip without your being compelled to work your way. After that, if you want to remain on water longer, you will feel more like working. What do you say?"

"I am certainly very thankful for your goodness," replied Arthur. "When may I start?"

"Whenever you please," replied the Messiah, rising as an intimation that the interview was at an end.

"Thank you, sir," said Arthur, very humbly. He then rose and bowed himself out with courtly dignity and grace. There was a very grateful feeling at his heart as he walked toward his humble quarters. So far as his preparations for the journey were concerned, there was nothing for him to do but to put on the Sunday suit of clothes which the Messiah allowed to every inmate of Zion. This he hastily did, and then, bidding farewell to his more intimate associates about the stables, he quit the Schweinfurth heaven forever. Naturally enough, the greater distance Arthur put between himself and the then fragrant fields of Eden, the more exalted his spirits became. Upon him, as upon most others, the invigorating air of freedom had a wonderfully revivifying effect. He had not walked with so buoyant a step for many a long day. Not only that, but his mind was clearer than at any time since his illness. He thought of poor Clara and the condition in which he had last seen her, and he was keenly pained. That he was capable of suffering in this way was the best possible evidence that his mind was fast coming out from under the stupefying cloud that had darkened his reasoning faculties.

He was not long in making his way to the city. It was nearly five and a half years since he had been there before, and in that time the changes in a progressive, glowing American city are many. Arthur scarcely knew which way to turn, and it was not with out some difficulty that he found his way to the bank where he had deposited his money and valuables before going to Zion. It was not a hard matter, however, for the officers of the institution to satisfy themselves of his identity, and what belonged to him was soon in his possession, though it took about all the Messiah had given him for traveling expenses to pay the rent of the vault for the long period he held it. That was of little consequence, though, for he had now a considerable sum of his own.

It will readily be presumed that Arthur lost no time in setting out for dear old Shelbyville. The trip around the lakes, which was but an inspiration of the moment, was thought nothing more of, and, as fast as steam could bear him, he sped onward toward the home of his youth, amid the rugged, precipitous and towering mountains of "old Kentucky."

The reader is already familiar with the events immediately preceding and subsequent to his return; the speedy death of the unfortunate young woman, the reticence of her parents as to her whereabouts during her protracted absence, and the attachment of Arthur to little Marcia, whom he visited daily and so often took to the grave of her mother on his evening visitations.

If Arthur was suffering from mental aberration when he left Shelbyville, in search of Clara, when all others believed her dead, it was clear now there was a "method in his madness," for he alone had been able to perceive the fallacy of the accepted theory of her death beneath the dark waters of the river. That he had been unable to profit by his clearer insight into the melancholy and mysterious affair was a great misfortune, though some charitable people were willing to concede that it was probably through no fault of his, seeing his mind was clouded when he went away and no less so on his return.

His parents were overjoyed to have him at home again, though he seemed to be so woefully changed; but Dr. Shannon said, and they believed it, that now, being assured the bright object of his adoration was no longer alive, he would soon regain his reasoning faculties, though he might, perhaps, remain to the end of his days a melancholy, taciturn man, far removed from the jovial, spirited, intelligent and keen-witted Arthur of former days.

This rather pathetic recital now brings us down to the evening when the young journalist, William Hatfield, listened to the entertaining story of the landlady of the tavern on the cliff, whose guest he was overnight and whose mission to Shelbyville was to ferret out the details of the unusual affair with which the reader has been made reasonably familiar. From now on he must be permitted to intrude a little of his professional acumen and have a share in whatever subsequent developments there may be.

Chapter XXVI
Surprising Disclosures

ANXIOUS TO BEGIN THE work which called him to this wild and picturesque region with the least possible delay, Hatfield rose early the next morning, partook of a hurried breakfast, and bidding his communicative landlady farewell, mounted his horse and rode to the village, a distance little greater than a mile. In the course of his investigations he met and had a long talk with Dr. Shannon. That gentlemen knew practically nothing of what had transpired during the absence of Clara and Arthur, and he did not believe the family of the dead girl were much better informed, for her statements after her return were incoherent and contradictory, he views of life being so completely warped and her mind so full of hallucinations as to require no commission to pronounce her case one in which the light of reason no longer remained. She was a complete mental and physical wreck, and nothing remained more than to make her progress to the grave as peaceful as possible. The doctor believed Arthur Fitzroy knew more of what had taken place than anyone else about the village, but he, poor fellow, was himself in a sorry condition and could not be induced to talk. The physician affirmed with much positiveness that Arthur's present affliction of mind would not be permanent, and that within a month or two he would again be a reasonable being, though he would possibly never drive entirely from his mind the events that had plunged him into so profound a condition of dejection. Mr. Hatfield would have to patiently await this change, and then, if still disposed to pursue his investigations, the doctor would cheerfully aid him in whatever way he could. After the doctor had promised to inform him by letter when a change for the better had taken place, Hatfield withdrew.

He next called upon Mr. and Mrs. McCoy. They knew nothing definite of what had befallen their daughter, but were anxious to learn all they could; therefore if Mr. Hatfield contemplated renewing his investigations when Arthur was in a condition to render some assistance they were able to spare something to further the work.

Thus the mystery remained as impenetrable as the authorship of Junius for the time being. Hatfield returned to the city and made a highly entertaining "story" of what facts he had been able to gather, for which he was personally complimented by his chief.

The day following the appearance of the article the managing editor of the paper received the subjoined note:

"Dear Sir:—If the young man who visited Shelbyville and prepared the report of the mysterious case of Miss Clara McCoy will call upon me at my hotel, not later than to-morrow noon, at which time I am compelled to leave the city, I can put him in possession of some further important facts from which he can weave a sequel vastly more entertaining than the article I have just finished reading in your paper."

The note was signed by Miss Ama Howard, the young lady detective who failed so ignominiously in her mission to heaven, and contained nothing further than the name of the hotel at which she could be found.

The note was handed to Hatfield with the intimation that it might be as well to call upon the lady at once and see what there was in it. Being more interested in the case than the journalistic magnate had any idea of, he hastened to pay his respects to Miss Howard.

He found her a bright, keen and rather prepossessing person of some twenty-three years of age, who, wasting no time in circumlocution, plunged at once into the matter on which she had called him into her presence. Most of what she said to him has already been imparted in these pages; but it was news to him, and such news that he could scarcely believe such transactions were possible in a civilized community. He was almost petrified with astonishment at some of her revelations, as almost anyone would be on first hearing them; at the same time they awakened the keenest interest in his mind. When she had finished he said:

"Miss Howard, I am little less than astounded. This pretended Lord must be capable of the profoundest depths of infamy. This seems to be a chance for a story, founded on cold facts, that will discount Haggard's wildest flights of imagination, if it does not rub shoulders with the alluring tales of the *Arabian Nights*."

"Truth is stranger than fiction," laughed Miss Howard.

"It assuredly is in this case," he replied. "I have already promised the friends of this unfortunate couple to investigate the case as soon as Fitzroy has recovered sufficient composure of mind to be induced to talk. What you have told me will enable me to set out at once on a tour of discovery. I will not delay longer than it will take me to get back to the office and get an indefinite leave of absence from 'the old man' before I go to work delving into this strange affair. Why, here's the data

Hatfield interviews the lady detective.

for an illustrated article that will enable me to carve my name several notches higher in the niche of journalistic fame, and—"

"Wait a moment!" interrupted Miss Howard. "You are starting out altogether too impetuously for success. You must move in this matter with the most extreme care, or you will drag yourself out at the small end of the horn, just as I did, or perhaps put in a good deal of valuable time to no purpose, as that poor fellow Fitzroy did for so many years, and as others have also done. Sit down again and I will enlighten you some as to the best course of procedure as far as I can from my brief but exciting experience."

Hatfield resumed his seat and the young lady related in detail the methods by which she had been enabled to become a member of the community and the means employed, as far as she could tell, to force her to disclose her identity without knowing what she was doing, and thus bring about her quiet but effectual ejection from the blissful abode of the redeemed before her mission was hardly begun.

Hatfield listened with earnest attention, and then, thanking her heartily for the information, said:

"I am free to confess, Miss Howard, that this man must be possessed of remarkable mesmeric power. His influence over his dupes must be complete. I wonder these women do not get jealous of each other and indulge in a hair-pulling matinee once in a while."

"Those who are not fully redeemed do exhibit this feeling occasionally and give the Messiah, I am told, no end of trouble; but I fancy those who have attained a pure and sinless condition are lifted above such earthly emotions. It is very likely their condition of mind is such that they are incapable of any but the one absorbing sentiment of slavish devotion to his man's powerful will."

"Perhaps so," mused Hatfield; "but if this brazen humbug gets his mesmeric work in on me he'll be even a cleverer rascal than I am yet disposed to give him credit for."

"And you'll be more clever than any who have preceded you if he doesn't give you cards and spades and then beat you out."

"Well, Miss Howard, I've made up my mind to give him a whirl anyhow. I shall not forget what you have said, however. Allow me again to thank you heartily for your information and valuable advice."

"Not at all," replied the young woman. "I am only to glad to aid in exposing the monstrous performances of the head of this sink of iniquity."

Hatfield then took his leave and hastened to the newspaper office, eager to obtain the coveted leave of absence and begin his investigations without delay. His chief, while he thought the story of Miss Howard greatly exaggerated yet believed it would pay to look into it, and consequently Hatfield was told he could go and turn himself loose on it. He made his arrangements accordingly, and two days afterward found himself at Shelbyville closeted with Dr. Shanon, Rev. James Brown and Arthur Fitzroy.

Arthur had improved rapidly under the care of the doctor, to whom the case was one of more than ordinary interest. Though unwilling to let even Mr. and Mrs. McCoy know the source of Clara's misfortune, his purpose being to keep it locked in his bosom as long as he lived, when he discovered how much Hatfield already knew, he was soon persuaded by the others to relate his whole experience from the time he left his native village until his return.

The frequent vigorous interjections of the doctor, coupled with many exclamations of incredulity, and the horrified expressions of the minister from time to time, plainly indicated how far astray they had been in the theories evolved to account for the long absence of Clara and Arthur. The astounding disclosures made during the conference by both Hatfield and Arthur revealed to them not only the existence of an institution of which they had no previous knowledge, but indicated a slavish subserviency on the part of a considerable number of apparently intelligent persons to the superior will of a monster of iniquity which seemed impossible.

When Arthur had imparted all the information possible he was allowed to retire, and Hatfield made further disclosures to his two friends that had the effect of putting them into such a condition of anxiety and disquietude that for a while they scarcely knew what they were doing or saying.

It was finally determined that Hatfield should proceed alone upon his investigations in pursuance of his original purpose, reporting to the doctor by letter or otherwise as often as he was able to do so, seeing that it was liable to take some little time, in carrying out the plan decided upon, before definite results could be reasonably expected. He should also, in the event of his pecuniary resources becoming exhausted, make direct and immediate application to the doctor for what funds were necessary to effectually prosecute his plans. Hatfield was, moreover, assured that if he succeeded in this important undertaking he would be liberally reimbursed for his time and efforts; while, if failure followed him, the doctor was willing to bear a portion of the expenses in return for the information he should obtain.

The discoveries of Hatfield, as well as his future movements, were to be kept a profound secret from all except themselves, even Arthur being excluded from a knowledge of their purpose. It was left to Dr. Shannon to reveal to those interested, or to the public as much as he thought advisable of what the future would bring forth. It was further understood that if either the doctor or the minister could be of any use to Hatfield as his plans progressed, they were to be notified at once, when either one, or both for that matter, would hasten to his aid.

Having thus settled the *modus operandi*, the conference terminated. The doctor, his mind full of what he had just heard, went to call upon some very impatient patients, who were at a loss to know what had come over the usually prompt and cheerful physician. Although he didn't intimate anything of the kind, the impression soon became general about the village that he had a critical case on his hands of which he did not care to speak.

Mr. Brown went directly to the McCoy home, where he greatly surprised the sad-eyed woman who welcomed him in by requesting a photograph of Clara. When she procured one for him that had been taken before the dear girl's disappearance he still further mystified her by declining to state for the present the purpose for which he required it.

Hatfield, before leaving the village, had another talk with Arthur, who, when he found the young journalist was going to visit heaven, earnestly tried to dissuade him from doing so, saying that if he valued his peace of mind that was the last place he should go to.

However, before the next sunrise Hatfield was well on his way to the branch home at Chicago, from which point he determined to begin his arduous journey Zionward.

Chapter XXVII
Seeking the True Way

THE FOLLOWING SUNDAY A young man presented himself for admission to the sacred precincts of the branch home at No. 1309 Walfram Street, Chicago, or more properly in Lake View, his object ostensibly being to hear the reading of the regular sermon with some extracts from the revised, newly-prefaced, overhauled and otherwise improved edition of the Scriptures.

The door was opened by an apostle whose face was wreathed in a smile that could scarcely be called saintly. He advised the applicant to ring the other door-bell, which summons was answered by a seraph of perhaps forty years of age, with a florid complexion, her hair combed high and a sanctimonious look upon her face. She was plainly dressed in black and held in her hand a Bible. She ushered the new-comer into a nicely furnished parlor and bade him, in a reserved, not to say suspicious, manner, be seated. The reader may as well be informed now as at any other time that the visitor was none other than William Hatfield.

After growing somewhat inured to the novelty of such sanctified atmosphere, the prospective convert ventured to scan the celestial furnishings. The room was very comfortably dressed out in Brussels carpet, plush furniture, large pictures, pretty rugs, with lace curtains draping the windows, and the walls neatly papered and crowned with gilt moldings and stucco work. The front room opened by a folding doorway into a spacious sitting-room equally well appointed, with the addition of a bay window on the east side filled with plants. Through a small room behind, occupying the southeast corner of the house, a handsome conservatory was visible, filled with bloom and a maze of green, whence issued the joyous duets and trios of birds trilling, probably thankful that the air they inhaled was of the finer essence of holiness instead of the common, smoke-charged Chicago article.

Seated on the sofa opposite were two children, a pretty boy of eight years and a girl of twelve in a rose colored dress with ribbons to match. Ranged around the room in comfortable arm-chairs were a dozen or more people, all sitting in a thick gloom of silence. Presently the silence was broken by a tread much like that of a cat. It was the cunning-looking disciple who first opened the door to Hatfield, and who, as he found later, was Wilbur L. Baldwin, the pastor of the Chicago branch of the Church Triumphant. He took possession of a great cushioned chair in the corner, before which stood an improvised altar, evolved out of a stand, a table-cover, a pile of books draped with a China-silk scarf, and a Bible.

The new-comer was made to feel keenly his low degree of caste and coarser clay, in that he was placed, not in the inner room in the enchanted circle, nor yet, what was worse—for the meeting lasted for hours—in a comfortable arm-chair, but outside the pale in one of those relics of the Inquisition, a straight-backed wooden chair.

Hatfield's attention was particularly attracted by another of the angelic throng, an old man with a stubby goatee and mustache of a nice shade of mouse color. One eye was gone and the other was cardinal-hued, making the glasses he wore give the unhallowed impression of a feline much disabled by many battles. He kept working his lips until Hatfield began to get nervous. As he sat in the bay window, back-grounded by greenery between the new convert and the light, the mustache and stringy goatee looked like mice chasing each other up and down the stem of the oleander behind him. It was all Hatfield could do to keep from "laughing right out in meeting" at this fascinating fancy. In the course of some remarks he afterward made, he said "the Lord had brought him up from the lowest hell," a statement which, from his appearance, was not really so difficult of belief.

The sermon was rather a disappointment to the prospective convert, in that it had nothing of the tables of stone about it, but was written with the machine used by very many ordinary sinners, a typewriter, and covered nearly three hundred pages of foolscap paper. It was read by Baldwin, and was the one preached by the Messiah in heaven proper the Sunday previous. Hatfield noted the point made that "nothing is so distasteful to the devil as divinity," the Messiah delegating in the most flattering manner the character of his Satanic majesty to the world in general and the divinity to himself. The rest was mainly an exhortation to his people to stand fast and obey in everything the will of the Lord— that is, himself. After a prayer of exactly twenty-seven minutes' duration by the watch the leader asked for responses to the divine discourse.

The first speaker was Miss Lily A. Raymond, one of Schweinfurth's favorites, at that time chief angel and assistant pastor at the Chicago branch. She was a young woman of about twenty-two and very pretty, with blue eyes, a good nose, firm, well-shaped mouth, finely-penciled eyebrows, dark brown hair, not very abundant, braided and worn on the crown of a shapely head, small white hands, and a pretty foot, small, slender and neatly booted. She wore a black dress, stylishly made, with white lace in the neck and sleeves. She talked in a sweet voice, enunciating very distinctly, but rather wildly, like one intensely in earnest but somewhat frenzied. She dwelt in extravagant terms on the goodness and mercy of "the Lord's holy anointed"—Mr. Schweinfurth—and said among other fanatical things that she would lay down her life for him if necessary, or her religion either; that she was redeemed, therefore would give her life, her love, her thoughts, her actions, all to the Lord, in the person of Mr. Schweinfurth. She spoke emphatically, using good language, seeming pure as a flower in her intents and purposes, but Hatfield thought in a mist of terrible delusion.

The next speaker was Dr. Marsters, the woman who admitted the new convert. She spoke with a nasal twang, pausing long between sentences. Remarks followed from each one in the experience meeting. After a few words the leader was about to dismiss the meeting when a man sitting near Hatfield arose and asked permission to speak. He was evidently a stranger, for he, too, was seated, not in the inner room, but in the doorway. He said:

"Friends, I do not wish to criticize anything that has been said, but the religion of my mother and her Christ, without the aid of a human God, are enough for me."

Then, amidst profound silence he took his Bible and left. He was a rather tall man, with blue eyes and light, sandy chin-whiskers and mustache, his light-brown hair combed low over a somewhat retreating forehead. He wore a silk hat and a brown overcoat, and carried a plain-case silver watch and a large Oxford Bible. The people at the branch never saw him again.

After the meeting was dismissed Miss Raymond went to Hatfield, shook hands with him cordially and began to talk with him about religion. He thought he had seldom met a more fascinating young woman.

"The attendance is not large to-day," she said, "for the reason that so many are at Rockford, where the Messiah lives. There is a special convocation of the redeemed there at present."

They talked together for some time, Hatfield giving the young woman to understand that he was not only very favorably impressed with the doctrines of the Church Triumphant but had considerable means at his command, which might find its way into the coffers of the church if he could persuade himself that was the right course to pursue. This of course made her the more anxious to influence him, and she said she was convinced he would be a good convert and would be very welcome. She said she would be very glad to see him as often as the wanted to come, and then he thanked her and left.

Hatfield noticed when he reached the street that the branch is a very fine piece of property. It is a commodious frame structure two and one-half stories in height, painted a light brown, and built to accommodate two families. The property is owned by Francis P. Ward, unless he has lately transferred it to the head of the Church Triumphant, as some say is the case. He is a carpenter and a hard worker who prior to the attainment of perfection, considerably augmented the income yielded by his saw and plane by renting the upper suite. He doesn't receive any rent now, that is certain. It is the abode of angels, and angels cannot be expected to pay rent.

Hatfield's next visit to the branch was the following Wednesday evening. This time the door was opened by Disciple James Wentworth, he of the mouse-colored mustache. The big shade-lamp was turned up to its fullest capacity, disclosing one of Sullivan's songs on the organ and the center-table heaped with books and papers. Comfortable chairs and lounges were strewn about in a way especially inviting.

Miss Raymond, in a pretty wrapper, read some extracts from the revised Scriptures. Baldwin, in slippers, easy-chair and a state of great tranquility, nodded approval now and then. After a while Apostle Baldwin spoke briefly, his remarks evidently having direct reference to Hatfield's case. He said:

"It costs much to be a member of the Church Triumphant. One may expect to give up all, everything, to the Lord, if need be; to hate father, mother, brother, sister, husband or wife, to yield our earthly all, our possessions and everything to further the holy cause."

He said much more in the same strain, while the convert-to-be bowed his head and at proper intervals emitted a heavy sigh. The apostle glanced narrowly at Hatfield from time to time to see how he was taking his medicine.

Miss Raymond then descanted for a few minutes on the joys that resulted from such sacrifice—the absolute perfection of character, complete happiness and the divine and boundless love of a living Savior.

After the meeting she again went to Hatfield and talked of the beauties of a perfect life. Finally he said to her:

"I have a fellow-feeling for the young man who accosted Jesus at Galilee, asking what he must do to become his disciple, and Christ said, 'Sell all thy goods, give the money to the poor, and come and follow me,' and the young man went away grieved, for he had great possessions. I can sympathize with him in a small way, being selfish and sordid enough to think of lands and money, and having the feeling that it would be a hard thing to give them all up and see the entire proceeds pass out of my hands forever."

At the mention of possessions Apostle Baldwin pricked up his ears and went forward to join in the conversation.

"It will not be required of you, my young brother," he quickly said, "to do so. The treasuries of the Lord are ever in need of gifts. All the giving you will need to do will be to the Lord. And if one is fully redeemed he will give himself and all to the Lord."

"Yes," interposed Miss Raymond, with her characteristic earnestness, "it is a simple question like this: Am I willing for my Lord's sake to wear the old cloak and let some one else have the new and pretty one? If I am completely redeemed and the Lord's I will say: 'Yea, Lord, and all I am and have shall be thine.'"

Although Hatfield was not at liberty to even given full rein to his thoughts just then, he could see quite clearly the corner of the garden where the serpent is fattening himself. He also noted with commiseration that Miss Raymond was in love, body, soul and mind, with Schweinfurth, and he resolved to break the charm if he could.

It was quite evident that Baldwin wanted money. Wentworth would like to be a villain, and a bad one, but did not have sense enough. The investigator thought he could stand a full-blown, double-duplex, dyed-in-the-wool villain, if he carried his plans into execution cleverly, and had perhaps some extenuation for his villainy, but the experienced a positive detestation for this little milk-and-water rascal, who wanted to be a boa-constrictor without the qualifications for an ordinary grass snake.

The disciple in chief, Wilbur L. Baldwin, is a very spare man, a little above medium height, with small hands and feet. He wears dark-brown side whiskers and mustache; hair of the same color, covering a well shaped head; has a fair forehead and a very long nose tipped, one might say if he were anything less than an apostle, with an incipient grog-blossom; a pendulous, somewhat protruding lower lip; small, keen blue eyes, with brows inclined to aspire heavenward at the outer ends; cheek bones noticeable but not prominent, and pallid complexion. He is a schemer and the nominal leader of the Chicago branch, but the real ruler is Miss Raymond.

Apostle Ward is a broad-shouldered, brown-whiskered, meek-appearing man of something over fifty years. He wears a full-grown squint, which extends its ministrations down his cheek and may find an ambush in the luxuriant growth of beard. Anyway it passes from sight on that border. When relating his spiritual experiences, and especially when informing his hearers how perfect he is, he is inclined to cast his eyes toward the ceiling, but, the squint, acting as a pulley, jerks them down again with such force that one almost expects the dull thud following after all falling bodies. Phrenological inquisitiveness receives an effectual slap in the face from the black skull cap he invariably wears. He is the possessor of an intolerable drawl.

His wife is a good old lady with a pronounced Swedish accent, thin hair strewn with gray and a protruding under lip. She is tall and not over sensible, but a neat housekeeper.

Dr. Marsters is an enthusiastic angle. She is a large woman with dark-brown hair, a generous nose, a "gift of gab," and an office on Madison street. She has a grown daughter who, with all her other relatives, became estranged when she adopted this creed. The little boy, Harry, is only an adopted child.

Apostle Wentworth seems to have been acquired by the church from the slums. Though an ex-debauchee he is a standard-bearer in the Chicago branch of the Church Triumphant.

The little girl is a daughter of "friends of ours", as Miss Raymond explained. Her name is Mary Burnett and she was placed in the home by her parents for the purpose of receiving an education. She was an attendant of a public school and was receiving violin lessons.

These were all the habitués of the place when Hatfield was "seeking the true way," except outside members of the church who came to spend a few days or weeks in the absorption of the holy atmosphere of the home and go forth girded for the fight, or perhaps a new fly who would get entangled in the web and stop a while ere being lured on to the main heaven.

After having been introduced to all these, and spending another hour discussing the doctrines to which they all gave such rigid adherence, Hatfield brought his second visit to a close, faithfully promising as he took his departure to be with them again on the following Sunday.

Chapter XXVIII
A Beautiful Angel

THE NEXT SUNDAY HATFIELD started for the branch at an earlier hour than was really necessary, his idea being not only to show a commendable promptitude but to have a few minutes conversation with Miss Raymond before the service began. He had frequently felicitated himself since his last visit that he was making very satisfactory progress toward a redeemed condition, and he was, so far as the people at the branch were concerned.

What was his surprise on boarding a street car to find Dr. Marsters also a passenger? She was on her way from a visit at her office to the same destination as he. Thinking to discover something of the general idea of Schweinfurth held by the women he took a seat by her side, paid her car fare, praised the little boy, and made himself as agreeable as possible.

"Dr. Marsters," he finally said, "you talk so interestingly—would you mind telling me about your conversion to this wonderful religion?"

She seemed to be much pleased by his skillful flattery, and in a short time was chattering like a magpie. She began by telling of her youngest brother, whom she educated at her own expense for the profession of medicine, and who turned against her when she joined the Church Triumphant. He declared he would have the Messiah in the clutches of the law. He cursed Mr. Schweinfurth terribly.

"And do you know," she added, in an awe-struck whisper, "six weeks from the very day he cursed our God he died! It was an awful retribution, wasn't it?"

This was followed by a series of blood-curdling incidents of terrible consequences to those who had dared raise a hand against their Lord.

"Why," she said, earnestly, "a man who declared he did not want lust removed from the world, and that Mr. Schweinfurth was a devil for wanting to remove it, was taken with typhoid fever the next month and died. Another who reviled the Lord was killed some time after. My own daughter, a young lady who had joined the church and backslidden out into the world's evil ways, was near death's door several times, but I was permitted to bring her back to life and health. When I think of this I am convinced the Lord must have some special work for her to do, for he usually spares only those for whom he has something to do to glorify his kingdom. I devoutly hope my daughter will be brought

Dr. Marsters astonishes Hatfield.

out of the wilderness of apostasy back into the fold. Why, I tell you," and she raised her hands impressively, "I would not raise one finger against our Lord if I was offered a title-deed to the world—nor would any woman who cares for her soul. And a good many don't think he is the Lord, either, I suppose, or they wouldn't say things against him as they do."

"I fear there are many who revile him," said Hatfield, with a sign.

"Yes, indeed; but you see they don't know. Retribution will come to them, all the same."

"But, as a physician, Dr. Marsters, do you believe it possible for women to bear children through purely spiritual agency?"

"Of course I do!" she rejoined, very emphatically. "Do you suppose I doubt the divinity of the Nazarine? It is the Almighty's original plan of peopling the earth. He never intended it to be populated in the way it is now. That came with the curse. Indeed, that is what the curse was. The reason God cursed Adam and Eve was because Adam frustrated the designs of God in relation to Eve. It was God's intention to be the literal father of all men, and then there could not have been sin in the world."

"I dare say you are right, Dr. Marsters," replied Hatfield; "but I am puzzled to understand why the sexes were created."

"I don't know of God's reason for all things, and I don't blasphemously stand and ask him why he did such as such a thing, either," she replied, showing some indignation, and at the same time glancing askance at Hatfield.

Then after a moment's pause she added, piously:

"He knoweth all things and doeth according to what seemeth best. It is only when a race of perfect women shall appear, eschewing the lusts of the flesh, and pure and noble in their lives, that the Holy Ghost will consider them worthy to consort with him. The highest privilege a woman can be allowed on earth is to bear children of the Holy Ghost."

"Then why is not Miss Raymond chosen?" said Hatfield, quietly. "Surely she is as noble a girl and as beautiful a character as any of the angels in the Church Triumphant?"

"O, yes; I do not doubt that some time the divine privilege will be granted her. But you see how it would be just now. The world would charge its paternity to some of the disciples at the branch. She will have to reside in heaven first. I tell you the Lord is going to do wonderful things for womankind. Old women will be fruitful and a new and pure race of men will spring up through them."

Hatfield glanced in horror at the woman who could receive with such complacency these outrageous and abominable doctrines, and predict with such calm and devilish satisfaction that Miss Raymond would in time be chosen as an instrument of the Holy Ghost.

They had now gone as far as they could by car and Hatfield walked out with a sickening pain at his heart. He had formed a liking for the fair girl, and he wondered to what extremes of religious fervor the human heart might not be carried.

On this occasion the sermon was read by Miss Raymond, Baldwin being absent at Rockford and Ward ill in the adjoining room, from which region issued the opening prayer.

When the meeting was over Hatfield began to talk to the boy, who was a really bright little fellow. He was giving a monosyllabic biography of himself when his mother spoke up:

"Don't you think it will be a beautiful thing to bring a boy up to manhood knowing absolutely nothing of sin?"

"Yes, indeed," replied Hatfield. "A most beautiful thing. He would be the most fortunate of mortals."

So he would.

Wentworth, who seemed to be a little suspicious this time, asked Hatfield what he came for.

"Curiosity to some extent, in the first place," was the answer. "But now"—with great vehemence and feeling—"I want something that will make me happy."

"Nothing but the Lord can make you happy," broke in Dr. Marsters with a joyous laugh and hysterical clasp of the hands.

Here Wentworth put in:

"We have been praying for you—"

Whereupon Miss Raymond gave him a look that might have wilted a banyan tree, and he quite collapsed. Hatfield had now no doubt where the seat of power lay. Then she said:

"We don't want to convert you, but if we have anything you want you are most welcome to it. We have been"—smiling pleasantly—"in your state of mind and know what you feel. But we never feel so anymore. We have found perfect peace in the perfection of our souls and in the love of our Lord."

"But," said Hatfield, thinking it best to make at least a feeble struggle before giving up, "is not my mother's religion enough for me?"

"That was under the old dispensation. A new one has now arisen."

Hatfield's doubts appeared to be silenced.

"Mr. Schweinfurth," she continued, "is one of the most persecuted saints the world has ever seen. When a Methodist, they did not like him because he preached against sociables. He said he did not believe in having kitchens attached to churches. Christ in his first coming had driven the money changers from the temple with a whip of small cords, and they should be treated in the same manner to-day."

"If Mr. Schweinfurth can give me the peace I am seeking I will follow him," said Hatfield. "I have about made up my mind to that."

Then for a while the two talked of books. Miss Raymond was fond of music; her favorite author was Mrs. Browning. She also talked freely of herself. She was an ex-school-teacher, having been engaged in that occupation several years at Rockford. She had been a member of the church for eight years—a perfect man-hater and child-hater from her childhood, having never loved a child until she saw Mrs. Tuttle's little girl at Zion, and heard the wonderful story of her birth.

Hatfield wondered how people with any degree of common sense could be so completely duped by what seemed to him such awful blasphemy, but he thought it wisest to say nothing, and Miss Raymond continued:

"The time is surely coming when the earth will be populated with sinless men and women and the curse will be removed. Of course women who are worthy of consorting with the Holy Ghost must have reached a high condition of purity and nobility of character. The teachings of Mr. Schweinfurth are so pure, so beautiful, so breathing of everything opposed to evil, that the stories told about him are dreadful to contemplate."

Her listener was almost petrified to hear this language from the lips of this beautiful girl. There was a tremor in his voice as he asked:

"You love Mr. Schweinfurth, then, with an all-absorbing love?"

"Yes; with all my heart, soul and mind. But it is a love purged and purified—a Christadelphian love, such as a girl may feel for her brother."

"I am sure it would be a pleasure to me to meet Mr. Schweinfurth," said Hatfield. "Is there not some way in which this can be accomplished?"

He hated to practice this deception upon this fair but deluded girl, and even doubted if he should disturb her peace of mind and happiness of heart; but he reasoned that he was actuated by a righteous desire to assist in erasing from the face of the earth an institution the stench of which is enough to blot out the stars and hide the gates of heaven, and no longer hesitated to prosecute the task he had undertaken.

"Yes," she said; "you can see Mr. Schweinfurth, if you desire. I will myself give you a letter of introduction. When would you like to go to Rockford?"

"I would go to-morrow if there is no objection."

At this moment Disciple Wentworth came into the room, just in time to hear the permission given Hatfield to go to Zion. Then he broke loose. He seemed very fidgety all afternoon and as Miss Raymond was about to speak again he cried, excitedly:

"I will speak, Miss Raymond; I don't care what you say! I feel lost, as though I hadn't a friend in the world. I feel as though I am bound straight for hell! My afflictions are more than I can bear. I need to be with my pastor. I want to go to him. Why can't I? I want to be folded to his breast. I can't stand it any longer. The Lord has deserted me and I am lost, lost!'

He almost screamed the last words; but Miss Raymond put in very quietly, with cold, steely precision, looking him squarely in the eye till he cowed down like a whipped cur:

"Mr. Wentworth, you forget what the Lord has done for you. You forget where we found you and from what depths we brought you. You forget what punishments await such open rebellion as you show here to-night. I say to you, Mr. Wentworth, you'd just better look out. Our god is a just and terrible God. He will not suffer such action to go unpunished."

The sharp-cut words fell until the old man quailed in abject terror before the savage young angel, and was silenced.

Then turning to Hatfield she said:

"Mr. Wentworth has given me such trouble several times, I some-times despair of ever bringing him into complete submission. When Pastor Baldwin is at home he behaves himself very well, but when he is away I have frequently to speak to him with some asperity to keep him in subjection. If you will excuse me a few minutes, Mr. Hatfield, I will write you a few lines of introduction to Mr. Schweinfurth."

As she spoke she rose and left the room, walking, as Hatfield did not fail to observe, with a grace as rare as it was natural.

"Fair, deluded creature!" he said to himself. "What would I not give to be permitted to carry you away from this wretched place!"

Directly she returned with the promised letter.

"Would you care to read it before I seal it?" she laughingly asked.

"O, no," he replied, with a heightened tinge of color in his face that looked much like a blush. "I am sure you have spoken kindly of me."

"I can assure you I have said nothing unkind," she replied, as she sealed the letter. "I hope you will like Mr. Schweinfurth, that he will like you, and that you may soon be numbered among the redeemed. You will then know, as we know, what perfect happiness is."

"I will endeavor to make him like me," replied Hatfield; "and I truly hope I may find the happiness I seek."

She gave him her hand as he left, and if he held it a little longer than even the cordiality of their relations required, he was not perhaps so very much to blame. If the girl noticed this at all she probably attributed it to an embryonic Christadelphian feeling just about to burst into bloom in the garden of his heart.

Shortly after that he might have been seen studying a railway time-card; and the first train that went to Rockford carried him Zionward.

Chapter XXIX
Higher Salvation and Fresh Vegetables

IT HAD BECOME QUITE evident to the Messiah, from the daily con-fessions which Clara felt herself impelled to indite, that she was mak-ing little or no progress in the direction of redemption. If anything she was becoming farther removed from the condition of divine purity to which he was extremely anxious to see her elevated. Stepping into the kitchen one day where she was at work he said to her:

"Emeline, I am greatly grieved to find you are a stranger to the celes-tial power of redemption. I had hoped that long ere this you would have passed from this merely external or nominal phase of devotion to a full realization of the higher beauties of spiritual life. You do not know how I have fought for you during all these years."

"I am very sorry, sir," she humbly answered.

"Your condition, Emeline, is one of great spiritual disorder. Every human being in a natural condition is in disorder. The mind, even when well cultivated and enriched by human learning, is a rude, chaotic, shapeless mass, destitute of light and life. Man walks in spiritual dark-ness, fancying meanwhile he is in a state of marvelous illumination. Your will and affections are now 'without form and void,' and dark-ness covers the recesses of your understanding. You have been ever and anon invited, and even personally solicited by your Lord to aspire after higher enjoyments than the world can offer. What have you done?"

"I have tried so hard to fully believe, Mr. Schweinfurth," replied the trembling girl.

"I am afraid you have not tried as you should. You have been as ear-nestly solicited by other invisible agents, who operate through the pas-sions, to reject the kind admonitory overtures of your real friends in Zion, and to descend still lower in the gratification of worldly desires. Thus situated, between two attractive powers, you are, by virtue of your free will, permitted to choose which course you will pursue, whether to obey the mandate of the Lord or remain the wretched vassal of your own natural and corrupt passions. If you were wise enough to choose the right way, and in time become a member of the angelic fraternity, you would then feel that your judicious determination and good res-olutions were constantly acquiring heavenly strength, and you would receive that spiritual light which is now withheld from you."

"I have prayed for this, sir," she said.

"You have been placed here in my private kitchen," he continued, "as the first stage of preparation which precedes redemption. This was rendered necessary by your recent contact with the world; for without being thus reduced to a state of humiliation few will consent to being led onward by the Lord, and consequently few would be saved. Divested of all earthly sources of enjoyment in which the heart has hitherto delighted, you are better conditioned to look to divine power for support, instruction and consolation. 'He who humbleth himself shall be exalted', for have I not said, in the plenitude of my compassion, 'Ask, and ye shall receive, seek and ye shall find; knock, and it shall be opened unto you?'"

"Yes, sir."

"I have given my angels charge concerning you, to lead you in a path which you know not; and I do sincerely hope, from this time forth, you will seek the illumination of divine knowledge to lead you into the way of righteousness and regeneration. What pursuit can be more profitable, what more commendable, than that of spiritual knowledge or a diligent searching for the treasures of divine truth?"

"I know of nothing, sir."

"I am about to transfer you, Emeline, from the laborious work of the kitchen to the supervision of the vegetable and dairy departments. Your labors will be comparatively light, though requiring your constant attention. You will be out of doors much more than now, which will be better for your health, and, in relation to the preparations of the vegetables for market, I want you to exercise your taste and ingenuity in arranging the products of our gardens in the most attractive way."

"I am very grateful for so pleasant a change, and I will do the very best I can," her fair face plainly showing the pleasure she felt.

"I expected it would please you," said the Messiah, with a bland smile; "and I am convinced you will do your best. The right spirit applied to your duties will be even as the prophet said concerning Tyre: 'Her merchandise and her hire shall be holiness unto the Lord.'"

These departments were innovations. The Messiah was continually contriving means to augment the revenues of Zion, which he disbursed with a prodigal hand. Lately he had added a kennel to his worldly possessions, not that he had absorbed anything of the Pythagorean theory of transmigration of souls, but because his great heart loved a valuable dog as it did a blooded horse or a thoroughbred cow, and the best to be had of any of these were only those which could grow sleek and glossy on the heavenly domain. The first canine acquisition which the Messiah held of especial value was a dog whose pedigree had really never become a matter of record. The animal previously belonged to a doctor residing at Rockford; but Schweinfurth, having seen and admired it, at once felt a desire to possess it. He sought the office of the owner that very day, and said to him:

"Good day, Dr. Mann."

"Good day, Mr. Schweinfurth," responded the other, who, like most every one else in the city, knew the Messiah well.

"What is that dog of yours worth?"

"Not so very much."

"What will you take for it?"

"What will you give?"

"I'll give you a milch cow."

"That's not enough."

"I'll give you two milch cows."

"I don't know, Mr. Schweinfurth, my family are greatly attached to the dog."

"And have a man get the dog and drive the cows to where you may desire."

"Well, take him," finally said the doctor.

The Messiah sent a disciple after the dog and the day following the cows made their appearance according to contract. After that dogs with pedigrees "as voluminous as an attorney's bill," and dogs with pedigrees as abbreviated as their cropped ears, found their way to the heavenly kennel, the last two purchased being valued at one thousand dollars each.

The additional outlay involved in establishing this new and markedly celestial feature required some means of recouping the treasury of Zion, and it was with that object in view that the Messiah set a disciple and an angel to selling vegetables from house to house in the city, and set about establishing a "milk route." It can be truthfully said in this connection that no finer vegetables or richer lacteal production found its way to the city than that which came from "the sweet fields" of the terrestrial Eden. The Lord found these new sources of revenue very satisfactory, and the departments have been continued to this day.

As superintendent of the work of seeing these products properly prepared and started to market Clara scored a marked success. The duties required her to be up earlier in the morning than heretofore; but she did not object to that, for it gave her added exhilaration of spirits to inhale the invigorating morning air and watch the glorious sunrise; and when the bright orb of day in its diurnal course sank from sight beneath the glowing western horizon her work for the day was done. She was then at liberty to "fix up" and go into the parlor, with the few others who were early at leisure, and enjoy herself until the Lord retired. When he disappeared for the night it was a silent signal for all others to do the same, and no one thought of longer remaining up, except those who were assigned to the regular guard duty.

One day the Messiah was hastily called away by some trouble at one of the branches. A man named George Ostrander had fallen from grace and made a demand upon the heavenly treasury for labor performed during his communal relations. Ostrander had been a member of the church for twelve years, being compelled to join when he was thirteen years of age by his father, who become infatuated with the doctrine as taught by Mrs. Beekman, the founder of the sect. Although so long connected with the church he had no faith in the divinity of Schweinfurth, and his dissatisfaction with the life he led continually manifested itself. One night before, he made up his mind to leave, and tried to do so. He started off across the country, slept out of doors that night, got soaking wet, and was so thoroughly disheartened in the morning that he turned around and made his way back. This time, however, he appeared to be gone for good. He left the farm near a branch where he had been put to work, walked ten miles, and, jumping on a freight train, rode until morning. Then he was put off and wandered aimlessly around until the afternoon, when he approached a farm-house and asked for something to eat, for he was penniless and hungry. He worked there for a while, and then went on to Chicago where he lived when a boy. There, meeting friends, he procured a position and dropped the alias under which he had traveled. Now, with the aid of a capable lawyer, he was endeavoring to procure some remuneration for six years of toil.

The Messiah started away the afternoon of the same day he was notified of Ostrander's operations. He went with a double carriage accompanied by one of his favorite angels, carrying with them what they required to eat and drink while on the trip, as it was not always easy to get what was good enough for an angel in an edible way on the road.

The very next morning after the departure of Schweinfurth the pretty young woman whose duty it was to accompany the vegetable wagon and the disciple salesman to the city was suddenly taken ill, and the disciple, not thinking of anything better to do, and knowing that those left in charge would not rise for some hours, invited Clara to accompany him. She knew the presence of a woman on the wagon was more to attract attention than for any purpose of usefulness, and the disciple promised to assist her in finishing her work when they returned. She knew, also, there were strong reasons why the Lord did not desire her to go to the city, although he had not said so, and she was persuaded that, were he at home, the visit would not be permitted. Still, she reasoned, someone ought to go, and, as there was just a little bit of independence animating her that morning, and the disciple continued his persuasions, she finally consented, though not without a feeling of trepidation. Making a few necessary changes in her apparel, she was soon seated by the side of the disciple on the vegetable wagon, bound for Rockford.

The morning air was fresh and invigorating and the roads good, and, alternately fascinated by the changing scenes of rural beauty along the way, and charmed by the prospect of again seeing those objects of the city with which she had grown familiar during her stay with the Belyeas, she found the ride a truly pleasurable one.

The disciple drove well into the city before attempting to effect any sales, so many of those living toward the limit having vegetable gardens of their own as to render it unprofitable to stop for what few sales might be made, unless accosted by someone as the wagon passed along.

They had been in town perhaps an hour, and their stock was rapidly diminishing, when something unusual occurred. The disciple had carried a basket of vegetables into a house some distance from the street, and had scarcely disappeared from sight when a young man stepped briskly up to the wagon and engaged the astonished girl in conversation. He spoke in a low but earnest tone, finally taking something from his pocket in which she seemed to be deeply interested. In a moment he was seen assisting her to alight, and then the two walked quickly away and disappeared around the nearest corner.

When the disciple returned to the wagon a few minutes later and found his companion was not there he was absolutely paralyzed, and was compelled to grasp the side of the wagon to keep himself from falling. The look upon the poor fellow's face when his returning senses permitted him to realize the misfortune that had befallen him was pitiful to see. Knowing the infinite misery in store for him if he returned to Zion without his charge, and trembling like an aspen, he covered his remaining vegetables, made his horse secure to a friendly hitching post, and set out in a half stupefied condition in quest of the missing girl.

That evening, when two anxious apostles went to the city to see what had happened to the twain, they found the horse had been cared for by an officer of the law and the frantic disciple was yet searching in vain for Emeline.

One apostle took the wagon and the half-crazed, trembling disciple back to Zion, while the other remained to institute a systematic search for the missing girl.

Chapter XXX
Out of the Slough of Despond

IT WAS LATE AT night when Hatfield reached Rockford and there was little he could do before morning to further the object that brought him there. Every resident to whom he addressed himself seemed to be familiar with heaven and its peculiar people—at least they considered themselves sufficiently well informed to speak with authority. He gathered much additional information, among other things the fact that, if he did not care to walk or patronize a livery man, he would probably have an opportunity of riding down to Zion with the apostolic driver of the milk wagon the following day, or, better still, going in the company of an angel on the vegetable wagon.

So he retired in a short time, that he might the better rise early in the morning. When he had breakfasted he began to look around in order to satisfy himself what should be his first course of procedure. He first saw the heavenly milk wagon and learned from the disciple in charge what hour he would leave the city and where he might be found when ready to go. There would be no objection to Mr. Hatfield's riding, the man said, and he was glad to know the stranger expected to become a member of the community.

Having considerable time to spare Hatfield then looked around for the vegetable wagon, having received from the disciple with whom he talked an idea of where it might be found. He told the man, as an excuse for searching for the other wagon, that he would like to avail himself of the privilege of whichever vehicle first left the city, as he was so anxious to see the home of the redeemed he was impatient of delay. Of course he was grieved to learn the Messiah was absent from home, but the disciple said that need not distress him, as there were those who would receive and welcome him.

In a short time he met the wagon, and was about to approach and accost the disciple when he observed the features of the young woman who accompanied him, and at once paused and looked intently at her. Then he withdrew a short distance, where he took a photograph from his pocket and studied that for nearly a minute. The inspection seemed to be satisfactory, if his face was any criterion. Placing it in a pocket where it would be readily accessible he turned his attention again to the wagon, following it at a sufficient distance not to attract the attention of the disciple and watching sharply for an opportunity to speak to the girl. A favorable chance did not present itself until the unwitting disciple carried a basket of vegetables into a house standing some distance back from the street, where, fortunately for Hatfield's plans, he was detained for some minutes while his forgetful purchaser found her purse.

"Now or never!" said Hatfield to himself. "Here's where I make a spoon or spoil a horn."

Stepping quickly up to the wagon he fairly startled the young woman, whose gaze was intently fixed on some object in the distance, with the abrupt exclamation:

"Miss McCoy!"

Clara turned to him with a look of alarm at thus suddenly hearing her name called. She riveted her wide-open eyes on the handsome face of the stranger and waited for him to speak again.

"Come with me!" he said, in a sharp imperative tone.

"Where?" she asked, too astonished to know what else to say.

"To your home at Shelbyville. They have sent me to bring you—father and mother and Arthur. Come quickly, before that man returns. Do not delay a moment—they are waiting for you—come! come!"

"But, sir," she hesitatingly said, "I do not know you."

"See! They gave me your photo so that I would know you," he went on eagerly and rapidly, at the same time drawing the picture from his pocket and handing it to her.

"That is my picture!" she joyfully exclaimed, looking at the card.

"Come!" he again urged, extending his hand to her. "Come at once, before the disciple comes back. When we reach the hotel I will explain everything to you. Let me assist you to alight."

The authoritative manner and tone, which he purposely assumed, influenced her more than his words. She permitted him to help her from the wagon, and, inspired by this words of encouragement, allowed him to almost drag her away. No one apparently observed them, except the ever-present street Arab who shouted as he saw them hurrying away:

"Say, mister, you'll get paralyzed if you run away with that there angel."

They paid no attention to the urchin but hastened around the nearest street corner and disappeared. They were not yet out of sight when the disciple emerged from the house. Had he been looking about him he might easily have seen them, but at that time he was carefully examining the money in his hand—probably to assure himself that he had not been overpaid.

In search of an escaped angel.

The boy, naturally interested in seeing a man carry off an angel, followed at a trot the fleeting footsteps of Clara and Hatfield for two blocks, doubtless with the expectation of seeing the man paralyzed. As this did not happen he suddenly wheeled about and trotted back to see what the disciple would do when he found the angel gone. It was necessary he should see somebody do something.

He found the disciple hastily making his horse fast and the keen eyes of the youngster quickly detected the distressed condition of the man's mind.

"Lose a angel?" was his brief query.

"Did you see which way the young lady went?" hoarsely asked the disciple.

"You bet I seen her!" replied the boy, eager to see a chase. "Skipped 'round that corner and then went two blocks that way—" indicating the direction with his extended arm—"and then turned down that way. Say, mister, ye'll have to get a move on ye ef ye ketch 'em; they was scootin' like whiteheads."

"Was someone with her?"

"Yes; a feller."

The disciple stopped to ask no further questions, but started off as rapidly as he could walk in the direction indicated by the boy, who, now thoroughly alive to the importance of the occasion, followed a short distance in the rear. Soon he saw another boy of his acquaintance across the street and shouted, without stopping:

"Come on, Tom. Here's a feller chasing a angel."

Tom did not understand what the other said, but he saw it was something that required his attention, and, forgetful of the errand upon which he had been sent, with an injunction to make haste, he joined in the eager chase. In ten minutes there were a dozen noisy lads at the heels of the panting disciple, and the strange procession became an object of deep interest to all who chanced to see it.

Meanwhile Clara and Hatfield hurried along toward the business section of the city. When the boy who was following them made up his mind to retrace his steps Hatfield said:

"I don't suppose there is any one in town you know?"

"Yes, sir, there is," she replied. "I know the Belyeas I stopped there for a while."

"Know where they live?"

"On Pine street."

"No danger of your being following there, is there?"

"No, sir."

"Then I'll stop this hack and we'll go there."

He did so, hastily bundling Clara in and as quickly following her, and the two were driven to the home of the friends from whom Clara had been torn by Apostle Mamby.

Mrs. Belyea was overjoyed to meet the unfortunate girl again, and not only congratulated her on her second escape, but had to know by what means she had been lured back to the infamous place, before Hatfield was given an opportunity to explain his business with the young woman. It was a source of extreme gratification to Mrs. Belyea to know that Clara was at once to be restored to her home and friends.

Leaving the two to talk together for a short time, Hatfield sought a telegraph office and sent the following message to Dr. Shannon:

"Have got Clara; will start for Shelbyville this evening.   HATFIELD."

The infamous and heartless plan of Schweinfurth to rid himself and Zion of the dying Angelica, and to effectually dispose of Arthur at the same time, is now made plain. When these two unfortunates met, Arthur mistook the young woman for his beloved Clara, whom he had not met during all the time he remained at Zion, and he was still unshaken in this belief. Not desiring to have Angelica die at the home, again calling in question his divine power of preserving life, he determined to avail himself of her remarkable resemblance to Clara. She was constantly told that her former name was Clara McCoy and that her parents lived at Shelbyville. In her deplorable condition of mind it was not a difficult matter to teach her to believe this, as well as to repeat, parrot-like, the names of her supposed parents and others of those with whom Clara had been on terms of intimacy when at home. When his shameless work had been thoroughly done she was told she would be allowed to go home for a while until she grew stronger, and the poor girl seemed to be pleased at the prospect of a change.

The daring outrage which the scheming head of the Church Triumphant perpetrated upon the unsuspecting parents of poor Clara, by sending another to them as their daughter with a child to account for, and which was successfully carried into effect by his fugleman, Mamby, gave that conscienceless individual no concern. The sufferings and humiliation of others were of small moment to him provided he compassed his ends.

Angelica remained at the branch but a few days—long enough to make it certain that no detail of the plan had been overlooked—and then Mamby took her and the little girl to Shelbyville, traveling by conveyance from the nearest depot. They entered the village after dark and the apostle pointed out to the young mother the house to which she was to go. He then assisted her from the carriage at a distance of a block from the house, to drag herself there with her little girl as best she could in her almost helpless condition. After waiting around long enough to make sure the plan had not miscarried—the news of Clara's return from her long absence passing through the village like wild-fire—he again entered his carriage and drove away.

Of course Arthur Fitzroy, feeling assured that the love of his life had left Zion to die in the arms of her parents, who already mourned her as dead, had no longer a desire to remain among the associations that had been so repugnant to him from the start, and the scheme to drive him from the place that had been the source of so much sorrow to him, was not difficult to carry into effect.

It was for the purpose of imparting what she knew of this affair to Hatfield that Miss Ama Howard, the young lady detective, summoned him to an interview at the hotel after reading his report of the mystery of Shelbyville. During the brief time she was at heaven she met and talked with Clara, learning her full name and where she came from. She also talked with Angelica, and was not a little puzzled to find her giving the same name and claiming to have come from the same place. Beyond nothing, however, the sad condition of Angelica's health, she paid no attention to her rather peculiar discovery until she read the graphic account of Clara's return to her home and subsequent death. Then the truth of the matter flashed across her mind and Hatfield was given a most valuable "pointer." Although Miss Howard failed of what she had undertaken, she doubtless felt amply repaid for all her time and trouble when she learned that Clara had been rescued from the deadly tentacles of the bewhiskered devil-fish.

Having sent his telegram and attended to some other matters, Hatfield returned to where he had left Clara. Mr. Belyea, who had been called home by telephone, met him very cordially. The two talked the matter over, reaching the conclusion that it would be the part of wis-dom to start for Shelbyville that evening. Hatfield would have very much liked to see the abode of the redeemed for himself, but Mr. Belyea argued that delay was dangerous as well as unnecessary in this case, for Clara, on the journey home, could tell him more about the place than it would be possible for him to learn by any efforts of his own. He was therefore persuaded to drop that part of his project, seeing the Messiah was absent and could not be seen anyway.

Before the conference ended Mr. Belyea, who declared, in language as emphatic as was necessary for any reputable citizen and father of a family to use, that he had never before heard of so diabolical and wicked an outrage as that perpetrated upon the McCoys, agreed to see a justice of the peace and procure the necessary papers for the recovery of Clara's effects held by Schweinfurth, while he would forward to her home as early as possible.

That evening the members of the family shook hands with Hatfield and bade Clara and affectionate farewell, and the two took a train for Kentucky. Mr. Belyea went to the station with them as a sort of body-guard.

Clara was supremely happy at the discovery that her friends would not revile her or her parents turn away in anger because of her misfortunes, as Schweinfurth had led her to believe, but would welcome her back to her home and happiness. When told that Arthur, faithful to his vows, had followed her to Zion and there remained a member of the community until he believed she was no longer there, her astonishment was unbounded; but when informed what disposition had been made of the miserable Angelica, her feelings found relief in a flood of unrestrained tears. Many things had transpired of late to shake her belief in the divinity of Schweinfurth. The crowning outrage perpetrated on her sorrow-stricken parents was the traditional "last straw." She turned her denunciation, feeble enough just then, against the shameless and heartless author of all this mischief, feeling indignant enough to have spoken her mind to the Messiah himself were they face to face.

After a time, when she became calm, she talked freely to her companion of the home. She told him much of what the reader already knows and a great many things that are not essential to her story. For a while she descanted upon the picnics which are a feature of the summer time, several of which she had been permitted to attend at times when Arthur was kept out of sight.

"Everything had to be done in style," she said, "and there would always be a parade. A fine repast is spread for the redeemed, but the others have to be satisfied with the ordinary fare, unless they can work themselves into the favor of the girls appointed to wait on table."

"Schweinfurth is the most remarkable humbug I ever heard of," said Hatfield. "I am convinced that he is the very personification of diabolism. He is an awful, blasphemous, scheming impostor. He is far worse than you are aware of, long as you have been with him, and his operations are much more extensive than most people have any idea of. He has many devoted followers who are such only in secret. Most of his women are, until they come under his direct influence, pure in thought and word. They believe honestly, strange as it seems, that their maternity is a direct impartation of the holy spirit. Some of his followers are petty fools, some of them are cranks, and some of them are deluded to the point of insanity; while all of them, I believe, old and young, male and female, are mere puppets, made to live and move and have their being that this man Schweinfurth may live in luxurious apartments and satisfy the debasing and consuming passions hidden beneath his smooth, magnetic and attractive exterior."

Thus the two continued to discuss the man, his doctrines and his community the best part of the homeward journey. Hatfield was soon familiar with the details of the communal life as far as Clara could tell him, for of course she was still ignorant of what transpired in the inner circle of those who had found redemption. On the other hand, she was constantly astonished at the revelations of the works of the Messiah as known to outsiders.

What means were taken to find Clara by the apostle who remained in Rockford to continue the search is of small account. It is certainly a matter of genuine satisfaction to know that his efforts were unavailing. Neither he, the Messiah, nor other members of the Church Triumphant ever saw more of Clara.

Were there time to investigate, it might not be uninteresting to discover what direction Miss Raymond's thoughts took when she heard of Clara's escape, and found that her prospective convert had failed to present himself and his letter of introduction at the heavenly portals.

And the unfortunate disciple who took Clara to the city, without authority to do so, and permitted her to escape! What of him? It is not hard to imagine the disgrace and humiliation to which he was subjected—the scorn and contumely of the faithful, a long season of penance with servile toil and meager fare, and hours devoted to committing to memory interminable pages of the Messiah's revised type-written scriptures.

Chapter XXXI
Hearts Reunited

HATFIELD'S TELEGRAPHIC MESSAGE REACHED Dr. Shannon about the middle of the same afternoon on which it was sent having been received by the nearest station agent in time to hand to the person who carried the mail to several of the smaller villages thereabouts. The doctor's eyes became greatly distended with the astonishment that took possession of him on reading the message. To tell the truth of the matter, both he and Parson Brown were very skeptical in regard to the story which Hatfield had heard from Miss Howard. There were several things, indeed, which they accepted *cum grano salis*, Miss Howard's story and the mesmeric theory of Clara's abduction chiefly awakening their incredulity. In several private conferences which the two held after Hatfield's departure they rather scouted the idea of such things, though they agreed there could be no question as to the existence of this pretender and his inexplicable power over his followers, and both fervently hoped the young journalist would be able to completely expose this agent of the evil one and his wicked doings. It was because they were dubious of much that had been related to them that the whole affair was kept a profound secret between the three. They had no mind to put themselves in the way of the ridicule of the villagers if it should ultimately be demonstrated that these tales were purely visionary.

Therefore, when the doctor was notified by this message that Clara had actually been rescued from the power of this iniquitous wretch, and would be on her way home that evening, his astonishment was unbounded. The news was too much for him to carry around alone for any length of time. A messenger was hastily dispatched for Parson Brown and another for Arthur, in order that the affair might at once be taken under advisement.

Arthur, who was the first to arrive, was sent into the doctor's private room and told to make himself comfortable until the minister came, when there was something important the doctor desired to say to both. Arthur, though somewhat surprised, obeyed the doctor's behest unquestioningly. He supposed the meeting had something to do with the establishment of Schweinfurth, but, not being in the secret of Hatfield's mission to the home, could not know the real reason for his summons. However, Arthur had well learned the lesson of patience and could await the doctor's disclosures with perfect equanimity. To all intents his mind had grown clear and strong again, leaving him with a settled melancholy that was plainly reflected in his features and a quiet, dignified reserve that kept him aloof from others. These peculiarities, the doctor and others believed, had become a part of his nature and would remain with him to the end. He brooded a good deal over what he conceived to be the miserable fate and sad end of her who had been his heart's choice, but he kept his somber thoughts to himself, are none knew how keenly he suffered. He understood that an attempt to seek satisfaction from the author of his unhappiness would only result in additional trouble for himself, so he calmly, to all outward appearance, bore his affliction, and uttered no word of complaint.

The minister reached the doctor's office soon after. As he entered the physician arose and greeted him.

"Read this telegram, Brother Brown, and see what you think of it," he said.

The minister adjusted his glasses in silence and then read the paper which the doctor handed him. He read it no less than three times, to convince himself that he was not mistaken. Then he looked at the doctor, who had been watching his face intently while he read, and both regarded each other in blank silence for a few moments. Finally Mr. Brown said:

"Is it not possible, Doctor, that this is a case of mistaken identity on the part of this young man?"

"Such a thing is possible, to be sure," answered the doctor; "but I believe it is highly improbable. This young man, Hatfield, is keen and bright. I do not believe he would permit himself to be deceived or that he would let his feelings incite him to unwarranted haste in an affair of such grave importance. If he says he has found and procured the release of Clara McCoy, the chances are that he hasn't done anything else."

"And we have been at sea in our conclusions?"

"So it would appear."

"Remarkable!" said the minister, meditatively.

"Very," replied the doctor.

Like most other men who, having once formed opinions, held to them pertinaciously, these two disliked to discard the conclusions they had reached. There was some human nature in both these good men.

"Arthur is in my private office," said the doctor, after a moment or two of reflection. "Let us go in and I will question him."

They at once joined Arthur, who was quietly perusing a medical journal which he found on the doctor's table. After rising and cordially greeting the minister he said:

"Here is an article, Doctor, on mesmerism and therapeutics that has greatly interested me as far as I have read. If I can borrow this paper I would like to finish reading the article."

"You can have the paper to-morrow, Arthur," said the doctor. "In the meantime I want to ask you some questions."

"I am entirely at your service, Doctor."

"You were in this institution called heaven about six years, were you not?"

"About that time."

"How much do you really know of what went on there?"

"Very little of what occurred in the house. I was seldom allowed inside, and never farther than the reception-room."

"Why were you excluded?"

"Because of my lack of faith, I suppose."

"It was a long time before you really knew Clara was there?"

"Yes; it was some time before I was really certain, and it was nearly or quite two years before I saw her."

"Are you sure you ever saw her?"

"Why, yes," said Arthur, his eyes opening very wide with surprise. "I do not think I will ever forget that meeting, Doctor."

"Arthur, I do not think you ever saw Clara there."

"Doctor," said the other, without the slightest trace of indignation at being thus directly contradicted, "I had complete possession of my faculties up to that time."

"Doubtless you think so. How did the young woman receive you when you met her? Was she pleased to see you? Did she recognize you?"

"She did not seem to know me."

"Just as I expected," said the doctor, as he and the minister exchanged glances. "Did you call her by name?"

"Yes."

"What then?"

"She said her name was not Clara. I remember I could not make her recognize me, and—" seized with a sudden inspiration—"why am I being interrogated in this way, Doctor? Has something impressed you with the notion that I was mistaken in the person I accosted?"

"Yes, Arthur; it was not Clara you saw, but a more unfortunate young woman who passed by the name of Angelica. Can you stand some good news?"

"I can stand anything," he said, rising to his feet. "Tell me what it is."

"Be calm, Arthur," said the hitherto silent minister. "Take your chair again."

"He's all right," said the doctor. "Good news never kills."

Arthur resumed his seat and Dr. Shannon continued:

"You remember young Hatfield, who was here a few weeks ago, and who went from there to Rockford?"

"I remember him very well. I tried to dissuade him from going."

Arthur spoke in a calmer tone and was less affected than either of the others.

"I have a dispatch from him," said the doctor, drawing the paper from his pocket. Would you like to read it?"

Arthur took the message from the doctor's hand and read it slowly. There was no gaging his feelings from his imperturbable features. He quietly said when he had finished reading:

"There can be no mistake about this, Doctor?"

"I have every reason to believe the young man knows what he is about," was the reply.

"I was aware my mind was sadly clouded for a season," said Arthur, in the same quiet, deliberate voice in which he always spoke; "but it seems I have been superlatively stupid from first to last. What shall we do?"

"You go and get Mr. McCoy and take him home. Mr. Brown and I will follow in a few minutes. Do not mention anything of this until we all get together. I think Mr. Brown or myself should break the news to the family."

"I will gladly do so," said Arthur.

He started on his errand at once, with a heart that was throbbing very rapidly, even if his face was no index of his emotion and his step was brisker than it had been since he walked the village streets in the old days.

"He will soon be himself again now," said the minister, when Arthur was gone.

"Yes," replied the doctor; "if the girl remains unchanged toward him."

In a few minutes they followed him to the home of the McCoys, first ascertaining that he had found the old gentleman.

What passed when they were all gathered together may be better imagined than described. As the doctor cautiously unfolded the particulars of the extraordinary affair his revelations called into play all the emotions of the human heart. The poor parents hung upon every syllable he uttered which seemed to them like a soul-inspiring melody sending its joyous echoes through the gloomy caverns of the heart. Every word appeared to be pregnant with gladdening glees. They could feel the buds of hope putting forth, and the future seemed fresh and promising. It must be such hopes as then animated the parents as are taken up and transplanted in the skies, there to bloom unfading forever.

Mr. McCoy insisted on driving over to the station in the morning, there to await, no matter what time it took, the arrival of Clara and Hatfield. The eager mother, of course, should accompany him, for the blessed rays of her maternal love, though obscured for a time by the intercepting clouds of grief, were in no ways dimmed by the circumstances of her daughter's absence. That love, like the sun in the eternal heavens, would glow with undiminished fervor while life lasted.

Of course when they met in fond embrace there were many tears— but they were tears of joy, like golden dew drops shaken from the wings of angels. Such a generous overflow serves only to relieve the heart overwhelmed and oppressed with grief.

Clara and Arthur were married three months later, when both, like the immortal Richard, were themselves again. To be sure, Parson Brown performed the solemn yet joyous ceremony. There was the old-time sparkle in the clear, fearless eyes of the quiet bridegroom, and loveliness again sat enthroned upon the face of the happy bride.

Doubtless when the evening of life draws nigh—though not forgetful of the six wasted years in the terrestrial heaven—it will find them with the leaves of connubial love still green and perhaps a joyous offspring surrounding and gracing the parent trees, like ivy entwining and adorning the time-scathed oak.

And what of the Messiah? He is still "doing business at the old stand"—more's the pity—deluding and luring the stray sheep of Christendom to osculate the hem of his unholy garment. If in the years to come the law can find no way to stop the infamous practice of this unblushing pretender, the relentless hand of time will bear him down with a weary load of years, and, old, decrepit and hopeless, in fear and trembling he will feel his feeble way with his staff to the cheerless tomb in the dull twilight of existence. Such a life as his must turn out poorly at the last. A sad change indeed in the space of a few short years, from the buoyant youth full of fervor, fire and righteous zeal, to the last winding path of senescence, with the flowers of hope few and unfragrant.

Indeed, dear reader, much of what begins well in this world must come to a comparatively poor ending, except TRUTH and VIRTUE. These put forth buds that blossom forever, and brighten in their bloom as eternity grows old.

Finale of the Modern Messiah.

THE END

www.ingramcontent.com/pod-product-compliance
Lightning Source LLC
Chambersburg PA
CBHW071132200626
46817CB00018B/2866